with no
Little Regrett

with no
Little Regrett

by
Janet Burnett Gerba

Janet Burnett Gerba

an historical novel
based on
the Journal of Madam Knight

Colonial American Press
Rutland, Vermont

Copyright © 1995 by Janet S. Gerba

All rights reserved.
No part of this publication may be reproduced
or transmitted in any form or by any means,
electronic or mechanical, including photocopying, recording,
or any information storage and retrieval system,
except for review purposes,
without permission in writing from the publisher.

Requests for permission should be mailed to :
Colonial American Press
P.O.Box 1416, Sta. A
Rutland, Vermont 05701

Library of Congress number: 95-70216

ISBN 0-9647752-0-4 (paperback)
ISBN 0-9647752-1-2 (hardcover)

Cover Design and Illustrations by Sue Thomas
Typeset by Write Stuff Communications
Printed by Daamen Press, West Rutland, Vermont

1995

Contents

Mortalitas	1
Præparatio	14
Exitus	32
Via Providentiæ	51
Deserta	72
Continuatio	87
Rudes Populi	101
Destinatio	117
Revelata	133
Inventorium	147
Divertere	158
Via Volcani et Bacchi	168
Lex Talionis	180
Meum et Tuum	196
Voluptas in Taberna	208
Dies Frigidi	221
Disputatio	233
Valete Dolor	243
Domi	255
Afterward	270

For help along the Post Road I thank

Barbara and Gene Burnett
Ron Bosco, Judith Barlow, Judith Fetterley
Dave King, Julie Perco, Patrick O'Connor
countless librarians and historians

and Vince, of course.

with no
Little Regrett

Mortalitas

Sunday, September 10, 1704

"We've washed and shrouded his body. Better lay him out downstairs with the windows open overnight. In this heat you'll need to bury him tomorrow." The older of the two nurses who had attended Caleb Trowbridge stood in the upstairs hallway holding a pail of cloudy water with the corner of her apron.

The other one headed for the narrow stairway with a bundle of soiled linens. "We'll pass by the coffin maker's and tell him to come," she said.

Sarah Kemble Knight nodded but said nothing. How could Caleb be dead? He didn't look sick when he appeared at her door several months ago. He would never have left his home in New Haven if he were suffering. His business problems in Boston wouldn't have been worth it.

Sarah looked at Mary Trowbridge, who was staring out the hallway window, her back to everything. Mary was smaller than Sarah, but framed in the midmorning light she seemed even more diminished in her sadness. In the last two years Sarah had been at her boarder's side through the death of her first husband, then her parents, and now Caleb. A second widowhood seemed incredible. And fast. Mary accepted Caleb's marriage proposal only a few weeks after he arrived. Increase Mather wed them in July. Then he came to pray with Caleb when he could no longer pass water and had grown too ill to rise from bed.

Now he was dead.

Sarah went to Mary and took her hand. "Let's go in."

They stepped into the newlyweds' bedchamber, avoiding the wet spots the nurses had left on the floor. For some reason they tip-toed; an odd thing to do, Sarah thought, in the room of a dead man. They had to sit atop a pine chest, which was the only piece of furniture, besides the bed. Mary had not even had a chance to furnish their chamber properly.

The heat and dampness closed in on Sarah. She noticed an odor, too, and wondered what part of death it was. The two clasped hands and stared at the distended shape. The silence made Sarah's ears ring.

"I thought the swelling . . . ." Mary sighed. "Well, that when he died the swelling would go down and he'd look as he did before."

There was nothing that Sarah could think of to say, so they just sat.

Finally Mary said, "I can't believe this has happened to me. What does it mean?"

Sarah knew what Mary was asking but did not have an

answer, so she prolonged the question. "What does what mean?"

"That I've lost two husbands before I'm even thirty."

"It's not your fault, Mary. It's poor luck, I guess."

Mary looked at her.

"Don't try looking for some negative providence," Sarah said. "And don't go asking the ministers, either. They'd probably just make you feel more miserable." She put her arm around Mary. "You're a good and dear person with bad luck, that's all."

Mary laid her head on Sarah's shoulder. "It's different this time. I'm in serious trouble, aren't I? I could tell when you were helping him with the will." She paused, but when Sarah said nothing Mary went on. "He was being evasive about something so I wouldn't be worried, but there's something the matter, isn't there?"

Sarah took a deep breath and exhaled slowly. How was she to explain what she had discovered the day before? Caleb was a businessman who took great risks, as did her own husband. The difference was, her cousin was known to recoup from failure with a number of successes, while Richard's response to failure was to jump on board the first ship out of Boston and disappear for a couple of years. Unfortunately for Mary, this time Caleb's kidneys gave out before he could recover his losses.

"Things don't look good." Sarah stroked Mary's hand a few times. "Last year Caleb made a deal with a trader here in Boston. The trader agreed to send Caleb nearly half of an entire shipload of English goods, even though Caleb didn't have the cash money to pay at the time. In return, Caleb promised the trader twice the amount of the value in molasses, if he'd wait a year for it." Sarah sat still for a moment. "I know you don't have a head for business, but do you understand what I've said so far?"

"Yes."

Now came the hard part. "Just before Caleb came here the molasses shipment was lost in a storm, and Caleb hadn't insured it because he was trying to make a greater profit—"

Mary tried to lift her head off Sarah's shoulder, but Sarah held her tighter. "Caleb said he'd been forced to sell the English goods at a low price because they'd been damaged in a leaky warehouse, so the trader hasn't been paid."

Mary wrested free of Sarah and looked at her. "Is there enough money in his estate to cover what he owes? How much is it?"

"I don't know. After I took down Caleb's will yesterday, I went to speak to the trader. They still hadn't worked out an arrangement. Caleb kept reassuring him that as soon as he was well enough to travel, he'd return to New Haven and get things straightened out."

"But how do we find out if his estate will cover it? I don't know anything about this. I mean we were married only two months. I just know how much money I had when we got married."

"When probate court does the inventory, then you'll know exactly what there is to liquidate."

"If I'm left in debt—this is awful. I can't...." Mary put her head back on Sarah's shoulder and started crying.

Sarah held her. Mary shook with sobs but made almost no noise. Over the years it had always been this way, Mary would grieve in her quiet fashion, never for very long, and Sarah would provide the shoulder.

Either Sarah was more impervious to pain or Mary simply had more misfortune, but it seemed Sarah was always the dispenser of comfort. She did rub a tear off on Mary's cap, though. Her friend's misery touched her more than her cousin's death did.

Presently Mary sat up and wiped her face. The two held hands and sat in silence until they heard the bumping of the coffin being brought up the stairs.

✱

Sarah used a brick to prop open the front door and a broom against the door at the back of the hallway. Then she joined her cousin, Robert Luist, in the parlor. He was raising the windows. Because the coffin had been placed there, they decided the house had better be left open overnight in hopes that an evening breeze off the bay might mitigate the effects of the unusually hot weather on the remains. Of course, that meant someone had to sit up through the night to prevent any animals from straying in while everyone slept, so Sarah and Robert had volunteered to keep watch over the coffin.

Robert removed his mourning coat, draped it over the high back of a wing chair and sat down across from Sarah.

"I didn't want to ask in front of Mary," he said, loosening his neckpiece, "but did Caleb make any final arrangements? You know, his estate?"

"He had me draw up and witness his will, but his situation's complicated. There's a business deal with a trader here in Boston that went awry. It may have created substantial debt."

"Oh, dear."

"Not only that," Sarah said, "Connecticut has the same law as Massachusetts—a will has to be registered at probate court within thirty days of death." She undid the top button of her bodice and pulled the damp wool away from her chest. "I'm assuming a will drawn up here is valid there. But even if it is, his family could contest it."

"On what grounds?"

"They might not consider a wife of seven weeks entitled to his estate." She picked up a fan from the table between the two chairs and tried to cool herself. "Don't forget, they may have just received his letter about getting married. It will take another week or two before they know he's dead."

"If they contest, does that mean Mary's left with nothing?"

"The court could decide either way. If they say she's entitled to the estate, then they could hold her responsible for his debts, which means she'd have to pay from the money her parents left her." Sarah was fanning with so much agitation that the silk made snapping noises. "Caleb took an enormous gamble with this last deal in Boston. Mary could be left with nothing but debt."

"That's terribly unfair," Robert said.

"Unfair? It could be disastrous. She'll have absolutely no future."

Sarah leaned back, untied her cap strings and continued

fanning. "Men look for wealthy widows before they'll court maidens, and they run the other way from widows in debt. You know that."

That was hardly kind of her, but Robert only gave her a knowing glance. The widow he had married provided him with profitable holdings across the Charles River. She even suspected that her husband, Richard, had been considering Amos Browne's widow until he discovered that her own father's wealth seemed more promising in the long run.

"The will's crucial," she said. "In case his business affairs can't be brought right, she needs clear title to his properties. Then she could sell them to satisfy the Boston trader and any other creditors that might turn up."

"Does she know the position she's in?"

"I've tried to explain, but it's hard to tell how much she can grasp at a time like this," Sarah said. She thought about sitting in the upper room with Mary and how tightly they had held each other's hand. Was that this morning or yesterday? So much had happened since then. She shook her head. "I don't know what to do. Mary's more like a sister than a boarder. I wish I could think of something."

Robert wiped perspiration from his face with a handkerchief. "Seems like she should take the next packet to New Haven and hire a lawyer."

"That's the last thing I picture her doing. She'd never leave those people she's caring for. Did I tell you Caleb had planned to move here eventually? He knew how important her charity work was." She put the fan down, muttering that it was useless.

"Anyway, she doesn't know anyone there. She hasn't even met his relatives, and she definitely has no head for legal entanglements."

Robert gave a grunt and nodded. "On second thought, there might not be any lawyers in New Haven. It's only half the size of Boston."

"Too bad Caleb wasn't from here." Sarah covered a yawn with the back of her hand. "I might've been able to handle it myself. I've recorded a number of wills. I even settled an estate by myself, once. It wasn't a very complicated one, but . . . ."

These words were like a seed planted in her mind. She did not hear Robert's reply or notice when he eventually dozed off. She would have to make some inquiries. There would be details to take care of. But it might work.

First she had to get Caleb in the ground.

✤

She dozed only fitfully during the night and was awake at daybreak. After preparing her family's breakfast, she went to ask the gravedigger about the burial time and the sexton about the hour to toll the bell. She arranged for the bier and pall cloth to be sent from the meetinghouse and purchased the mourning gloves for the bearers and black crepe for shawls and armbands for the mourners.

All the while she went about these affairs, the idea to go to New Haven grew in her mind. By the time the small group of mourners had committed the remains of Caleb Trowbridge to the earth and was walking home, Sarah's plan was complete. She would begin its cultivation on the morrow.

Tuesday, September 12

There was another customer in John Hayward's shop when Sarah entered. Once he had been served, she could make her inquiries in private. She hung back by the door, pretending to read the broadsheets from England and shipping schedules tacked to the walls. Finally she had the postal agent to herself.

"I've come for information about overland travel to New Haven," she said. "If one weren't disposed to travel by packet, what alternative would be possible?"

"Uh, the western post riders go there twice a month. They're commissioned to, uh, to escort travellers. Few gentlemen choose to go that way, though. Riding to, uh, New Haven's more a punishment than a journey."

He spoke so slowly that she nodded at each piece of information, trying to encourage him to press on.

"What do you know about accommodations?" she asked.

"Uh, nothing, except they have regular stops where they pass the mail to the, uh, next rider or eat or sleep."

"How long does it take?"

"This time of year? Uh, anywhere from four to six days depending on the weather and rivers."

Just the mention of water made her shiver. "What are the departure dates?"

He picked up a stack of letters and began tying them in a bundle with a string. "Uh, the first and third Mondays. And they leave New Haven for Boston on the second and, uh, fourth. But tell the gentleman I really don't, uh, recommend travelling by land. Too long, too taxing and too dangerous."

"If I return with a letter to my cousin in Charles Town, is there someone who can take it across today?"

He nodded. "Long as it's here before three."

"And I've brought a letter for New Haven. What's the quickest way to send it?"

"A packet ought to be, uh, sailing tomorrow. That'll probably be quicker than the, uh, post."

"I'll be back with the letter for Charles Town," she said, and she handed him the letter containing the news of Caleb's death. It was addressed to Thomas Trowbridge, New Haven.

Thursday, September 14

Sarah shifted on the seat at her writing desk. The customer in the stationery shop she kept in the front room of her house was dictating a letter of complaint to a shipping agent in Jamaica and had reached the point where he was sputtering. When one bead of spittle landed alarmingly close to the writing paper, Sarah moved away slightly. No wonder his face was red. He had long ago outgrown his collar, and his neck and head were all one, like a large squash.

Something caught her attention through the window above her desk. Her cousin Robert was coming up what the neighbors had agreed to call Moon Street. She was not surprised; she had expected he would come in person.

She turned to her customer. "A brief protest is more effective. If one goes on too long the recipient loses interest. We have the main points here." She took the customer's arm, so he rose from the chair. "I'll write a closing and take it to the post for you." She had him at the door by the time Robert entered. "Thank you so much. I'll collect from you later," she said and closed the door on the bewildered man.

Robert seemed to attend very carefully to the tail of his coat as he took a seat in the stationery. Then he cleared his throat and his Adam's apple popped up above his collar. "I know you," he said. "We've grown up like brother and sister. And so I know when you send me a note saying you're going to New Haven and need help, it'll be a struggle to dissuade you."

"You're entirely correct." She could not help smiling.

"Nonetheless, I seriously object to this adventure. A woman just doesn't board a horse and ride off to New Haven." He flung one arm in the general direction of Connecticut Colony. "Have you ever heard of such a thing?"

"No."

"Can you name a single woman who has even ridden past Dedham?"

"No, but the post rider does it twice a month, and I'm sure gentlemen have accompanied him before. So if no woman has, then I'll be the first."

He just stared at her.

"Care to come along?" She was careful not to smile.

"I would not. I'm expecting three ships to arrive within the month." He moved to the edge of his chair. "This is silly giving you excuses for something so ridiculous." He leapt up and began pacing. "People travel to New Haven by packet boat."

"Well I don't. I'm terrified of the water. Boats are out of the question."

"It's nearly two hundred miles. Two hundred."

Although he paused to gauge what effect this had, Sarah furnished him with no reaction. He was so dear in his attempt to be stern.

"Hire an agent to go there and act in her behalf," he said.

"The relatives could send an agent packing more easily than they could me. Besides, I'm capable of acting in her behalf. I've worked in probate and witnessed more wills than I can remember in the last seven years. You think I can't handle this?"

"I don't question your experience in public affairs at all. It's just—" He let out a long sigh and began deflating before Sarah's eyes. "Aren't you afraid of what might happen to you on such a journey? What if—"

"I've thought more about what might happen to everyone here. Boston's not such a safe place, you know. Mr. Corey was gone a fortnight and returned to find his family dead and a quarter of Boston burnt to the ground. And smallpox can arrive on a ship and sweep through here in a trice."

She began putting away her writing equipment. "At worst Mary could be imprisoned for debt, Robert. She's the one facing real danger, not me. A few days on a horse; how bad could it be?" Robert sighed again, which seemed to have left him empty because he collapsed into the chair the customer had occupied. "As I reckoned, you'll not be dissuaded."

"But you've done your cousinly duty in trying, and I thank you," Sarah said. "Now that's established, let's discuss the horse. Can you find me one?"

He stared at his boots. "I stable mine with Mr. Pemberton.

He has new horses on occasion. And Judge Sewell trades in horses from Narragansett, I believe." Then he looked up. "When was the last time you rode?"

"Before Father died. Fifteen years. I was a good rider. You used to compliment me, remember?"

He nodded. "You could probably still control a reasonable, well-trained horse. But the horse is the easy part. How are you going to present this plan to your mother and mine? And what about Elizabeth? You'll just wave to your daughter and ride off?" He marked his challenge with raised eyebrows.

Sarah had anticipated that convincing the family would be the most difficult part of the preparations. She had won over Robert. She would have her way with the others too. But it took some time for her and Robert to arrive at an adequate strategy.

Præparatio

Monday morning, October 2

When Sarah awoke on the day of her departure, her bedchamber was gray. The color looked like seven or seven-thirty. The sky she could see outside her window was also gray, the early gray when one could not tell whether the day would be overcast or clear. Where would she be sleeping that night? She rolled over and hugged her sleeping daughter, who for nearly all her fourteen years had shared the bed with her.

Yesterday one of Sarah's boarders said he once had to share a bed with a man who snored fiercely. Mr. More had said the Salem Ordinary had only one room for guests and only one bed. She wondered what a woman traveller was supposed to do in those circumstances because she had no intention of sharing a room, let alone a bed, with a stranger.

"Is it morning?" Elizabeth's voice came from beneath the featherbed.

"Yes, it is. Let's get the fire going and the chores finished. I want to be able to sit down and enjoy dinner before I leave."

The chill of the room made them hurry to dress and straighten the bedclothes, and their conversation and laughter carried upstairs, bringing down the three male boarders, Mary Trowbridge and Sarah's mother.

Sarah crossed the hallway, which divided the house from front to back, and she opened the door to the room that claimed the whole opposite side of the first floor. Everyone called it "the hall" because that was the name her father had brought from England. She met the accumulated smells of twenty years of family life: baking, pipe smoke, laundry roasted dry and the hot breath of long conversations. She opened the shutters of the window at the back of the room. A beam of sunlight struck the top of a sand-scrubbed, white pine table in the center of the kitchen area then settled in fragments on brass pots and pewter platters lined up on open shelves. She went to the fireplace and picked up a small shovel. An iron crane, hooks and trammels, three-legged skillets and long handled frying pans all hung in blackened silence, waiting. She scooped a heap of ashes aside, stirred the coals and watched them bring life back to the room again.

Her boarders, Mr. More and Mr. Corey, entered the room with their arms full of wood while Mr. Richardson helped Sarah with the fire.

Elizabeth squeezed between two wainscot chairs to open the shutters at the front of the house. She straightened some cushions on the settle and came back by the fireplace. She lit a lamp and put it in the center of the long dining table. It shone on the oak, which had been worn smooth by years of elbows.

"What's your weather report, Mr. More?" asked Sarah.

"You're going to have good weather." He and Mr. Corey stacked the firewood near the fireplace. "Frost the last few nights has firmed up the ground. That'll make it easier for the horses."

"I'm glad of that," Sarah said. "Did you hear about the horse that got stuck out near the ferry last week? The rider fell headlong into the mud, and it took ropes and planks and several men to rescue them. That's not the way I want to leave Boston."

With the fire revived and the milk heated, the boarders and Mrs. Kemble took their places at the table. Sarah waited with the milk pitcher because Elizabeth was still arranging chunks of leftover bread into seven porringers. All the chunks had to be crust down.

"Grandma and Mary just drop the bread in any which way," Elizabeth had whispered to her mother one day. "And it doesn't taste the same when you have to turn them over with the spoon, because then the tops have soaked up most of the milk."

That is why she hurried to help her mother in the morning, to make sure the bread got in the porringers in the right direction. Since Elizabeth's birth, Sarah had never been away from her. An ache spread through her whole chest.

The seven porringers were passed down the table. Spoons clanked and scraped, and there was the usual slurping. Sarah looked at her mother and then Mary. They were both subdued this morning and seemed overly occupied with their milk pudding. It was just as well that they were. Her mother did not want her to go. First she proposed that such a journey violated the behavior expected of Boston women. When that had failed, she objected on matters of physical hardship. Perhaps now she had given up, or maybe she was searching for a new tactic in the final hours.

Of course Mary was grateful that Sarah was trying to save her from ruin, but she also regretted being the cause of the contentious journey. Every time Mrs. Kemble mentioned another obstacle or danger, Mary sagged a bit more from the added weight to her burden of guilt.

The men pushed their chairs away from the table and offered Godspeed and a safe journey to Sarah before they left for the docks. She shook hands with each one.

Through the hallway door she saw them pass Mrs. Gridley, who was entering with food parcels precisely at eight, as she had done every weekday morning for the last five years. Her dependability as the cook and housekeeper was one of the items on the list Sarah had composed to justify leaving her home and business. Robert would come to serve her customers three mornings a week and Mary would start the fire and get breakfast every day. Elizabeth had her responsibilities too.

"I could watch the shop by myself," she had said the day before. "I could even make breakfast."

"You probably could," Sarah had said, "but Mary has to feel that she's doing something for me in return, and Aunt Hat would nattle Robert no end if he didn't come over here to tend the family. You'll just have to let all of them help you."

Every day Sarah had run through this list of who would do what, to reassure her mother that the household and Boston would continue to function for a few weeks without her. But

Sarah's list included some items she disclosed to no one. At the top was her desire for adventure. It prickled inside and sometimes made it impossible to sit still. She frequently had to force her attention back to the matter of the estate. There was also envy, which she readily admitted to herself. Whenever men returned to Boston with stories about cities they had visited around the world, Sarah hoarded the details in resentful silence. Now she could picture the admiring townspeople seeking her out to hear accounts of people and places beyond Boston.

"Morning, Madam. It's going to be a fine day." Mrs. Gridley had hung her cape on a peg near the kitchen door and was standing next to Sarah, looking at her.

"Good morning. Sorry, I was thinking about something."

Then the cook saw Elizabeth with her grandmother near the fireplace and said, "Morning, Mrs. Kemble. And how's my Lizzy this morning? Reading to Grandma? I see you got the men fed and off to work."

Elizabeth came to the kitchen worktable to greet the cook and inspect her food parcels.

Mrs. Gridley asked Sarah, "How many for dinner this afternoon?"

"Mother, Elizabeth, me, Aunt Hat, Robert . . . ," Sarah looked at Mary.

"I won't be home until supper time. I'm just leaving to sit with Mrs. Weatherby for the day."

"Her husband's still away, is he?" Mrs. Gridley dumped the oysters she had brought in a wash pail.

"I'm afraid so. And she's worse. She seldom wakes anymore."

How can she do that, Sarah asked herself. Mary was only twenty-five, had already lost four loved ones, and she could still go sit with people who were also going to die on her. Sometimes Elizabeth joined Mary in the afternoons. Elizabeth was more like Mary. They had tender hearts and concern for others. Sarah felt guilty knowing she usually thought about herself first. Well, at least she had a sense of humor and a generally pleasant disposition, and she knew everyone regarded her with affection. She hoped that this basic selfishness, which was so apparent to her, seemed to go unnoticed by others.

Mary finished tying her cape and hood. "What time are you leaving, Sarah?"

"At three. I have to meet the Providence post rider in Dedham. He gets there about four and spends the night." Sarah handed Mary her sewing bag. "Robert says it'll take us an hour to ride to Dedham. If we leave at three, he can see me there and return to Boston before dark."

"You'll pass by the Weatherbys', won't you? I want to see you aboard your horse." Mary gave her a hug. "Thank you again for taking this risk for me."

"Sh-h-h," Sarah whispered. "Don't get Mother started."

Mary leaned next to Sarah's ear. "I'll pray every hour for a safe journey. And tell Caleb's family I hope to meet them one day." Then she left on her charitable mission.

"Give Mrs. Gridley a hand," Sarah told Elizabeth. "Grandma and I have to pack my things."

Light filled the diamond panes of the bedchamber window. Draped over the arms of a tall chair was a large double saddlebag Robert had delivered yesterday. She lifted it off so her mother could sit down, then placed it across her lap. "One side's already full with my writing box and journal, so what I'll need for the next few weeks will have to fit in this other side." She unlatched it and looked in. "Guess I'll have to rely on charm and wit instead of a wardrobe."

Although her mother attempted a smile, Sarah saw defeat on her face. Her mother had never been able to curb her determination—not when she was a child and not now that she was thirty-eight. Her mother sat in silence, so Sarah tried to distract her while they packed.

Sarah went to her clothes chest. "I'll have to present myself in New Haven society in scarcely one change of clothes." She took out the seven items she hoped to fit in one side-pocket: an embroidered satin bodice her mother had made, a trimmed blouse that went under it, her warmest linen dressing gown and a pair of black kid dress-slippers. She had a roll of gauze for her monthly inconvenience. "At least I won't be travelling when that time comes. I'll be in New Haven by then." She also chose an extra pair of drawers and a pair of stockings. "Not much variety, is it?"

"You won't be there long enough to need any more. It's just for two weeks."

Her mother always did that. She would say something was so, thinking that would make it so. Sarah decided to divert the conversation toward her father's travels. "This reminds me of the times we packed for Father. I used to wish I could go with him. The first time he went to London, it seemed he was gone forever. I was much younger than Elizabeth, wasn't I?"

Mrs. Kemble nodded. Sarah detected a slight blush and knew why. When Father had returned from his first voyage, her mother had run out the front door to greet him. Sarah recalled waiting in the doorway, trying to remember the father she had not seen for nearly three years. In his elation he had embraced her mother, lifted and whirled her around, set her down and given her an affectionate pat on the bum as they entered the house.

Unfortunately this joyful reunion had occurred on the Sabbath and in view of the constable, who reported her father to the magistrates. She could still hear her father quoting their charges in a resounding voice whenever he had had too much rum. "Lewd and unseemly conduct in saluting his wife at the step of the door, on the Sabbath day, when he met her after three years' absence." They condemned him to stand two hours in the stocks for being happy to see his wife, and he, in turn, refused ever to set foot in another Sabbath meeting. She missed him.

She pressed down on the folded pile of clothing, and her eye measured with satisfaction the size of both the pile and one pocket of the saddlebag.

Then they heard the knocker at the front door.

"It's probably someone for the stationery," Mrs. Kemble said. "Go ahead. I can finish this myself."

When Sarah entered the hallway, she saw Elizabeth letting in Rosy Parker, who, upon first sight of Sarah at the other end, began her most subtle and ingenious method of inquiry.

"I only heard at meeting yesterday that you were departing on a journey today. When I told my husband, he said I should stop by the stationery first thing this morning to get additional supplies, since we don't know when you'll return."

Sarah had discovered long ago that Rosy's method was one of indirection. She never asked questions; she just made statements contrived to evoke a desired response. Whenever Sarah detected what information Rosy was after, she took delight in predicting Rosy's half of the conversation a second before Rosy spoke. Sometimes she would spare Rosy the difficulty of her elaborate ritual by providing her with a thorough account. But when she felt perverse, as she did now, she offered Rosy little nibbits, one at a time, and paused between them to watch Rosy plan her next move.

"I'll probably be away no more than a month, but you needn't worry about storing up paper or quills. I've arranged for my cousin to be here from nine to ten forenoon, three days a week, for my regular customers." She led the way into the stationery.

Elizabeth opened the curtains to let in some light. Sarah just stood and smiled at Rosy. She wanted Rosy to work for her information, so she waited for Rosy's next move.

"My husband said to me, 'I surely hope there's no tragedy calling her away so suddenly.'"

Sarah was intrigued by the constant movement of Rosy's

eyes. They swept and darted about, meticulously searching for a facial expression, a movement of a hand, or any other tiny detail that might augment whatever she managed to learn from her non-questions.

"No. No calamity. It's just that when my cousin Caleb died, he left properties and a business in New Haven, and he hadn't yet registered the will I drew up for him. That's why I'm going to New Haven—to settle the estate for Mary, before his family decides to do otherwise with it. Now what is it you've come for?"

"In that case, I'll just have half a ream of foolscap and a dozen blotting papers." But not to be diverted, Rosy pressed on. "My husband said, 'There's no ship sailing tomorrow. How could she possibly go on a journey tomorrow? You must've got it all wrong,' he said to me."

Now Sarah watched Rosy's face to see what reaction her next nibbit would produce. "I'm going on horseback."

Sarah was triumphant. She rendered Rosy unable to control her bulging eyes and drooping mouth. Behind her, Sarah heard Elizabeth giggle then quickly try to disguise it by rustling in the paper cabinet.

Rosy only managed to repeat, "On horseback!" Then slightly recovering, she continued. "I—well, I don't know how one rides off into the forest and expects to find New Haven."

"I don't need to find New Haven. The post rider directs travellers. I just follow his horse." Sarah took the paper from Elizabeth and handed it to Rosy. "Here you are." She gestured toward the stationery door to indicate Rosy should leave.

Rosy seized her last opportunity to comprehend Sarah's

incredible plan. "But, it must—it must take days and days. I should be terrified to sleep at night in the forest where Lucifer and all the beasts are bedded."

"It's only four days' ride, and there's no reason to sleep in the forest. Post riders know the best taverns for baiting and lodging." Sarah led Rosy into the hallway and opened the front door. "But when I return, I'll be able to tell you more."

Rosy gave Sarah a final stare. "May God be with you." Then she bustled off to report her findings to her husband.

Back in the stationery Elizabeth was wiping the dust off a small glass case, which contained a display of ink pots, quills and pen knives.

"Poor Mrs. Parker." Elizabeth laughed. "You gave her such a shock that she was speechless."

"When she gathers her wits about her she'll be back. I bet she'll come once a week to investigate." She looked around. "Where are the books Robert's to help you with?"

Elizabeth pointed to one of the three small writing tables arranged near the fireplace, opposite the stationery door. "I put them there so he can listen to my lessons when there aren't any customers."

The two of them sat and talked about Elizabeth's history and French lessons and about the Odyssey, which she had just finished. When the clock on the mantelpiece struck noon, Sarah got up. "Robert and Aunt Hat will be here soon." She went to the mantel, fingered for a key under the clock, then inserted it into a tiny square above the six. "You'll remember to wind it for me every other day?"

Elizabeth nodded as she placed markers in her books and pushed them to the corner of the table.

"We should see if Mrs. Gridley needs help," Sarah said, "but first I have a gift for you." She removed a book from a cabinet and handed it to Elizabeth, who opened the unmarked cover to find empty pages. She let the gold-edged leaves brush past her thumb.

"A journal book like you have." She sounded delighted.

"I was hoping you'd keep a journal while I'm away."

"It won't be as interesting as yours," Elizabeth said.

"Of course it will. You know how I don't like to miss anything that's going on around here. Whatever you write will interest me," Sarah said.

Elizabeth gave her a hug.

"Go ahead to the kitchen. I'll be there as soon as I mark the Parkers' account and tidy up."

Sarah went to her desk and removed the cap from the inkwell. She made the entry in her ledger and left it in the center of the desk where Robert would find it. Then she replaced the cap and put all the articles for recording legal documents in a drawer, out of his way.

While straightening the chairs at the writing tables, Sarah noticed a dried spot of ink left by one of the young children who had recently come for a writing lesson. She wet her thumb and rubbed it off.

Sarah pulled the curtains, stood in the doorway to take a last look at her favorite room, which she had so carefully furnished to conduct her several enterprises, then closed the door.

She was in the hallway when Robert called from outside. The household hurried to the door, where they saw a procession approaching. A group of children was skipping alongside Robert. He was leading two horses. In his left hand he held the reins of his mare, in the other were the reins of an enormous sorrel horse. Atop that horse, wrapped in courage and a black cloak, sat Aunt Hat. The commotion arrived at the front door.

Reaching the end of her tolerance for such attention, Aunt Hat said, "Set me down, Robert. I've been a spectacle long enough." He complied, and she withstood the embraces and commendations from everyone.

Then Robert turned to Sarah, patted the horse's flank and said. "Madam Knight, may I present your travelling companion."

"She's a beautiful color." Sarah stood back to take a better look. "I hope she's got a good nature."

"She hasn't complained so far," Aunt Hat said.

"I'd hate to have a difference of opinion," Sarah said. "She's so big."

"I'm assured she's very gentle," Robert said. "Is dinner ready?"

"It is," Mrs. Gridley said. "Come inside."

They went in, everyone talking at the same time.

※

The meal began with oyster stew and talk of horses.

"It was really fortunate, my finding this horse," Robert explained. "Two of them just arrived in Charles Town last week. Some say the breed originally came from Spain. Andalusia. Now they're being bred in Narragansett and trained to pace. The broad backs are supposed to provide the smoothest ride. Do you agree, Mother?"

Aunt Hat wiped her chin. "Of course it was smooth, as slowly as we were walking. I can still feel the saddle, though." She shifted in her chair.

"You don't have the padding I do," Sarah told her aunt. "It looks like a new saddle."

"Almost," Robert said. "The trader's wife has used it. He said he'd buy it back when you return. He said he'd even buy back the horse if you haven't worn her out."

The conversation was interrupted when Mrs. Gridley entered the room with a large platter of roast pigeons, pumpkins and apples. She placed it in the center of the table and took some plates from the sideboard.

"I should take along Mrs. Gridley's instructions for roasting," Sarah said. "Not many people know how to roast fowl. In New Haven they probably stew everything in a pot." Sarah broke off a browned corner of pumpkin and ate it. "And who knows what sort of food there will be between here and there."

"Who knows if there'll be any food at all, Madam." Mrs. Gridley began filling the plates and passing them around the table. "You should let me pack enough food to keep you alive for four days."

"I've no place to put it. My saddlebags are full."

Mrs. Gridley shook her head disapprovingly.

"Look at me. You can see I'll be in no peril if I have to fast for four days. Anyway, the post has been delivering mail for a number of years now, so there must be ordinaries along the way where people eat."

Sarah was enjoying this last dinner with her family. Although she participated in the conversation about learning to ride, about relatives and acquaintances who had settled in New London and New Haven, and about whether the Trowbridges had received the letter telling of Caleb's death, she also felt detached from the gathering, as if she were off to the side of the room observing herself and the others, or as if she had already gone and were recalling each sound, smell and taste of home.

When the family had eaten the last of Mrs. Gridley's molasses cakes and dispensed the final praises and thanks, Robert took Elizabeth outside for her first horseback lesson. The women went to Sarah's room to help her dress for the departure.

※

As soon as Aunt Hat shut the door she began scolding. "I know you've made up your mind, but I just want you to know how exceedingly distressed I was when Robert told me about your plans." She stood in front of Sarah, who was taking off her chemise and slippers. "I couldn't very well say this in front of Elizabeth, but what about Indians? The war with Metacomet may be over, but there's still violence. A family was murdered not long ago in the Narragansett country."

Sarah said nothing. She put on the sleeveless, quilted

underbodice her mother handed her and tugged at the front hooks to close them over her ample midsection.

Her aunt continued. "You've read Mary Rowlandson's account of her captivity. Worse things than that have happened to some women. You're not worried about your safety?"

"I haven't spoken to any post riders myself," Sarah said, "but Mr. Hayward didn't say anything about anyone being molested by Indians."

Her mother gave her a pair of stockings and garters, then she added her protest. "The post road follows Indian paths for much of the way, Sarah. How could you not come in contact with them?"

"Problems arise with settlers, not travellers." Sarah rolled the stockings up her legs. "Of course, our good minister says Indian attacks are God's punishment for wearing periwigs. I should be safe enough, since I don't wear one." Her laughter failed to draw a smile from the older women. They shook their heads knowing their words were wasted.

Sarah stepped into a linen underskirt and pulled it up then tied a pair of pockets around her waist. To escape further protestations she hurriedly stuffed the pockets with a pile of coins, a bottle of lavender water in a shagreen case, a hairbrush with a carved wooden handle, a linen night cap and an embroidered handkerchief.

Sarah heard herself babbling about the rest of her wardrobe as she finished dressing.

"I decided to wear this brown kersey petticoat—the color of dust is practical, don't you think?" She picked up a brocade bodice. "Do you recognize my this, Aunt Hat? It's from the fabric Robert brought back from London."

Sarah jammed her arms into the full sleeves and hooked the front. She put on her French hood, tied the ends in a quick knot and grabbed her cloak.

"I appreciate your lining this with silk." Sarah fastened it at the neck and rattled on to her mother, "It'll be good and warm. So will these." She stuffed her winter mask and gloves into her muff and put the muff strap around her neck.

"I have to get my shoes by the fireplace and say good-bye to Mrs. Gridley," Sarah told the women. "Meet me out front. Robert should be back with Elizabeth by now."

Sarah crossed to the great room. She felt relief with a hallway and a pair of doors between herself and the disapproval of the two women.

Mrs. Gridley set down the stack of clean dishes when she saw Sarah all dressed. "Madam, you can surely fit this small brick of chocolate in somewhere. A hot drink after a cold ride will be just what you need."

"There's a little room left." Sarah opened the cloak and lifted her petticoat so Mrs. Gridley could place the neatly wrapped packet in the left pocket. She sat down to lace her shoes. "I'm grateful to you for so much. If it weren't for you, I couldn't go. And thanks for the wonderful dinner."

"Oh, Madam." Mrs. Gridley mopped her eyes with the corner of her apron. "May God be with you on your journey." When Sarah stood, Mrs. Gridley crushed her in a good-bye embrace.

Sarah stopped in the hallway to get the safeguard she had

left on a chest. It was not a proper one, made in the English fashion. Her mother had improvised with a large piece of gray rugging. Sarah had sat on the edge of the table, as she would sit on her saddle, and her mother had cut it so it would wrap completely around from Sarah's waist to her feet.

"The people in the woods between here and New Haven won't know if I'm wearing the latest riding habit or not," Sarah had told her mother. "I just need to keep dry and warm."

Sarah put the safeguard over her arm and opened the front door. She turned to look down the hallway. The doors to the lower rooms were all closed. Mrs. Gridley's cape hung on a hook, and Elizabeth's green brocade house slippers were below. Particles of dust floated in a slant of afternoon light coming from the doorway. She stepped outside and shut the door to her home.

Exitus

Monday afternoon, October 2

Elizabeth returned from her lesson with enthusiasm. "I love riding. I wish I could go with you. When you get back, may we keep her so I can ride again?"

Sarah saw the alarmed looks on the faces of her mother and aunt and decided to ignore the question altogether.

When Robert set Elizabeth down, the envious neighborhood children surrounded her. "I even thought of a name," she said. "How about Athena? She brought back Odysseus." She looked at her mother to see if she understood then added. "Like your journey. She'll bring you back."

"I like it. That's what we'll call her." Sarah thought a prompt departure would be best for everyone. "And you picked the name just in time because we need to leave."

The moment she put her arms around Elizabeth her eyes began to burn. "I'll miss you very much." Sarah tilted her head up because tears were filling her eyes, and she did not want them spilling over.

The two older women embraced her, each silently and tightly. Then she turned to Robert, who was pulling hard on the girth strap. That was how her throat felt.

"How are you going to get me up there?" she managed to ask.

"We'll use the mounting steps next door." He led the small crowd to the neighbors' house. Once aboard, Sarah placed her right knee over the pommel and arranged her skirts.

"Let me lower the stirrup slipper one notch. You're a bit taller than Elizabeth," Robert said. "Try that. Your heel has to be lower than the rest of your foot to maintain the pressure. Otherwise you'll topple off before we even get to the mill creek drawbridge."

When Robert went to get the saddlebags, he told the group of children to stand back. Sarah did not know what to say to the three faces staring up at her. She felt flushed as she gave her attention to pulling on her gloves. She adjusted the fingers, some more than others, and all of them more than necessary.

Robert returned with the saddlebags, and while he was securing them she gave equal attention to how the reins should loop around her hands.

"Lead the way," she said when he mounted his horse.

As the horses took their first steps south on Moon Street, she heard some of the children question Elizabeth.

"Why does your mother have to leave town?"

"Did she do something bad?"

"Where is she going?"

"You ever see her again?"

Sarah looked back.

Elizabeth watched her mother as she spoke. "My mother has chosen to go to New Haven on business. She'll be home in a few weeks."

Sarah had forced her daughter to defend her. She stifled the urge to cry, by holding her breath until they rounded the corner. Then she would no longer be able to see her aunt and mother holding each other. She would not hear their repeated God-bless-yous, and she would not see Elizabeth's eyes.

⁂

They joined the usual dust and noise in North Square, where most of the pedestrians and wagons were headed in the opposite direction after a day at the market. Sarah was disappointed not to see anyone she knew so she could wave good-bye.

Beyond the meetinghouse they turned onto Middle Street. Sarah was annoyed to be caught behind an empty firewood cart. The wheels on the new paving stones made a deafening clatter that echoed off the buildings lining the narrow street.

They had to stop at the mill creek drawbridge, where another cart was rumbling toward them. Then they waited for the knot of people detained behind it.

"I always feel fortunate if I arrive here at incoming tide." Robert glanced upstream toward the butchers' shacks. "The stench can be unbearable."

Sarah pulled Athena to a stop and stared at the rickety drawbridge. "I know, but I hate when the tide is high enough to wet the planks like this."

"Why are you so afraid of water? You don't even like to come to Charles Town on the ferry."

He asked the question she often thought about. "Do you remember one winter when we were small and two of my neighbors drowned? They fell through the ice while trying to cross the Charles on horseback."

Robert nodded.

"I didn't see it happen," she said. "But an older boy deliberately terrified me with his description of the horse. He said it screamed and thrashed for a long time after the people disappeared, and it made a big hole in the ice before it sank. For a long time after that, every time the boy saw me he would scream like the horse."

"How terrible."

"I saw when they brought the bodies, though. In the spring. They hauled them up Moon Street on a cart like that." She nodded backwards.

Robert looked over his shoulder at the creaking vehicle.

As the way cleared for them to cross the drawbridge, Sarah eyed the water. Her fear had increased over the years. She remembered her resentment toward the ocean early in her childhood. It had deprived her of her father's company for long periods. As she grew up, his descriptions of shark attacks, piracy, storms at sea and shipwrecks were stored away in her imagination.

She was still too unnerved to tell Robert about being at the docks recently, when a missing sailor had been pulled from the water. Clinging to the partially eaten flesh had been dozens of crabs that dropped off and dove to the bottom. Her memory of the body caused her to shudder in revulsion.

She had also seen crabs tear at the butchers' offal tossed into this creek on the outgoing tide. Every time she crossed this drawbridge, she looked into the water and knew they were down there.

Robert called back to her as he turned off Middle Street toward the town center. "Mary's up ahead."

Her cousin's widow waved from the Weatherbys' door. She came out and walked alongside them as they passed the small houses that were squeezed so close together they spilled over the street. "Your horse is beautiful. You look firmly attached. No problems so far?"

"We seem to getting along," Sarah said. "I don't know what will happen when we reach The Neck and can put on some speed. Elizabeth named her Athena."

"What an odd name." Mary gave no indication she knew what it meant. She stopped and shielded her eyes with her hand.

Robert called to her as they continued. "I should be back by seven with a report of her horsemanship."

"Godspeed, Sarah," Mary called. She waved again.

They passed through the dock square and entered Cornhill Street. She saw the town house ahead. Only a few country people and small merchants remained in the market area on the ground floor. They had been coming to the open gallery since before she was born. She looked up at the windows of the second floor and was again disappointed. There were no town officials who could see her departure.

They plodded alongside without speaking.

Near the covered outside stairway, at the far end of the

structure, stood a whipping post and stocks, like the one in which her father had been punished. Not in use at the moment, she observed. Her father's experience was not at all unusual. Nearly everyone she knew, women as well as men, managed to run afoul of the laws of either the town or the church sometime in their lives. There were so many that sooner or later one could not help being caught in some sort of trespass.

It was maddening to go so slowly, but there were fines for riding fast. They passed the other meetinghouses, Judge Sewell's new brick home, Wheeler's Pond and the common cow pasture, which they could smell before they actually got there.

Between Frog Lane and the fortified gate, the peninsula was the narrowest. Large numbers of seagulls squawked overhead, and she could hear more of them screeching in the tall phragmites that grew along both shores.

Robert stopped outside the gate. "Dedham's about six miles from here. We should put on hard to get you accustomed to the saddle. Be sure to keep your shoulders square ahead and your left knee pressed in."

"Take up the rear, where you can watch me," she said. "But not too close. I don't want you tromping over me if I fall off."

She snapped the reins and Athena broke into a pace. Sarah pressed her left heel down and her knee into the saddle skirt. Then she remembered her back and shoulders. She straightened her upper body, trying to maintain a centered position, but whenever she concentrated on one body part, the others did as they pleased. If she continued to joggle in the saddle like this, she would never make it to the end of The Neck, let alone New Haven.

Robert caught up to her. "Relax. Feel the rhythm of the horse. Listen to her feet." A few moments later he added, "Now let yourself join her rhythm."

When her various body parts coordinated their efforts, Sarah regained the confidence she had felt the last time she rode. She had come this way with her father when he ordered firewood. He had always boasted about how well she rode sidesaddle on her own mount.

But after she had married, Richard had said it was not proper for his wife to ride alone. He was going to put a pillion behind his saddle. She told him she would rather walk or stay home than sit on a pillion. There had not been much opportunity or necessity to go anywhere on horseback since she had married anyway. Most of Richard's unsuccessful business ventures had kept him out of Boston for long periods, so she had to busy herself at home with her various enterprises and with Elizabeth, her mother and the boarders.

Even now she was not sure where Richard was. In his last letter he said he was going to London to establish himself in shipping, but that was more than a year ago.

She wished he would write. It was easier to forgive his financial failures when he wrote nice letters. He knew how to charm her, and she knew when he was trying to. She did not mind being manipulated so much because that was the sign he was coming back. What bothered her most was the prospect of being known as an abandoned wife.

"We're near to Dedham," Robert called out. "If you don't slow down, you'll miss it."

"We're in Dedham already?" She realized how long she had been absorbed in her own thoughts and in the pleasure of riding. She was also aware of the tightness in her lower back and irritation where her right knee wrapped around the pommel.

Robert led her down a slight embankment and across Wigwam Creek, where the water was not deep enough to cover the largest stones. After a right turn at a road crossing, they arrived in the center of Dedham, which comprised only three buildings—the meetinghouse, the minister's house next to it and Fisher's Tavern. Sarah was to meet the post there.

In front of the tavern, next to a large wooden water tub, stood a pole with an iron ring. Robert dismounted and tied the reins to the ring. Sarah looked around and discovered why she was not relieved to reach her first destination.

"There aren't any horses here," she said.

He reached up to her. "Someone in the tavern is sure to know when the post is expected." He grunted as he lowered her to the ground.

Sarah centered her skirt with a tug and gave her cloak a shake to remove some dust. She followed Robert into the tavern. They stood in the doorway for a minute while their eyes adjusted to the dark room. The hostess approached them. Sarah thought she was carrying a small bundle until it leapt from her arms with a meow and ran to a far corner.

"Good afternoon, sir, madam," she said, brushing hair from her sleeves.

"We've come to meet the Providence post rider. They assured me in Boston that he'd be here mid-afternoon to meet the Hartford post." Sarah was aware that she had begun abruptly and was annoyed that her voice sounded slightly high-pitched and excited.

"Sometimes he comes in here, sometimes he don't," the hostess said. "There's no mail for him to pick up today anyway, and if he ain't got mail for Dedham and he meets the post going the other way, then he just passes on by here." She wiped the dust from a tabletop with her large, wrinkled hand and gestured for them to sit.

"What is it you suggest we do, then?" Robert asked.

"Have a sit and wait to see if he turns up. If he ain't here by six or seven, he ain't coming here at all. You hungry? You want some cider?"

"No thank you," Sarah replied. She was too disquieted to sit and said to Robert, "I want to go outside."

When he closed the tavern door, she took his arm. "Not an hour from home and a problem arises. Let's walk while we think."

"I'm sure he'll come." He took her arm. "I'll wait with you. If he's very late, I'll stay at the tavern and return to Boston in the morning. And if he doesn't come at all you can go home with me."

These words stung. It would be humiliating to ride back into Boston the day after she had said good-bye to everyone.

Sarah realized they were in front of the minister's house. "If Reverend Belcher's in, I'd rather wait here than in the tavern. Judge Sewell said if I saw him to tell him he's coming to Dedham to hear the Wednesday lecture and visit his daughter."

※

When Mrs. Belcher opened the door, Sarah recognized her from the last time the Reverend had lectured in Boston. She was wearing a plain black dress, but her cheerful face rendered the black incapable of solemnity. Even the close-fitting black cap, tied under her chin, failed to restrain several curls that had sprung out and bobbled when she spoke. She was as charming as Sarah had remembered.

"Please come in," she said, after Sarah explained the circumstances that brought her and Robert to the Belchers' doorstep. "The family's in the kitchen."

Mrs. Belcher served cake and cider. The couple listened with amazement at Sarah's proposed journey, but in the end they promised Robert they would assist Sarah. They even convinced him to depart at once so he might reach Boston before dark.

"I'll tell them at the tavern that you're waiting here and ask them to send a messenger when the post arrives." He embraced his cousin. "I can't believe I'm telling you good-bye. I don't know what to say." He reached for her hands and held them for a moment. "Have the safest of journeys," was all he could manage.

Sarah and Mrs. Belcher waited at the door until Robert emerged from the tavern, mounted his horse and waved. With his departure Sarah felt her final separation from Boston and a sense that she was really at the beginning of her journey—

except she could not proceed without a guide. Her hosts' conversation did not prevent her from growing more anxious.

About six o'clock a young man, who came from the tavern, confirmed Sarah's greatest fear. The post rider had not come. She was stranded.

The Belchers suggested she stay with them for the night. "Then on the morrow you can try to hire someone to accompany you to New Haven and back, instead of trying to keep pace with post riders from one stage to the next."

Sarah shook her head. "I don't think I could find an escort with enough experience. Post riders make the trip twice a month, so they know where they're going and where accommodations are. Besides, they're required to guide travellers." She thought for a moment. "Well they're required to, even though everyone keeps telling me no one travels that way."

To herself, however, she admitted her confidence in post riders was waning. In all her preparations she had never once thought the post rider would just not show up in Dedham. She refused to give up because the plans went amiss; she would just alter the plans. "Thanks for the offer, but I'd like to go to the tavern. Someone must know where else the post might have stopped."

"Then let me come with you and see what can be done," Mrs. Belcher said.

※

In the tavern, men were seated on stools and chairs near a large stone fireplace. Sarah must have been too preoccupied earlier to notice whether anyone had been there. The cat, apparently unperturbed by the noisy conversation, now napped alone on a settle by the fire. The low, rough-hewn beams that ran to the other end of the room were draped in smoke. There at the far side she saw a pewter apparatus for making malt liquor. Next to it was a high desk where the hostess was entering figures into an account book.

"Mrs. Foxe," called Mrs. Belcher, "we'd like to ask your help."

She put down her quill and approached them. "Evening, Mrs. Belcher. Madam. Sorry about the post."

"Mrs. Knight feels it's important to ride on and find him. Do you know where he might've stopped for the night?"

"Probably Billings' Tavern, in Stoughton. But it's nearly dark and that's twelve miles south of here."

Sarah looked at the men by the fireplace. "Is there someone I could hire to take me there?"

The hostess laughed. "Them? They've had their noses in their beer too long. My son, John, could ride you there." While she was pushing a couple of chairs back to a table, she must have figured out what a valuable offer she had just made. "But he wouldn't go out the door at this hour for less than three pieces of eight, what with the dark and the danger and all."

"Three pieces of eight! That's extortion!" Sarah said. "I could hire a guide to take me all the way to New Haven for three pieces of eight."

"Oh, no. Three it is." Mrs Foxe did not look the women in the eye. She began rearranging chairs around another table.

"He has to walk over to the field and catch his horse and saddle up. And he won't get back here before midnight. Besides, there's wolves out there. It's fearsome. Three. No less than three."

A man who had been watching the women from a doorway to the back of the tavern walked over to them and asked, "What you offering for me to guide you?"

"Are you John?" Sarah was surprised because the man appeared to be no younger than the elderly hostess.

"I am, for want of a better name." His enormous belly shook as a wheezing chuckle escaped his mouth.

"What price do you ask?"

"Half a piece of eight and a dram of rum."

Upon hearing his offer his mother glared at him and snorted.

"You shall have it with my gratitude," Sarah said.

"I'll be in front of the tavern in twenty minutes." He turned and walked away with his mother, who scolded him on behalf of his wife, for agreeing to such a price.

✤

When Sarah took leave of the Belchers, it was dusk. She waited next to her horse for her guide. How would an old man, who was shorter and heavier than she, manage to get her up on the saddle?

Foxe came leading a gaunt horse, which he tied to the ring. He found a wooden pail near the tavern entrance and upended it for Sarah to step on. But from there she was still too low to get her left foot in the stirrup or her right knee over the pommel. To her amazement her guide bent over and positioned his rump, which resembled an upturned pumpkin, against Athena's flank.

"Here you go, Ma'am. Just put your trotter on my backside and hop aboard."

Since he was bent away from her and wore a floppy, large-brimmed hat, she decided her modesty would not be compromised. She stepped onto his back. "I hope I'm not hurting you."

"I'm strong as a stone wall." He went to mount his swaybacked jade, over whose protruding bones were stretched the dirtiest hide she had ever seen.

Sarah settled onto the saddle and arranged herself. Several tender places reminded her of the earlier ride. Robert would be back in Boston by now, sitting with the family near the fire, while she was wandering from Dedham to Stoughton at night in search of a post rider. She recalled her last conversation with Rosy.

Sarah followed the bouncing pumpkin and his fencepost of a horse. They kept at a moderate pace along the cart path, splashing through several harmless brooks, until they were a couple of miles south of Fisher's Tavern. By then, tree branches were reaching up like feather dusters to brush away the last faint traces of daylight. She noticed that John's horse had slowed to a walk and wondered how the sad-looking thing was able to lift one tired foot after another.

John soon provided the explanation. "My horse, here, is a smart one. Knows it ain't good to travel fast after dark. Takes it nice and careful at night, she does. That way she don't stummle over no fallen limbs or such like." He paused for a moment of silence. Sarah supposed it was for her to appreciate his beast's intelligence.

"One night a young lad what lives near here was racin home and got throwed when his horse stummlt. Left a big dent in his forehead, and he ain't been right since. No ma'am, can't be too careful round here."

He went on to describe every accident and Indian incident, every mystery and crime that was reported to have occurred during his lifetime, and even before that, on the road they were travelling. Sarah suspected that night-vapors excited his imagination, and the tales which were billowing forth in the dark would lose their strength in the light of day.

"Now this here's the beginning of the swampland." The horses' hooves made sucking sounds in the muck, and the fog became so thick that there was nothing left of her guide but his voice, which Athena followed. The Voice expounded on all the animals that he and everyone else he knew thought they had seen in this swamp.

"Came upon the hugest snake I ever saw in here one day. Had the back half of a water rat stickin out his mouth. The front half he swallowed made this great big bulge in his neck."

Every few paces they disturbed some animal. One made great protests and thrashed away in the tall weeds. Sarah felt the skin under her hood crawl. "What's that?"

"Makes enough noise to be a bear, but I ain't really seen a bear since I was a kid, so it's probly just an old fox. Magine he was tryin to sneak up on a heron or somepin. Must be mad at us for chasin his supper away." While his reply to this and other queries increased her alarm, hearing his lengthy descriptions of venom, teeth and claws were better than hearing no voice at all in such an ominous place.

After an hour's ride they emerged from the mist. Her learned guide motioned toward the left where Sarah saw a faint light an indeterminate distance away.

"Now over there you have the last farmhouse fore Wolomolopoag Pond and the tavern. Not a lucky place, that one is. In seventy-six the rigional house was burnt to the ground and all the occupants was killt. That's when Metacom's men came through here, burnin their way to Medfield. But the old Indian never touched the tavern. He was friendly with the elder Mr. Billings."

"Then in eighty-five, almost on this very spot, lightnin struck and killt two peoples on horseback. The horse, too. They say if you pass by here in a storm, you can still smell burnt horsehide ahanging in the air."

The thought disgusted Sarah. She searched ahead in the darkness for sight of the tavern where she would be relieved of this Professor Sylvanus, who, she supposed, was now silent out of respect for the terrible ground upon which they trod.

Without the distraction of his lecture, she became aware of her aching back and sore legs. For all the disarrangement and discomfort of this first day, and only half a day at that, she was not sure how she would react if there was no post rider at Billings' Tavern either. Then what would she do? She did not have the strength to search any farther. If she must abandon her plans to travel to New Haven, she most certainly did not want to spend two more hours retracing her steps with friend John. But if she stayed overnight at Billings', how would she get home?

Her speculations were interrupted by John's announcement that the tavern was just ahead. She first saw three dim squares of light, then the dark figure of a building against the evening sky.

They rode up to a wooden post near the door. John slid down from his horse. He tied the reins, placed a set of mounting steps below Sarah's feet, then stood slapping his hat against his leg while she had to dismount and contend with her unsteady legs herself.

"Go on in." John pointed toward the tavern door. "I'll water the horses." Then he walked away.

Sarah stepped into the public room and found only a dying fire to greet her. She gave a hello. Presently a young woman appeared and gaped at the sight of a lone woman in riding clothes. This made Sarah feel quite a spectacle. Before she could offer an explanation of what she realized must have been an unprecedented occurrence, the young woman set forth with one question after another.

"Law for me, what are you doing here this time of night? I never seen a woman on the road so dreadful late. Who are you? Where are you going? You're alone?"

John's entrance interrupted the barrage. "Good evenin, Zipporah." He nodded, drew a stool to the fire, turned his back to the inquisitress and took out his tobacco and pipe.

"Lawfull heart, John. Is it you? How d'ye do," she brayed.

"Where in the world are you going with this woman? Who is she?"

John sucked on his pipe and ignored her.

She turned back to Sarah. "What are you doing out in the Devil's darkness? Where did you come from?"

"This is rude treatment, indeed," Sarah interrupted. She drew herself up to the fullest measure of preeminence her small stature provided. "With great difficulty, I've come from Boston looking for the Providence post, whom I wish to accompany tomorrow, and you've not offered me so much as a chair or an opportunity to ask if he's here."

"He's gone upstairs to sleep." The unchastened hostess placed her hand on a chair, posed for Sarah to notice half an armful of clinking bracelets, then she pulled it out for Sarah.

Sarah took the seat, much relieved that she had found her post rider. "My guide will have a dram of rum before he goes." She removed her gloves and untied her cloak while Zipporah clattered off.

"The silly creature thinks to impress me with her bangled arm," she said to John's back. "A new nose-ring in her grandma's pig would affect me as much."

He gave no response.

She lifted her petticoat and removed a coin from her pocket to settle the contract with John. He said he would unsaddle her horse and bring in the saddlebags before he left.

Zipporah returned with John's drink and set it down, rattling her bracelets. Then she came and stood near Sarah and looked her up and down unabashedly.

Sarah felt cross because she was exhausted. She had no patience for an unmannerly hostess. "Where am I to sleep?" she asked.

With a flutter of her jeweled arm, the maiden indicated a doorway at the other end of the room. She lighted a lamp and led Sarah into a small lean-to attached to the back of the tavern.

The yellow glow revealed a windowless room, half-filled with a bed on high posts. Under it rested a white chamber pot with a cracked lid. The young hostess left the lamp on a narrow table and returned with the saddlebags. Sarah told her to knock when the post rider came down.

She lowered herself onto a chair, whose seat had more hole than cane to it, and untied her shoes. Each one clunked on the floor. She unbuttoned her bodice but did not remove it. Then she pulled out the journal and writing box from her saddlebag. She had resolved to write every night before retiring and did manage a few lines. She stared at them. Why was she doing this? She put her pen away and capped the ink pot. The rest had to wait. Maybe she could wake up before everyone else and do it in the morning.

A brief toilette was all she could manage. Then she stepped on the rim of the chair seat to climb onto the bed. Still in her bodice and underskirt she stretched out her tired limbs and lay back on a sad-colored pillow. What was she doing here?

Tears escaped from her closed eyes. This had not been the day she had imagined.

Via Providentiæ

Tuesday, October 3

There was a scrape of metal. Sarah opened her eyes and looked toward the dim light coming through the doorway into the public room. The scraping... it was probably that saucy girl stirring up the fire with a coal rake. What time must it be? There were no voices. At the thought of the post rider she sat up and bumped her head on a rafter. Her back was sore, so she twisted and stretched toward her toes before climbing down from her perch. Her foot struck the chamber pot and the lid clattered on the wooden floor. Missy appeared at the doorway with a candle.

"You'd best light the lamp before I destroy this wretched little room or myself," Sarah said. "What time is it? Is the post rider about yet?"

"It's half past six. He asked to be called at seven. I'm just getting the fire started. When the water's het I'll fill you a basin." Zipporah returned to the public room.

The floor was so cold Sarah laced up her shoes before beginning her toilette. She brushed her hair back into a bun, secured it with hairpins and put on her cap.

It took some shifting on the bottomless chair to find a spot on her rear that did not hurt. She read the few words written in her journal the night before then dipped the quill and continued with her experiences at the tavern in Dedham.

. . . tyed by the Lipps to a pewter engine.

She was very pleased with this description of the men who were too drunk to help. Her quill scratched as she told about the quarrelsome madam who tried to negotiate the outrageous amount for her son's services as a guide.

Madam held forth at that rate for so long, that I began to fear that I was got among the Quaking tribe, beleeving not a Limbertong'd sister among them could outdo her.

She decided to compare John with Parismus and the Knight of the Oracle.

I didn't know but I had mett wth a Prince disguis'd, she wrote. *But nothing dismay'd John: Hee had encountered a thousand and a thousand such Swamps, having a Universall Knowledge in the woods; and readily Answered all my inquiries wch were not a few.*

Zipporah entered with a copper kettle and filled a small basin on the table. "You can come write by the fire if you want to. I'm fixing breakfast, and no one else is ris."

"Thank you. Have you a towel?" Sarah asked.

Zipporah stared with her mouth open for a moment. She set down the kettle, handed Sarah the cloth that had been wrapped around the handle, picked up the kettle with the corner of her apron and left. Sarah looked at the towel, which seemed to be clean.

❧

At a table near the fireplace Sarah sat with her back to the girl, hoping to discourage her from resuming her interrogation. Dipping and scratching with the quill, Sarah took delight in recounting her arrival at Billings', while its hostess, unaware she was the subject of Sarah's entry, rattled about behind her. Encouraged by Zipporah's presence, Sarah felt each new line was wittier and sharper than the last. She finished then read the entire account of her first day. It pleased her very much.

She looked up when heavy clumping came down the stairs. A man, younger than she, entered the public room wearing boots up to his knees and a greatcoat down to his ankles.

"Does all the clattering mean breakfast's ready?" His smile was not inconvenienced by many teeth. "I might could get an early start, for once, and beat the western post to Attleboro."

"Wouldn't count on that," Zipporah answered. She waved a spoon at Sarah. "This lady came in last night and wants a guide for her journey."

"You're the post rider?" Sarah knew she was not successful in disguising her disappointment at his confirmation of the fact. Her image had been of a gentleman, older than she, who wore a uniform that befit his royal appointment. In the years since Charles II's orders, had some standard not developed? Now the Queen's post was carried by toothless youths in their grandfathers' clothes. Sarah saw he was no less disappointed. He seemed to be calculating how much difficulty she would cause.

She wanted to prevent another inquisition. "I'm on my way to New Haven. I'm sure I'll be no burden. I have a good

Narragansett pacer. And I'll pay for your drink and board." Then in case he was susceptible to sympathetic appeals she added, "My dear cousin has died and I am making this sorrowful journey to help the family settle his estate."

Zipporah placed bowls and mugs before them. They busied themselves with eating and exchanging comments.

"Is the Narragansett a lively one?"

"Oh yes," she confirmed.

He took a long drink from his mug. "I certainly hope so because there's five hours of hard riding to the next stage." He scraped the bottom of his bowl then sucked on his spoon. "You ready to leave immediately?"

"Yes, and would you be so kind as to help me with my saddle and saddlebags?" She hurried to deposit her writing materials in one of the pockets and put on her outer clothing. While he brought the horses around, she settled her account with the hostess and was in the saddle and on the road before she had time to speculate on what the day might bring.

※

Sunrise revealed land that was flat and unremarkable. The post rider kept a fast pace, but he often looked back. When they had first left, she felt every sore place from the previous day. Then she loosened up a bit.

The ride provided plenty of opportunity for contemplation. Sarah frequently pictured what must be happening in her household at the moment she was thinking of it—Elizabeth reading her lessons in the stationery at mid-morning, Mrs. Gridley calling everyone to the table at noon, Mother dozing in her chair after the meal. As the pain in her back increased, she even considered what she would be doing there, had she not got this torturous idea into her head.

After several hours she was tired and growing more occupied with every part of her body that hurt. When they slowed to pass through a marshy area that bordered a large pond, her discomfort was so great she was compelled to suggest a stop. He looked for someplace she might dismount and eventually headed toward an embankment at the pond. The horses stood knee-deep in water at the point where she could step onto the ground. She groaned and rubbed as many aching places as she could reach.

"More difficult than you imagined, eh?" His toothless grin annoyed her immensely.

She shot out an angry finger in the direction of her horse. "Set yourself on a horse sideways, screw your body half way round, hang on with one knee and see how you fare after half a day's trot." Her face was hot.

He turned to watch the horses drink. "It's less than an hour's ride to the stage where we bait. If the New Haven post hasn't arrived, you'll get a rest there. Must say, though, this has been the easy part. There's yet again as far to go afore the next tavern, and you'll be crossing one river after another."

She could not see his face to tell if he were pleased about imparting this bit of unwelcome news, but she knew hers must look grim upon hearing it.

✤

The Attleboro tavern rudely presented itself when they

came around a wooded curve in the road. Sarah eyed it while her guide fetched the mounting steps. It was small, of weather-cracked wood, with windows so tiny they could not be of much use, and it was surrounded by trampled dirt. A narrow chimney reluctantly issued pinches of smoke. "It would have been better to arrive here at night too," she grumbled aloud to herself.

After her eyes adjusted to the dark room, she found the inside just as inhospitable—a single table with no lamp, one rough-cut bench beside it and the backsides of two people at the fireplace. When her young escort entered, he called a name she did not understand and one of the figures turned. She learned, with disappointment, that he was her next guide, already arrived and eager to depart after they ate.

Her new guide was more than disappointed, however. "She's not coming with me. I'm not poking along with a nagging lady at my back."

"I didn't say she nags. She complained a bit. She's not even that slow. Took me only three-quarters of an hour longer than usual. Made just one stop the whole way."

"But it's after two," the older one said. "I have to reach Havens' tonight. That's twenty-two miles and three river crossings. How do you think she'll take to bobbing across the Providence River?"

Several times they glanced her way and pointed but never addressed her. She had never heard anyone say such things about her before. Without acknowledging Sarah's presence, the hostess put three bowls on the table, motioned for them to sit and returned to her pots at the fireplace.

The older man continued growling. "Take her back home where she belongs. I never heard of such a thing as a lady wandering off to New Haven alone."

Her young guide pulled a knife from his boot. "I'm headed for Bristol. I won't be back through here until next week." He sawed off the end of a loaf of coarse Indian bread, stabbed it, then passed it to Sarah on the end of the blade.

"Well, you're not leaving her here," croaked the hostess as she set a large bowl on the table.

"What's this?" demanded the older post rider.

"Pork and red cabbage." She returned with a twisted white mass on a board and tugged at it. "I'm not feeding anyone for a week."

Sarah stared at the heap of meat, bone and cabbage that sat in a purple sauce, shiny with grease. She would rather ride home alone than remain here for a week and eat from someone's dye kettle. The woman kneaded and tugged at the white cable. Perhaps it was dough. When it reached a softer capacity, she placed a wad in each dish and covered it with the purple concoction.

The hostess continued her scolding. "Your charge is to escort travellers. It don't say, 'Escort men who ride fast and don't complain.' It says 'travellers.'" The brim of the woman's bonnet extended four inches, and with a large bow concealing her chin, the woman's face was only visible when she lifted her head and looked directly at someone. "Quit your blustering and escort the traveller. That's what you get paid for," came the voice from inside the bonnet. She banged three wooden spoons on the table and left the three of them to gnaw on the meal in silence.

Sarah poked at the food on the plate, tasted a bit of the cabbage and decided it was safe to swallow. Avoiding the meat and the mysterious wad in the bottom of the dish, she lifted each spoonful of cabbage and tilted it to drain off the greasy sauce. Half-a-dozen bites were enough, though.

She rose from the table with painful effort, stifled a groan, put some coins on the table to pay for the meal and went outside.

The sunlight did little to brighten her spirits. Sarah assessed the toll this adventure had taken on her body so far. The backs of her upper arms were sore. She had chafed hands, but gloves had prevented blisters from the reins. Her entire lower back and buttocks ached, and there was a shooting pain between her shoulder blades and neck. Her calf muscle was strained from pressing her heel down in the stirrup. Of particular concern was the raw feeling inside her right knee where it went around the pommel. She dug in the saddlebag for the roll of gauze. She could wrap her knee; that would prevent a blister, if there were not one already.

In the confinement of the outhouse Sarah struggled with the layers of clothing. Even if there had been enough light to see, it was not possible to bend over to examine the back of her knee, so she secured the gauze around the tender spot, quickly finished her affairs and quit the unpleasant place.

Sarah had been so self-absorbed that she had not given any thought to the condition of her mount. Robert had given no instructions, and she knew nothing about caring for a horse whilst on a long journey. So far Athena's care had been left to the escorts. They had done whatever one does with a horse. And what would that be? Some food and water? Taking off the saddle and putting it back on again? Did horses get sore spots? Sarah leaned against the warm neck and stroked it while waiting for the riders. She wondered what the hostess' tirade had accomplished.

When the two men emerged from the tavern, Sarah had already fetched the steps, rolled and tied the safeguard to the back of the saddle, it being unnecessary in the mid-afternoon sun, and was seated with all her tender and aching spots in place. She and Athena were at the ready as a final precaution against being left behind.

The men finished with the outhouse and walked toward her, fumbling with the buttons on their pants. The younger post rider swung up on his horse, gave a couple of clucks with his tongue and rode away, without a word, in the direction she assumed was Bristol. That left her with the older rider, who now sat in his saddle, staring at her while struggling to dislodge a bit of supper from between two molars. He wiped grease from his beard with the sleeve of his coat.

"You'd better keep up." He snapped the reins and his lithe, black horse galloped off.

Sarah urged Athena on but discovered that her graceful, steady gate was not nearly fast enough. The narrow, black rump and the slight figure with flapping elbows grew smaller as the distance between them increased. It was fortunate that the Attleboro terrain was flat and the path was straight so she could keep them in sight.

After a quarter-of-an-hour she noticed the post rider had stopped ahead near a couple of small buildings at the edge of a river. A ferry was tied to two trees. A man and a young boy came out of the nearest building and went to the ferry, which was open at both ends, had railings on the sides and was large enough to accommodate a horse and wagon.

The post rider dismounted, came to her and reached for the reins. "You stay up there. He's got no mounting steps to get you down." Then he led Athena up a ramp and tied the reins to one railing.

Panic stirred in Sarah. "What if my horse is frightened and rears up? I could be tossed off into the river."

He ignored her and sucked his teeth with his tongue, still struggling with the pork.

She tried again. "I'd really feel more comfortable standing down on the deck."

Without a glance in her direction he went to fetch his horse, tied him to the other side, leaned on the railing and stared out toward the far bank.

The ferryman's son untied the ropes, tossed them on board and scrambled up the ramp. They both pulled the ramp onto the ferry, and each one began working a scull. The river was wide and slow-moving. Sarah guessed from the color that it was deep.

The ferry ride was smooth and Athena was still, but Sarah was so uncomfortable on her perch high above the water that she held tightly onto the pommel. She kept quiet, as well. The scolding she had in mind might cause him to abandon her altogether.

"What will the tide be at Weybosset Neck?" the post rider asked.

"Should be about half tide and going out," the sculler replied.

"The lady'll appreciate being high and dry on a ferry when her horse is paddling across the next ford."

The men laughed.

This piece of news kept her imagination occupied long after reaching the far bank.

They rode hard again. The cabbage Sarah had eaten earlier now served as her cud for the afternoon. The post rider kept well ahead on the road, which skirted a great swamp. Indignant geese and ducks rose from the marsh grass and squawked their complaints.

On the right, beyond a burying ground, appeared a river—a narrow one, she was relieved to note. She could tell that the post rider had slowed. They passed a couple of taverns and mills, a meetinghouse, then a small gaol with stocks. It must be Providence.

Just when she decided that fording the river here did not look as frightening as the post rider had suggested, and that he had tried to alarm her and have a laugh at her expense, the river widened. The farther south they rode the farther away they got from the opposite bank. Surely he did not intend to have the horses swim across at the widest point. She wanted to shout at him to stop, but he was beyond the reach of her voice.

The path became the town street, which was busy with the end of the day's activities. It curved to the southeast. When she rounded it, she found the river narrowed again, bringing the opposite bank within sixty yards of where her guide was waiting.

"You're lucky the tide's no higher than your horse's chest," he said.

Sarah's stared at the rapid current, which carried leaves and bits of refuse past them. "I can't do it," was all she said.

"Come on Missis. We got a long ways to go before we stop for the night. We can't draw rein at each river cause you get the flutters. There's rivers and streams ever half mile or so from here to New Haven. I've rode across here twice a month for leven years. Don't you see me sitting here as proof?"

But Sarah's eyes were fixed on the swirling water, which flashed golden white from the reflection of the late afternoon sun, and she never noticed he had jumped down with a mumbled curse and stomped off toward a nearby house.

"I can't do it," she repeated to no one.

He returned with a young lad, who carried a paddle and some mounting steps. "Come on down from there and get in his canoe," her guide ordered. "But don't think they'll be one of these ever time we come to a riverbank."

She disengaged her right leg from the pommel and slid onto the steps unassisted. The boy had pulled a small dugout canoe from the weeds and pushed it partially into the water. He steadied her as she got in and lowered herself onto a doubtful-looking slat that served as a seat. The craft wobbled when he pushed off and hopped in.

The boy's paddle sliced the water with deep, quick strokes. Sarah grabbed the gunwales, which were so low to the water that her fingers got wet. She dared not speak, nor move her tongue, nor move her eyes for fear she would upset them. Her canoeist, however, worked his tongue from one corner of his mouth to the other with each stroke. She prayed to God, whom she was unaccustomed to entreating, for their safe passage.

Her guide rode across, leading Athena. When the outgoing tide churned around the horses' bellies, the post rider held his feet out to keep them dry. He was correct about the depth though. Only her slipper stirrup was below water.

The canoe bumped onto the shore, and the lad stepped out to pull it part way out of the water. When Sarah let go of the gunwales, she could hardly straighten her aching fingers. She leapt from the canoe and started running away from the water's edge before her fear subsided and she could stop herself.

While the lad waited for her guide to ford the water, Sarah retrieved a coin from her pocket.

"Right generous of you, ma'am. Sorry there aren't any mounting steps on this side. I'll give you a leg up." He locked his hands together and explained how she should step onto them with her left foot. With some misgivings regarding the lad's strength, but nothing else to stand on, she availed herself of his kind service.

"I do apologize," she said, when she saw the mud her shoe had left in the palms of his hands.

He gave them a shake. "I can wash them in the river. I never saw a lady travelling by herself before. Where are you going?"

The post rider answered for her with great impatience. "She's going to New Haven, but we've got fourteen miles to go before we stop for the night."

The young canoeist just whistled. His amazement compelled her to ask her guide about the rest of the road.

"Some of the way's even, some's woods and hills. And we ride through one river that's so fierce sometimes a horse can hardly stem it." He gave his horse a kick and added, "And there's no canoe."

She knew he said this just to torment her, but he rode off without waiting to relish the effect it had. She nudged Athena in the side. Black scenarios kept pace with her horse... Athena stumbles on a boulder in the river... she falls into the water... the post rider, far ahead, finally discovers her riderless horse... she is swept out with the tide... or she falls from the saddle with her foot trapped in the stirrup... she hangs upside-down from the side of her horse, her submerged head dashes against the rocks of the riverbed.

Her teeth were set hard, and waves of fear radiated from her chest into her neck and arms. If she fell in, would it be possible to swim or struggle to shore when all her clothes were wet? What would it feel like to have cold water flood her lungs? Would it kill her suddenly or would she struggle and suffer?

When Sarah discovered she was holding her breath, she tried to time her breathing in rhythm with Athena's steps, but shortly lost concentration. Would anyone find her body? If it washed out to sea, how long would it take for there to be no body left to find?

To force her runaway imagination to cease, she stared at the spot where the sun had just set. The glow through the phragmites and marsh bushes gradually expired, allowing the first stars to appear in the cloudless sky. Ahead, the post rider was nearly lost in the darkness. What was she to do now? Another nudge made Athena quicken her pace. The way was trodden to a cart's width. She hoped her horse could see this path and keep to it.

Riding on, Sarah focused only on the spangled sky. More than half an hour had passed since the ford at Weybosset Neck. The post rider would surely wait to help her. He had both times before. And if he had to wait, why did he ride so far ahead? Maliciousness, she decided. What angered her even more than his barbarous treatment was having to remain politely mute about it. She was preparing a withering reproof to deliver upon their arrival in New Haven when Athena slowed to a walk. A sudden whinny next to her made her jump and cry out.

"Scared you, did I? The Devil himself could sneak up on you in this darkness," the post rider said with a chuckle.

"Then I guess I should be grateful that you check on me every hour or so," she said with more sarcasm than was probably wise.

"Follow right behind me."

They entered a thicket of trees and shrubs that caught on her cloak. Athena shook her head and snorted. Sarah grabbed the pommel when she felt the little catch in the step that horses make when going down an incline. Then she heard her guide's horse splash in the water, followed by her own.

He stopped. "This is the river I told you about."

"How deep is it? I can't even see where the other bank is. Are there rocks my horse might stumble on?" She strained forward in an attempt to see something. "I don't think I can do this."

"Tide's favorable, but you'll probably have to lift your leg and all them skirts. The bottom's gravel. Takes only a minute to t'other side. If you're coming across, I'll stay next to you upriver. If you're not, you'll have to find your own way back to Providence."

With no choice other than to proceed, Sarah gathered her clothing up with her left hand, gave rein to her horse with her right and went forward. It was too dark to determine the depth of the water, so she extended her stirrup foot in front of her. In that awkward position she rode as motionless as possible. She did not realize she was holding her breath until she gasped for air. The water slapped against the two horses, but they strode across without effort or complaint.

"Now you're in Narragansett country. It's wooded for several miles. Mind the branches."

"How am I to know the way when you're so far ahead?" Her voice sounded high and thin, like a little girl.

"It's a narrow path. Your horse will keep to it."

"And how much farther to the ordinary?"

"Eight miles. About an hour's ride."

Athena followed the receding form. When the first low branch smacked Sarah, she bent forward behind her horse's head and was reminded of the soreness in her back. Soon her right leg fell asleep so she sat up, but another low branch greeted her face. She could no longer hear the rider ahead. The terrifying darkness encompassed her. Lifeless tree trunks with shattered limbs appeared to be the armed enemy. They would kill her. This was the night she would die. Every particle of her body vibrated with fear. When an attack failed to happen, she had to admit that the enemy was her imagination. Then a stump became a ravenous devourer ready to spring upon her.

She had been foolish to believe she could make this journey. The terror of being alone in the woods at night was as bad as her fear of water. The only difference was she had not spent a lifetime developing it. She need not have been so critical of John's phantasmagoria the night before. She could produce her own.

Sarah was angry at everything. Herself. Her own impulsiveness and vanity. At the outrageous insensitivity of the post rider. And at the boughs and limbs that attacked her. The anger, helplessness and fear, made her sob. It was so loud she startled herself. "I don't expect we'll be riding after dark," she had told Rosy. She had been so sure of herself then. "I only have to follow the post rider." She could hear nothing over her own crying. And she could see nothing either.

When Athena began stumbling and struggling up a steep incline, Sarah grabbed the pommel with her left hand and the rim of the saddle with her right. "Steady, girl. On you go." Her words came in hiccups after crying so hard. "Steady," she urged Athena, not knowing what else to say or do that would help.

Ahead, Sarah could make out the crest of the hill because an illumination grew behind the trees. After laboring to the top, she was amply recompensed by the appearance of the full moon, just then advancing above the horizon. It gave light to a smooth and even path ahead. The relief brought a joy that she had to express, but she was alone. She began composing rhymes . . . *a light to see, the passage free . . . moonlight through the trees, visions of spires and balconies. . . .* At the next stage stop she would note in her journal how this new guide had rescued her from despair.

The post rider's horn interrupted her composition. He had sounded his arrival at the stage somewhere ahead. That music was as welcome as the light of the moon.

※

"Bless you, Madam. Coming all that way. And in the dark, no less. I'm Mrs. Havens. Let me help you with your riding clothes." A tall woman with a spotless white apron greeted Sarah at the door. "Mr. Fleer's the most ill-natured rider who comes through here. I'll wager he wasn't such pleasant company for you. But he's usually on time." She hung Sarah's cloak, muff and hood on a peg. "May I get you some supper?"

"No thanks. My stomach hasn't settled yet from a very disagreeable dinner."

"Perhaps something hot to drink then?"

"I have some chocolate with me." Sarah retrieved Mrs. Gridley's package from her pocket.

"Chocolate. How lovely. Please have a seat while I get some milk." She left the room with a small copper kettle.

Sarah sat at the only table in the kitchen end of the busy tavern. Oil lamps made the whitewashed walls bright. At two tables in the adjoining room were half a dozen men, who went back to their mugs and conversations after scrutinizing Sarah and whispering their speculations to each other.

Mrs. Havens explained the arrangements as she grated the chocolate into the kettle. "We're just a small ordinary and the post rider and another traveller are occupying the bed upstairs. You can have the room off the kitchen to yourself. The bed's a bit hard but the linen's clean."

When she finished heating the chocolate, she poured it into a mug and set the kettle on the table. "I'll light a candle in your room and pour you a basin of water, then I'm off to bed myself. Mr. Fleer will be wanting to leave early." She brought Sarah a bowl of sugar chunks and a spoon. "If you need anything, my husband is tending the town topers in the other room," toward which she nodded with forbearance.

Sarah stared at the copper kettle as she sipped the chocolate. She loved its shape. Lamplight caught the curve at the base. A sense of safety and well-being reflected from the dear little thing. She could not take her eyes off it.

Loud voices from the other room intruded. They soon drove Sarah to her room, where she set out her writing materials and recorded her day's journey. She composed several couplets that could be reworked into a poem of tribute to the moonrise, and she was especially proud of what could serve as the opening:

> *Fair Cynthia, all the Homage that I may*
> *Unto a Creature, unto thee I pay;*
> *In Lonesome woods to meet so kind a guide,*
> *To Mee's more worth than all the world beside.*

As she readied for bed, the conversation in the tavern became louder. Only a thin partition separated her from the voices raised in dispute.

"A fart on you," one man shouted. "I happen to know Narragansett means nothing of the sort. I hunted once with old Scars-On-His-Arse, and he showed me this briar that grows to the size of a house, and he said, 'Nar-ra-gan-sett.' Just like that. 'Nar-ra-gan-sett.' He pointed to the briar, then pointed to hisself and two friends and said it again. They's all named after a damned sticker bush." The remarks were punctuated with a hawk and spit.

His explanation of the term met with much protest.

One man out-voiced the others. "There's briars in your bunghole."

A roar of laughter arose, then he continued.

"Narragansett means hot and cold." With each adjective he pounded on the table. "It comes from a spring south of here. I been there, myself. The water comes out hot in the winter and cold in the summer. Narrag-Ansett. Hot and cold." Two more blows on the table. "The tribe came from near the spring originally. That's how they got the name."

A call came for another dram for every man, and that only oiled the fire. With sleep impossible, Sarah picked up her pen again and composed her vexation in the following manner:

> *I ask thy Aid, O Potent Rum!*
> *To Charm these wrangling Topers Dum.*
> *Thou hast their Giddy Brains possest—*
> *The man confounded with the Beast—*
> *And I poor I, can get no rest.*
> *Intoxicate them with thy fumes:*
> *O still their Tongues till morning comes!*

And her wishes were soon granted. The dispute ended with another dram, the men departed for home, and the hard bed had no effect whatsoever on her falling asleep.

Deserta

Wednesday, October 4

"Madam." Mrs. Havens shook Sarah's shoulder. "Madam. Mr. Fleer's chafing to go."

Sarah had been so soundly asleep she could not comprehend what was happening or where she was.

"If you aren't ready quickly, he might leave without you."

Sarah sat up but was not sufficiently awake to think clearly.

"Make a hasty toilette while I gather up your riding clothes and bring you a hot drink."

Then Sarah flew into action. The bastard was trying to sneak out without her. She was buttoning her bodice when Mrs. Havens returned.

"Four in the morning. The man has no propriety," the hostess said. She put the cloak over Sarah's shoulders while Sarah stuffed her writing materials in the saddlebag. "Drink your milk while I lace your shoes. He and a French doctor have just gone out to saddle up. Mr. Havens is preparing your horse.

He'll detain them a while." She fastened the flap on the saddlebag. "I'll take this and your muff; you put on your hood."

They hurried across the kitchen and out to the side of the tavern, where Mr. Havens' lantern maintained a feeble orb of light in the chilly blackness. He helped Sarah onto the saddle and Mrs. Havens secured her saddlebags and safeguard. The two men set forth, so Mr. Havens gave Athena a swat on her rump. Sarah was off in pursuit before she even thanked or paid the kind proprietors.

The men put on furiously. She could not keep up with them, but now and then they stopped just until they saw her. The road was poorly furnished for travellers, forcing them to ride until well after sunrise, at which time they drew rein at a stream.

"We'll water the horses here," Fleer said. "They need to cool down." He and the doctor dismounted and went off into the bushes to relieve themselves. They left Sarah aboard her horse with no such opportunity.

When they returned she asked, "How far have we come?"

"Twenty-two miles in less than three hours."

"And where in this God-forsaken tract are we to eat? I've hardly had anything in a day's time."

"A few miles further is the Davils' place. He'll accommodate us."

She kneaded the small of her back with both hands. "The Devil's? I seriously question whether I ought to go to the Devil to be helped out of my affliction."

The men ignored her comment, and, like the rest of the

deluded souls who post to the Infernal Den, they made all possible speed to his residence.

It was the only structure she had seen since daybreak, a mean building with an overhanging second floor. The hinges of the tavern door creaked as a woman stepped out. She was followed by another, who resembled her both in features and habit. They shielded their eyes; only their noses and chins protruded into the morning sunshine.

"Is your father within?" Mr. Fleer asked.

"Aye," said one, but neither of them moved.

"We've ridden from Havens', near Frenchtown. We haven't eaten this morning." He waited, but the noses and chins remained motionless. "Call him out, then," he hollered.

At that moment the Old Sophister appeared.

Since no greeting was forthcoming, Fleer repeated, "We left Frenchtown at four and we haven't eaten. Can you accommodate us?"

"No," Davil replied.

"You have no breakfast to offer?"

"None." The corners of his mouth lifted slightly, then he turned and led his daughters back into the house. The door creaked shut.

Fleer shook his head in puzzlement. "They're strange ones, but they never turned me away before."

"What do we do now?" Sarah was thirsty, and pains occasionally gripped her empty stomach.

"An old lady runs an ordinary a couple miles farther on, near Ninigret's Pond."

❧

Under the signpost of the Haversham Ordinary they tied up next to six horses and an oxcart. In the smoke-filled dining room, patrons ate at every table.

Mr. Fleer spoke loudly to the ancient hostess. "Let the lady take the seat here at the fireplace. The doctor and I'll sit over there."

The old woman hobbled after them trying to get a good look at the Frenchman. "He's a doctor, you say?" When they sat, she leaned toward him. "You a doctor?"

He drew back and nodded.

"Mrs. Cloggin." Fleer shouted to get her attention. "We'd like some breakfast."

She soon produced three trenchers for them, saving the doctor's until last. She hovered near his ear while he ate. "I have very little hair left under my hood."

All the diners heard her confidence.

"So I made *aqua mellis* last spring. Three parts honey to one part juice of vine pulp. I've rubbed it on regularly, but I don't see any results."

Fleer turned to the men at the next table. "It won't matter that she's deaf as well as bald. The doctor doesn't speak English anyway."

She did not hear their laughter and continued her consultation. "Should I try something else?"

The doctor noticed her voice rose in a question. He shrugged his shoulders because he did not understand what she said.

Taking that as a lack of confidence in her tonic, she

pursued. "Maybe I should try an Indian metsin I heard tell of. Dried ground worms, snails, hummy bees and fire flies mixed in milk."

Groans and laughter came from the diners. They looked at the beleaguered doctor to see how he would respond. In embarrassment he smiled and nodded back. Mrs. Cloggin, however, interpreted his gesture as approval of her second remedy and went happily back to the kitchen.

Sarah had finished her meal and decided to quit the smoky dining room. She wanted to record her morning's experience. While she settled her account with a man behind the serving bar, she could hear the hostess resume her medical conference. She was describing how she had finally cured her insomnia.

"The hot poultice of camomile, bread crumbs and vinegar on the soles of my feet didn't work. The smell kept both me and my husband awake. Finally I tried two little bags of aniseseed steeped in rose water. I bound one to each nostril and fell right to sleep."

*

Sarah removed her writing materials from the saddlebag and went to a bench in front of the ordinary. She composed a verse to warn poor travellers of falling into the circumstances she had at the Davils'.

> *May all that dread the cruel feind of night*
> *Keep on, and not at this curs't Mansion light.*
> *'Tis Hell; 'tis Hell! and Devills here do dwell:*
> *Here dwells the Devill—surely this's Hell.*
> *Nothing but Wants: a drop to cool yo'r Tongue*

Cant be procur'd these cruel Feinds among.
Plenty of horrid Grins and looks sevear,
Hunger and thirst, But pitty's bannish'd here—
The Right hand keep, if Hell on Earth you fear!

It was rough and would need refinement, but just drafting it relieved her resentments. She then packed her things and sat back to let the midmorning sun warm her tired and aching body.

⁂

By noon they were underway again. For the first time since she left Boston Sarah could see the ocean. A thin strip of land lay about a mile out. The shore birds of various sizes and colors were thick between the sandbar and the beach road. Apparently her escorts enjoyed the sights as much as she because they proceeded at a leisurely pace ahead of her and often pointed at one thing or another and nodded. She wondered what words they had in common.

Just before the path swung away from the shore, she spotted the sails of a ship so far away she could not tell whether it was sailing south with her or north. It was such a tiny, stationary shape, fixed on the flat, unwavering line of the horizon, that it made her feel foolish about the mental picture she always had of sailing—waves crashing across the bow and herself clinging to a cabin railing. The passengers out there were probably seated on cushions, watching the shore, while she battered her hind-quarters on a saddle.

The path now skirted a swamp to the right. A flock of geese rose from a pond and organized itself into a squawking, southbound chevron. Then, ahead, appeared the wide mouth of a river. Fleer was waiting at the bank. He had turned to watch her discover it.

"It's the Pawcatuck. High tide," he said when she rode closer.

She leaned forward to look up the river.

"There's no other way but horseback. No ferry, no canoe, this time," he said.

A wave of panic again washed over her. It was becoming a frequent sensation since she left her doorstep.

"It's two hundred paces across," Fleer said. "The horses can walk all except the center channel. That's where you'll get your drapery wet."

"I can't cross when it's that deep." She was not happy that her voice exposed her fear. "If it's high tide couldn't we wait until it goes down?"

Fleer pulled a timepiece from his pocket. "It's one o'clock. I have to be in Stonington by two and New London by three to make Saybrook by dark. It'll take three or four hours for this river to go down. I can't wait. Got to go now."

"But I'm so tired, Mr. Fleer. I haven't the strength to struggle across. You know I have little courage in these circumstances. Please don't leave me." She made a sweeping motion with her hand. "There's nothing here."

"There's some raggedy creatures in a hut over yonder. You can stay with them till the tide goes out. Or come with us now; it's all the same to me."

The Frenchman had been looking back and forth between the two disputants and appeared puzzled. When Fleer kicked his horse to urge him toward the river, the doctor asked him something. Sarah regretted her French was barely sufficient for reading, but she thought she heard the word *abandonner*.

Fleer just shook his head, gave a dismissive wave toward her and said, "Let's go," to the doctor.

The doctor glanced back and beckoned to her with his hand. "*Venez*," he said.

But she shook her head, and the two men rode out into the Pawcatuck. As they approached the center of the river they drew their legs up and balanced themselves carefully, but their feet and bottoms got wet anyway. When they reached the far bank, only the Frenchman looked back.

The two of them rode off in great haste.

She stared in disbelief at the curve in the path where they had disappeared. She gasped several times; each one was marked with a small sob, and each sob vanished in the vastness of the landscape. She gripped the pommel and twisted both ways in the saddle. Where was she? She was not sure if the Pawcatuck River was on the map she had been too impatient to study in the Boston post terminus.

What had Fleer said? It was one o'clock. There was a town he had to reach by two, but she couldn't remember it, and he must arrive in New London at three. So New London was a two-hour ride from here. If she could get across at low tide and find the path, perhaps she could reach friends in New London by herself before dark. Dark.

"Oh, God," she cried. And that too vanished.

Then she remembered Fleer had mentioned people,

raggedy creatures. She glanced around. The only indication of a human hand was a stack of timbers, barely visible in the bushes and undergrowth. A child peered out at her from an opening, and Sarah realized the wood pile was actually a hut made of undressed timber clapboards. She wiped the tears from her face and turned Athena around. The child withdrew.

Sarah called, "Hello, the house," as she rode toward it.

A bearded man stepped out, followed by a woman and two small girls. They made no response, but they looked her over as she approached. She did not know if they had seen what had transpired, so she explained her predicament.

The father burrowed through his beard to scratch his chin before he spoke. "Tide'll be down in a couple of hours. You can come in and wait." He brought her a piece of tree stump to dismount onto. "Then I'll see you acrosst."

"How deep will it be at low tide? I just saw my escorts in water over their saddles." Sarah straightened her clothing while the father tied Athena to a tree branch.

"You won't get wet."

In uncomfortable silence she and the family examined each other. Only the smaller daughter smiled at Sarah, but she pressed close to her mother and grabbed her hand.

"Well, I'd appreciate your help," Sarah said.

"Get her a seat," the father told the children.

They hurried into the hut. The door hung askew; she had never seen leather cords used for hinges. She bent to avoid hitting the lintel. The children offered her one of the two tree stumps that served as stools. At her feet, stones circled a single log that rested on a bed of coals. There was no hearth or mantel or chimney, and there were no windows. Smoke hung in the cracks of light where the clapboards did not quite meet. What protection was this from the cold or blowing snow?

The father sat on the other stump, and his family crowded next to each other on the edge of a bed. It and a table completed the furnishings of the hut.

"Where've you come from?" he asked.

"Boston. I left there two days ago." She did not know how to continue conversing with four people dressed in layers of tattered clothing. Of what importance were her complaints of mistreatment or her aches and pains to a family whose only possessions consisted of four pieces of rude furniture? A cup and basin that contained several corncakes sat on a wide board with cut limbs for legs. She saw nothing else to eat once the cakes were gone. There was no pantry. She could not complain to them about hunger based on her experience in two days of travel. So with nothing to say, she just smiled. Then they all stared at the father, who was stirring the coals with a charred stick.

The sound of a horse's hooves and several whickers relieved them of their silence. The younger girl went to the door with her father. Sarah heard an exchange of names. They let in a savage young man with a headband around his long hair and a shaggy hide vest. He remained in the doorway, staring at Sarah and awkwardly scratching the toe of his moccasin on the dirt floor. Then he nodded and sat on the stump next to her.

His odor overpowered the smoke in the air. He took a long pipe from inside his vest and fumbled some junk from a pouch into the bowl. He dipped this into the coals, and when the junk began to glow he stuck the pipe beneath his crusted moustache.

In several sidelong glances Sarah caught him as he sucked noisily on the stem. The six of them were crowded into the hovel with the sounds of scratching, occasional rattling coughs and the man sucking on his pipe.

The father finally asked, "How does Sarah do?"

Sarah was startled to hear the name. She looked directly at the newcomer, awaiting his answer. Just when she decided this was the longest time she had ever spent next to an Indian, she realized he was a white man.

"Well as can be spected. Soon as she can hang on the back of me, we'll ride over. She says you should name your first grandson."

"Where you headed now?" the father asked.

"Crosst the river to the fulling mill. Got some bags of wool on my horse."

Sarah quickened. "Could I hire you to guide me to New London?"

He regarded her with one eye, the other went off toward the wall. "Can't be gone that long. I could take you to Saxton's Inn, right near the mill. You might could ride with somebody from there."

The mother said they should have the corncakes. She broke them into pieces, which the girls distributed. Sarah declined, with the excuse that she had just recently eaten. The family exchanged other news between bites of cake, chewing, and licking their fingers.

When the men decided that the tide had receded enough to cross the Pawcatuck, the son-in-law rose from his stump and brushed cake crumbs from his lap into the fire. They all followed him out into the mid-afternoon sunshine. The fresh air made Sarah aware of how much the smoke had irritated her eyes and throat.

The son-in-law pulled himself up on a bedraggled horse. He had no saddle, but two bulging bags were fastened over the rump. The father came from the far side of the hut leading a dusty mule with a work harness. After helping Sarah mount, he vaulted onto the mule's back and grabbed Athena's reins.

"So's you won't be afeared, I'll lead you t'other side," he said.

Sarah thanked the mother and daughters.

They said nothing. The smaller girl waved then covered a smile with her hand.

The Pawcatuck was wider than the crossing at Providence, but the water was slow-moving. Sarah guessed the level had dropped two feet, and at the center it barely came up to Athena's belly. She observed the son-in-law ahead of her to determine the depth. The father rode beside her, clicking his tongue and speaking softly to both animals all the way to the other bank. Sarah was so absorbed in this she had no worry for herself. She rewarded the father with a coin, then she proceeded with her tatter-tailed escort.

The way was stony and uneven, which slowed their travel.

"Was the town of Stonington named for the condition of this road?" she asked in jest.

He appeared to give the question serious consideration. "Don't believe it was. The town's in a meadow near a landing place. No stones to be seen there."

"What do you know about the road from Stonington to New London?"

He spit away from the side where she was riding. "From Mystic to the Thames the road's four yards wide. You never been here, I take it?"

"I've come from Boston."

"Oh, yeh? Some seaman from Boston came here two years ago. He brought the smallpox. Lot of people died. Some cousins of mine, too. Wouldn't tell no one I was from Boston. They might lock you up."

She pondered that news briefly then figured, since she now had a guide who was willing to converse with her, she should pursue a less provocative topic. "It's been a pleasant fall. I've had fair travel weather so far."

"Aye. No hurricanes or nor'easters yet. It will cold up soon, though. Cold's the worst. A hurricane will blow through in a day but the cold just sits." He looked back to check on the bags of wool. "Winters is bitter here. In ninety-eight the ocean froze. I rode my horse acrosst the sound from Stonington to Fishers Island."

"We suffered in Boston too. The Charles River and Boston Bay were frozen solid."

They rode with their own thoughts until they reached a brook.

"This be the Anguilla. Mostly rocks and noise at this point. Comes out at Stonington. We're almost there." He took the reins from her and led Athena across in a crooked course that avoided the largest boulders.

West of the brook, on the left side, stood a silver-weathered building with a gambrel roof. Chimneys rose at either end, and the third story had four gabled windows. Such a fine building was common in Boston, but here, after two long days without seeing many habitations of any sort, Sarah found it a marvelous sight. A relief carving of a three-masted bark hung from one end of a covered porch. In black letters below, it said Saxton's Inn.

"You've delivered me from a dark moment, and I'm very grateful," Sarah said. She withdrew a second coin for the son-in-law. "I hope I haven't detained you."

"No ma'am." He bit the coin then put it in his vest pocket. "Much obliged."

She watched him ride off with the bags of wool bouncing on his horse's rump.

"Welcome to Saxton's." An elderly groom with stiff, bowed legs came waddling toward her with some mounting steps. "You're alone?"

"Regrettably so."

"Where are you headed?" He assisted her to the ground.

"To New London and New Haven. Would there be anyone here going that way?"

"No one here at the moment. Mr. Polly said he'd probably

be back through here tomorrow. He passed by this morning on his way to fetch his daughter out of the Narragansetts. She ran away again. They're a bit rough, but if you're looking for company, they'll be riding to New London."

Sarah removed her gloves and used them to assault the dust and dried mud on her garments. "I've had nothing but rough guides since I left Boston. I'm not in the position to be particular. I'll follow anyone at this point."

"You rode here from Boston?" He came around the horse for a second look at her and for confirmation of this news.

Sarah nodded.

"Well, now that's really something. All the way from Boston. Captain Saxton was born there. He'll be pleased to entertain you." He escorted her to the door and opened it for her. "You go right in. I'll take care of the horse and bring in your bags."

The captain and his kind wife made good the groom's prediction and installed her in a spacious room on the second floor, from which she could look out on the front lawn of the inn. Her riding garments were taken to be beaten and brushed, her basin filled with hot water, and she had a supper of carbonado and cider with the host and hostess. When she retired early, the old woman who had served dinner was sent up with a candle lamp and bed warmer. Sarah had returned to civilization.

Continuatio

Thursday, October 5

Having fallen asleep early, Sarah also rose early. She carried her journal down to the fireplace in the dining room, where the same elderly servant brought her toast and milk pudding. Perhaps she was the wife of the groom. The woman returned later to remove the dishes, then Sarah read over her entries. All that had transpired in two and a half days consumed nearly a quarter of the pages. If she were able to return home in two weeks, this one book might suffice. If something delayed her until the following postal run, she might have to buy another.

Returning home. The implications just occurred to her. She would have to do this all again, the same rivers, the same desolate stretches. And the worst of it was she might have the ill-fortune to draw Fleer as her guide again. In that case, she decided, she just would just remain in New Haven for the next post rider.

Sarah stared at the fire and was reminded of the hut by the Pawcatuck. "Raggedy creatures," Fleer had called the family.

They lived as she imagined Indians lived, although she had never been in a native village. The farther the English moved from Boston, the farther from any town, for that matter, the less they were touched by civility. She was sure the greatest danger for the English was the wildness of this country. Growth of towns and cities was the best way to prevent regression into savagery.

What was incomprehensible was why these English people would choose to live in such isolation. Their poverty pained her. She had scarcely a change of clothes with her because a piece of luggage would have been a burden; they had no change of clothes at all. There was no chest or wardrobe in the hut; what they were wearing was all they owned. Neither was there a pantry. She wondered what they ate after the meal of cornbread.

"Would you like anything else?" The woman had come to sweep the room.

"No, thank you. I'm going to my room to write."

"Then I'll bring up a foot stove. It's chilly in here this morning."

※

Sarah took a seat at the secretary, arranged the foot stove under her skirts, then lowered the secretary door and laid out her writing materials. She sat in comfort, looking out at the morning sunshine. The last time she sat at her own desk she had looked out to see Robert riding up. Maybe he was with customers in the stationery at this moment.

She wrote about the afternoon in the Narragansett country and her abandonment at the Pawcatuck.

So takeing leave of my company, tho wth no little Reluctance, that I could not proceed wth them on my Jorny, Stopt at a little cottage Just by the River, to wait the Waters falling.

She recalled the shock when she stepped inside. *This little Hutt was the wretchedest habitation for human creatures I ever saw. All and every part being the picture of poverty. Nowhere in Boston did people live in such degraded circumstances.*

Sarah decided to compose a couplet that might express how the encounter had affected her sensibilities. Within the hour she had a poem of six couplets that suited her sentiments.

> *Tho' Ill at ease, A stranger and alone,*
> *All my fatigu's shall not extort a grone.*
> *These Indigents have hunger wth their ease;*
> *Their best is wors by halfe then my disease.*
> *Their Misirable hutt wch Heat and Cold*
> *Alternately without Repulse do hold;*
> *Their Lodgings thyn and hard, their Indian fare,*
> *The mean Apparel which the wretches wear,*
> *And their ten thousand ills wch can't be told,*
> *Makes nature er'e 'tis midle age'd look old.*
> *When I reflect, my late fatigues do seem*
> *Only a notion or forgotten Dreem.*

Having got to Saxton's in her journal, Sarah packed the writing materials and went back down to the public room. Half-way through a mug of cider she noticed a couple riding up to the inn on a sorry-looking horse. The groom helped the young woman down from a thin bag that served as a pillion behind the older man's saddle. She burst into the public room holding her bottom.

"I been four hours on that bony beast. I'm so joggled and bobbled my insides is mush." The girl tossed a long braid of greasy brown hair over the shoulder of her homespun cape. "Even my teeth hurt." She scraped a chair over the hearth stones to sit as close to the fire as possible.

The servant brought the girl a steaming mug. "If you stayed home, Jemima, you'd spare your bones a beating. Here's a hot drink." The old woman took a woolen shawl from a peg near the fireplace and put it over the girl's shoulders. "You rest a bit. Dinner will be ready soon."

When the man entered and saw Sarah, he removed his battered beaver hat. This exposed a woefully neglected periwig. A belt drawn tight around the middle of his cape made his body appear like two sausages.

He approached her table. "You be the lady Mr. Cobble says is going to New London?"

"Yes, I am."

"I'm Epsilon Polly."

"Sarah Knight."

"You can ride with me and my daughter over there. We'll be leaving after we've et."

He sat with Sarah, and they discussed where each had ridden from. He complained in a hushed voice about his wayward daughter, who disappeared whenever a certain trapper from Narragansett came to town with his pelts.

"I've near wore out my ol' horse going to fetch her. This

here's the fourth time. I swear, I'll lock her up when that furry rascal shows up again. The swamps and rivers of Narragansett's no place for a woman to live, specially one who's not strong in the head." He nodded toward the girl, who was huddled at the hearth and apparently indifferent to her father's complaints. "You shoulda seen where I found her this trip. Not even savages live in a hole in the side of a hill."

His bluster was interrupted by the arrival of a tureen filled with sliced meat and vegetables in gravy.

"I been dreaming bout this since I left yesterday, Mrs. Cobble. Haven't et since then," he said.

Jemima joined them for the meal, which they ate without the bother of conversation. By three o'clock they settled their accounts with the inn. Mr. Cobble helped the sour-faced girl onto her bag of a pillion and Sarah onto her saddle. The three set off at good speed. Jemima began to groan at once.

"Oh, lawful heart, Father! This bare mare hurts me dingily."

"Poor child," her father said.

The mare was a hard trotter, Sarah had to admit. It had enormous feet and looked like it was better suited to the plough than the path. The girl bounced with each beat of its hooves. Since the bag had no handles and foot-rest, staying aboard was all the more strenuous. Jemima had to cling to her father.

"I'm direful sore, I vow," she howled a short while later.

"She used to serve your mother well."

"I don't care how Mother used to do. She's killing me."

"We have to ride like the dickens to get to the New London ferry before nighttime." Polly kicked the beast in the sides and laughed. Poor Jemima jolted ten times harder, her braid flopping from one side to another.

Polly had explained they would swing away from the coast to avoid several bays and river mouths. About an hour west of Saxton's they crossed one river. Polly told her the water would not be above her horse's legs, and he was correct. He said the small settlement at the river was called Mystic. A wonderful name, she thought, because the lowering sun was cast into glinting fragments on the surface of the water. It also lighted the back of the silver-brown plumes of phragmites that rose from the wetlands, making them look like glowing torches. The dried stems and leaf blades of these reeds swayed and rustled in a strong breeze.

Jemima did not appreciate the landscape. She continued with her loud and bitter complaints, adding to them the insults she was now suffering from the wind.

The sky held the last light of day when the party came to the Thames River embankment. The water was worked into white-capped waves. Below them a large ferry bumped its dock. They descended to a cabin nearby, and Polly rousted the ferryman. Although the ferry was of heavy timber construction and had enclosed sides as tall as their horses' shoulders, Sarah was not encouraged. A windswept river lay between her and the opposite shore. She could see light coming from the windows of the homes of New London atop a cliff that rose above the shore. A ferry ride separated her from the warmth and shelter of her acquaintances and relatives who lived there.

"I was left on the east bank of the Pawcatuck at high tide yesterday because my courage failed me. And it wasn't windy and almost dark," she told Polly and the ferryman.

"No fear here," Polly said, "The tide's going out and the wind's blowing in. It'll be choppy, that's all. Anyway, the ferryman here claims he won't never cross if there's any risk to his ferry, but the real reason is he's a scaredamouse."

The ferryman ignored the barb and tossed out his own. "So, you're back again, Jemima. Didn't take your pa long this time. You two're keeping me in business. Nine pence, Polly. I won't charge extra for your bag of wind."

He slipped the coins in his pocket then turned to Sarah and pointed to a sign nailed to the side of the ferry. It read, "6 pence for a man and horse. 3 pence for a man."

"And how much for a woman?" Sarah asked.

"Six pence. Same as a man . . . unless she can't keep her horse quiet, and it tears up my ferry."

She retrieved a coin from under her skirt. The ferryman put it between his teeth and led the horses aboard.

"I'll tie your horse down good," he mumbled around the coin. He tied one rein to a loop on the right rail, the other to a loop on the front rail, then pocketed the coin.

"Will I have to stay up here?" Sarah asked.

"She'll stay quieter if you do. Just lean over and talk soft in her ear. She can't move her head, so she won't rear on you." He walked back to the tiller.

Polly held his horse's reins in one hand and a rail loop with the other. The ferry pitched, and Polly's horse began to caper. Jemima had only the edges of the bag to hold on to.

"Tell her 'So-jack,'" she demanded.

The horse reared her head and pranced to the opposite railing, jolting Jemima so that her braid swung around and hit her face. "Pray sooth, Father, are you deaf?" she roared. "Say 'So-jack' to the jade, I tell you." She spat hair from her mouth.

Thus chastised, Polly leaned forward and grabbed his nag's ear. "So-jack, so-jack. Quit your prancing."

For good measure Sarah also patted Athena's mane and said, "So-jack." She sympathized with the young girl, whose fear and rage had produced dark circles around her eyes, a flushed face and a white ring of anger around her mouth.

*

"You got family here?" Polly led both horses off the ferry.

"I have a relative and some acquaintances, but they aren't expecting me. I don't even know where they live."

"I'll take you to Mrs. Prentice's. She knows everybody in these parts."

Polly and daughter led the way along the bay, past the shipyard, a wharf and some warehouses. Near the end of the bay, the street curved back and began to climb the hill. Across the water, a mill and overshot wheel were visible in the growing darkness. The street led up to a square, bordered by homes, the meetinghouse and a few shops. They stopped in front of a two-story residence that bore a green shingle that simply said Prentice's. Polly slid down and went in to announce their arrival.

❧

"Goodness gracious. I don't recollect ever greeting a lone woman traveller from Boston before." A tall, thin woman came outside and pulled a fringed wool shawl around herself. "The mounting steps are at the corner of the house, Mr. Polly." She watched the proceedings. "Please come in, madam."

Sarah stepped into a room that was heated by a fire in a painted brick fireplace. Pairs of matching wall lamps hung on each of the four walls. Light and warmth; Sarah inhaled them.

"I'm Mrs. Prentice. Let me take your wrap. Would you like some supper?"

"Can you feed the three of us? I'd like the Pollys to be my guests. I'm in their debt for delivering me here."

"Of course. Join the others in the dining room. Have you anywhere to stay? I'm afraid I can't accommodate you. The *John and Hester* is overdue, and I have awaiting passengers here."

Sarah started upon hearing the name. "I, uh . . . no. Not yet. A cousin lives here, and I know a few families. But they don't know I've come. I might shock them to death if I appeared on the doorstep at this hour." She and the Pollys followed the hostess across the hall and into the busy dining room.

"Let me bring you your meal, then we'll see to your accommodations."

❧

How many ships could be named the *John and Hester*? It had to be the one Richard had taken. He said in his last letter a year ago that he planned to quit the ship in England. "I have decided to remain there until I establish myself in the shipping community," he had written. "I am optimistic of brighter prospects there."

Brighter, indeed, she had thought. He had put his candle out with his last adventure in Boston. To pay off furious investors in a failed scheme to ship ice to the West Indies, she had had to sell a small shop she inherited from her father. But the longer he had stayed away, the more willing she had become to forgive him. All it would take was a letter.

What if he had never left the *John and Hester*? What if he were to sail into New London tonight . . . if he were to walk into this tavern where she sat eating?

Polly's chuckling interrupted her. "Imagine the look on your kinfolks' faces when they open their door and you surprise em." He rubbed the greasy hair of his beard. "They'll probly say, 'I just can't believe my eyes. Just can't believe em.'" He chuckled again and poked Jemima, who was staring at the table and dusting it absent-mindedly with the end of her braid. She made no response.

"Set it there, Ralph." Mrs. Prentice indicated where the pale lad should put a tureen. "Get bowls and spoons, dear." She explained to her guests, "This is oyster stew, and here are goose pasties."

Sarah watched the son set out the dinnerware with trembling fingers. They were the same color as the ivory spoon handles. His narrow shoulders shook when he coughed.

Sarah asked the hostess, "Would the ship you're expecting be the one that sailed from Barbados to London a year ago?"

"Aye. A year ago June she left for New York, then Barbados and London and returned by November. She's never been to Boston. How do you know her?"

"Someone wrote me from Barbados that he was taking the *John and Hester* to London. I never heard from him again. I'm trying to determine his whereabouts." Not wanting to reveal any more, she busied herself with the soup young Prentice had delivered with a dribbling trail to her bowl.

"She was my late husband's ship," Mrs. Prentice said. "Named after him and his first wife. Now my stepson's the captain. You could talk to him when they arrive."

Sarah placed a pasty in her empty soup bowl. "I'm afraid I can't wait. I need to get to New Haven as soon as possible."

"How long will you be there?"

"I'm not sure. Two weeks, I hope."

"You're in luck, then. My stepson has to be in New Haven next week. He's a deputy to the General Assembly. You can ask him about your missing friend. I'll write his name for you, and the name of the family he'll be staying with." She left to do that.

"I appreciate this. Tell him I'll look for him," Sarah said when Mrs. Prentice returned. "Now I need to find somewhere to stay for the night. Do you know where Mary Christophers lives? She's my cousin."

"Her house is down on Town Street but she's away. What about the families you mentioned?"

"I knew Gurdon Saltonstall when he was at Harvard Seminary some years ago. His late wife was a childhood playmate of mine."

"He lives just across the street. Ralph, go tell the minister. May I get you anything else? Mr. Polly?"

"Not for me." Some flakes of the pasty crust adorned Polly's beard. "The girl and me have two miles to go yet. Much obliged to you for the supper, madam. Good luck in your travels." He scraped his chair away from the table. "Let's be off, Jemima."

※

"Sarah! From what Ralph said, I knew it must be you." The modest divinity student Sarah remembered, now stood before her wearing an emerald satin cassock, and of all things, a fine white peruke. The Boston clergy would be astounded. He took her hand to lead her across the street to his exceedingly curious family, who waited at the door step. "You won't recognize Elizabeth and Mary. They're young ladies now. Sarah was born after we came here. And this is my wife, Elizabeth."

Sarah shook her hand, then she took another glance at the minister's hairpiece.

"Our son Rosewell is sleeping," his wife said, "but baby Katherine is still up to greet you. Come in. Come in. We'll send our man for your things."

The whole family moved into their great room and gathered around the seat they offered their guest, who imparted one amazing adventure after another. When Sarah concluded with her triumphal entry into New London behind the Pollys, she was quite pleased with the applause.

"So you feel you must leave in the morning?" her hostess asked. "You can't stay and rest yourself?"

"If I don't get to New Haven by Monday, my trip will have been for naught. Which brings me to my present predicament, can you find me an escort? I really need someone who can leave tomorrow?"

"Let me think." Saltonstall rose. "It's nearly ten. I'll have to do it in the morning."

"How long is the ride?" Sarah asked.

"I've never gone by horse. The way's too rough for me. I'm not an accomplished horseman at all. I should imagine a couple of days on horseback, though. Most of the way is primitive Indian path. You should go by packet. That takes only a day. I could inquire about the next sailing."

"I don't travel by water. I'm firm about that. I'll have to find a guide."

"Gurdon will take care of it tomorrow," said the minister's wife. "Let's figure out the sleeping arrangements for tonight." She addressed her oldest stepdaughter. "Mrs. Knight can share the bed with you, and I'll make a pallet for your sisters."

That being decided the family prepared to retire.

⁕

"You used to play with my daughter," Sarah told her bedpartner.

"I did?"

"Yes, and her name is Elizabeth also. Your mother and I both liked the same name. She was my best friend, your mother. She was so pretty. Do you remember her face?"

"I don't think so. I dream about her sometimes, but I only remember her hair."

"You must miss her."

They were quiet for a while. The house was dark and a dog barked in the distance.

"My Elizabeth is also fourteen. You're taller than she."

"Do you miss her too?"

Sarah realized that until she saw Elizabeth Saltonstall she had not once thought of her daughter the entire day.

"Yes, I do." Her face felt hot with shame.

Rudes Populi

Friday, October 6

The girls' upstairs bedroom was under the slant of the roof and had no window. No light and no stirring came up the stairway. Somewhere a rooster was announcing the dawn, but darkness and anxiety enveloped Sarah.

Perhaps most New Londoners felt as Gurdon did about the route to New Haven. If people always travelled by packet, there might not even be anyone who knew where to go, no matter what she offered to pay. Fleer would have departed yesterday, so there would not be another post rider for two weeks. She certainly did not have the courage to ride alone, although it seemed she had come much of the way on her own, for all the company the post riders had provided.

These difficulties churned in her mind until a lamp was lit below and she heard voices. She slipped out of bed, dressed quietly so as not to waken the girls, then joined her host and hostess in their kitchen.

"We were hoping not to waken you." The minister's wife

sat in a chair before the fire. She talked over her shoulder, which was draped with a blanket that concealed her nursing infant.

"I can't sleep in such an uncertain state," Sarah said.

"I'm leaving shortly to see if there's anyone familiar with the route who could escort you." Gurdon adjusted his cravat then the sleeves of his black bombazine coat.

In the presence of such an impeccable host, Sarah plucked and patted her rumpled clothes. "I'm prepared to consider any price asked." The Dedham tavern negotiations came to her mind. "I'll even consider extortion, at this point."

※

The family was gathered at the table when Gurdon returned with the report of his mission.

"I've located a guide. At first I thought it was impossible because a group of men had just left to hunt wolves at the swamp." Gurdon removed his coat and sat down. "But Joshua Wheeler was home. He lost his spectacles and couldn't hunt. Anyway, he knows the way to Saybrook."

"He knows the way, but he can't see?" Sarah asked.

"Well, he can only see close up. He said if you're willing to describe the route ahead, he'll accompany you. Of course Saybrook is only a third of the distance to New Haven, so he can't be any more than a companion and protector the rest of the way." He smoothed his peruke with both hands then took the breakfast his wife handed him.

"How will Mr. Wheeler get home then?" Sarah asked.

"He'll sail back. He said if you would pay all the expenses, including passage for him and his horse, that would be sufficient."

"Well, at least he won't ride off without me, since he can't see. And I should consider it a boon if he's either courteous or civil."

"You needn't worry on any count. Wheeler's a reliable and honorable young gentleman. He'll be here as soon as his wife gets him ready."

After the minister's household finished breakfast, Sarah completed her toilette. She was thankful that an escort had been found, but she greatly regretted having to leave before the captain of the *John and Hester* arrived. She would be in a turmoil by the time he came to New Haven for the General Assembly. There was nothing she could do now but go back to the kitchen and wait for her myopic guide.

*

Joshua Wheeler and Sarah Knight rode side by side out of New London. The road swung north.

"We have to go around Niantic Bay," he said. "There's no ferry across."

Wheeler was tall, and she admired how erect he sat in the saddle. He made trotting look so graceful. All that, and he could not even see where he was going. Sarah wanted to be graceful too, but she could not possibly feel as relaxed as he looked. She had to force her aching muscles to remain poised. They had been riding only half an hour, and her arms already sagged with the weight of her sleeves. This would be a long day.

"Past this farm I can't see where the road is," she said.

"That's because there isn't any. We pass through an

orchard at the end of the farm. From there to the bay is just a rocky path through hills. We are headed for the orchard, aren't we?"

"Less than fifty yards. What misfortune befell your eye glasses?"

"I was attacked by a wayward bale of wool being loaded on my ship. It fell from the loading wagon and struck me on the back. I'm told the spectacles flew off into the water. I couldn't see that, of course."

"And I assume there's no lens maker in New London. We have none in Boston."

"There isn't. I've sent messages out with every packet. Something suitable should arrive before long. Or I might find some glasses in New Haven."

At the far end of the orchard Sarah took the lead. The horses began to strain and lurch up a rocky passage that was dense with foliage.

"Does this distress you?" Wheeler asked.

"I've been through worse terrain, and in the dark to boot. Climbing's very disagreeable to my tired old carcass, though."

For an hour they went on at a moderate pace, without conversing; the only sounds were the horses' labored breath, occasional snorts and their hooves clacking on stones.

Then Sarah heard running water. "Do we cross a river?"

"The Niantic at the head of the bay. We should be at the cascades. It's eight miles north of New London."

"Cascades? I'm terrified of rivers. How am I to manage crossing cascades?"

"You'll see a log bridge shortly. It's about thirty feet long."

"How wonderful. In four days of riding I've never crossed a bridge. There've been fords, canoes, ferries. I'm impressed there's a bridge so far from any habitation." Then she gasped.

"What's the matter?" Wheeler reined to a sudden stop. "What's there?" he asked.

Sarah lowered her voice. "Five natives are on the bridge. What shall we do?"

"How are they dressed? Are they carrying weapons?"

"Their faces are painted, one side black, the other yellow or red. They haven't much on—capes and leather wrappings on their feet."

Wheeler raised his eyebrows.

"Their privates are covered, but I've never seen such a sight. They're carrying something, not guns. They see us." Her whisper came out high and pinched. "What'll we do?"

"Now they've spotted us, we shouldn't retreat. We'll ride up to the bridge and greet them and hope they're in a peaceful mood."

"Greet them? How do we greet them?"

"I'll say 'friend' in Pequot, then point across the bridge. If they're of good temperament, they'll let us pass unmolested. It depends on what's transpired here recently. Sometimes they're slow to realize when they've been done in by the English. When they do, they devise their own unique retribution."

She dared not ask for examples. "So we might have to suffer for some woodhick's newest parcel of land?"

"We'll hope not. Have you anything to offer them in case they hold out their hands?" He felt his pockets. "I usually carry some trinkets of pacification when I travel, but I forgot in my haste this morning." He drew out his tobacco box and fingered inside it. "I haven't enough to satisfy five men."

Sarah patted the bulges her pockets made. There was the remainder of Mrs. Gridley's farewell gift. "Do Pequots know what to do with chocolate? I also have some coins." Her mind raced through the contents of her saddlebags. "A hairbrush, lavender water, pen and ink. I can't imagine what they'd do with them. Some clothing. That's it."

"Look unperturbed and nonthreatening, and don't say a word." He motioned to proceed.

Sarah nudged Athena's side. They neared the bridge, and she stared as intently as the Pequots did. A claw held together each cape under the chin. Necklaces of bones and teeth hung out below. The sides of the men's heads were shaved and the greased bristles of hair on top were decorated with feathers.

Such men did not walk in the streets of Boston. Natives who were domestics wore European clothing, and the few Massachusetts or Wampanoags who wandered in to trade were required to clothe their bodies. Here, a few paces before her, was naked savagery—bronze skin, muscles, dark nipples, ribs, navels, knees—parts she had seldom seen on her own husband.

She pulled her cloak tight. Her heart beat against her arms. She held her breath to contain the panic.

Each man had a basket-shaped object made of sticks. Over one man's shoulder was a leather thong, on which he had threaded a dozen or so fish, mouths agape and blood-red wedges of gills exposed.

"Look unperturbed," Wheeler had said. Her face was stiff. Even if it managed to look composed, they could surely see fear escaping from her eyes.

"*Netop*," Wheeler said. There was no reply, but one nodded. Wheeler pointed ahead. The Pequots stepped to the edges of the bridge, making the riders pass between them.

Wheeler took the lead. His horse's hooves made muffled thunks on the wet logs. Sarah followed immediately behind him. The bridge was so narrow that she had to pass within a foot of the bristles, bones and teeth. Any one of the Pequots could have touched her.

Half way across, a hoof of Wheeler's horse slipped into the curve where one log met another. He balked in fright then bolted ahead across the bridge. This startled Athena. She reared, squealing. Sarah was thrown down on her hands and knees. Athena reared again, this time she pranced backward, and one back hoof slipped off the bridge altogether. Sarah screamed.

Two Pequots dropped their baskets, lunged forward and caught Athena on either side of her neck. They pulled her to the end of the bridge where Wheeler was quieting his horse. Two others rushed to help Sarah up. Each grabbed an arm to keep her from slipping on the algae-covered logs. The fifth, the one with the fish, picked up her muff and safeguard.

When Sarah, with a Pequot on each arm, came into Wheeler's range of vision, he leapt down from his saddle. His sudden movement startled them, but they had hoisted her up onto her saddle before he reached her. They fled back over the bridge.

"Stop!" he shouted.

They looked back but kept running.

"No," Wheeler shouted. "I want to thank you."

They grabbed their baskets and fled into the woods.

"Can you see them?" Wheeler asked.

The two travellers stared at the empty bridge for several moments. There was the sound of water rushing over rocks, but nothing else stirred or gave evidence that anything had happened there. Except Sarah could still feel the pressure of the two men's hands on her arms and waist.

"We're alone." She shivered. "Just behind you is my muff and safeguard."

He gave her his pocket handerkerchief to wipe herself off and picked up her things.

"I'm terribly sorry for frightening you and your horse, and even them." He handed her the muff and helped wrap the safeguard around her. "If we could only communicate, we might prevent so many problems. I think I'll try to learn their tongue. There's a man near here who knows it. His father was a minister among the Pequots. Who knows, it might even give me the advantage in trade."

Sarah was not convinced of the benefit, however. She had heard two natives speak once. It was barbarous noise to her. She could not imagine herself making such utterances. She rubbed the spots where her rescuers had touched her. They had responded as any Englishmen would have; they saved her and Athena.

Maybe she could just learn "thank you." Also, "please." Then she wondered if savages even had such words.

※

For half an hour they followed a stony path, slowly descending from the cascade. They entered a cleared area and passed in front of a farmhouse. At one end a man stopped cutting wood and rested his axe on the chopping block. He waved.

"A farmer is hailing us," Sarah told Wheeler.

"He's always glad to see someone passing by. Hello." But Wheeler waved toward the opposite end of the house, where a buck was hanging upside down from the branch of a tree. The white blaze showed from the drooping tail, and the deer's tongue dangled above a wooden pail on the ground. Sarah looked away and did not inform Wheeler of his mistake.

In a few moments she saw the ordinary where Wheeler had said they would compose themselves. It was the first painted building Sarah had seen since she left Boston. Even Wheeler could spot the white walls at a hundred yards.

"Hello, Mrs. Caulkins," he called. He dismounted and tied the horses to a ring on a water barrel. "Mrs. Caulkins, are you there?" By the time they were secured, a woman with a cane opened the door.

"Mr. Wheeler. How nice. It's been an age."

"I'm escorting a woman to New Haven. We had a near calamity at the bridge and could use some refreshment."

"Oh my. Poor dears. Come in. Come in. You'll have some brandy, then." She led them into the social room, tapping the way on the polished floor with her cane. "Have a seat in the sunshine there." Her trembling hand pointed to a table by a large window with rows of small glass panes. "I have applesauce bread, baked this morning."

As Sarah settled herself, the woman looked her over thoroughly. It was not an intrusive examination; more like a grandmother surveying a beloved one. She smiled. Her head trembled in concert with her hands.

"This is Mrs. Knight from Boston. She's ridden all the way here on her horse."

"Oh my," she said again.

"I told her she'd receive the best entertainment here."

"Yes. Yes. I'll have a tray brought in." She left to get her serving girl.

"Mrs. Caulkins is the repository for all news and travellers' tales between New London and New Haven. She never forgets a detail. You'll be known around here in short time too." The aged chronicler rejoined them. "What's the latest hereabout?" Wheeler asked.

She lowered herself stiffly onto a chair. "Moses Griswold's wedding. A fine groom at age sixty-eight." She was overcome by a tiny attack of mirth. "Poor Moses. He did poorly as a widower. Wife died of putrid fever last spring."

The tray arrived and refreshments were served. The three saluted Moses and then each other and drank down the brandy.

"So he found himself another wife." Wheeler poured a second glass and took a slice of bread.

Mrs. Caulkins nodded. "And this sent his three sons into a passion. She's not only the same age as the eldest son, she has two sons of her own. The Griswolds imagined their inheritance would shrink from thirds to fifths, so they protested to the magistrate, calling the new wife a schemer and opportunist."

"How selfish," Wheeler said.

"Oh, but the judge saw through them well enough. He chided their self-interest, as well as their ignorance. They weren't clever enough to see that the new wife's estate passed on to their father. They stood to inherit an additional mill, two land parcels, twenty dairy cows and a house."

"Was their behavior grievous to the father?" Wheeler ate a second slice of bread.

"It had no effect on him. He was a giddy groom. I took great offense on his part, though, and condemned them extremely. I said their father had a right to whatever portion of happiness was left in his time on earth."

"You spoke the truth," Wheeler said.

They finished their second glass with a toast to truth. Wheeler again refilled the glasses and had another slice of bread.

"And what about a portion of happiness for you?" he asked. "Have you found a suitor?"

It took some moments for the woman to recover from this amusement. "I've outlived all the possibilities. There's not a man left my age. I can't even entice someone younger with my ample property and the great probability he'd soon be a widower." She paused to laugh again. "Enough. Is your husband still living, my dear?" she asked Sarah.

The shift of attention to her, and especially the question, caused Sarah to hesitate. "I think so. We're a May-December marriage like the Griswolds." The brandy encouraged more elaboration than she otherwise would have provided. "But he's been at sea since ninety-eight, and my last letter was a year ago."

"What a pity to be left without your helpmate."

Sarah would not have thought to call her husband a helpmate. "With him away for much of our marriage, I've learned to help myself."

Mrs. Caulkins looked off toward a portrait by the fireplace. "My husband and I were never apart one day in forty-three years." Her comment seemed more a reminiscence than an intentional comparison.

The three of them withdrew briefly to their brandy and private musings.

Sarah had no such portrait of Richard, and sometimes she had to concentrate to recall his features. At times she even had difficulty hearing his voice.

Then Mrs. Caulkins said, "So, tell me what it's like to ride here from Boston. I can't even imagine it."

Another round of drinks and the rest of the bread were required in order to apprise them of the nature of her business and to relate the major events of her journey, concluding with the incident on the Niantic bridge.

"This is truly remarkable. It's my pleasure to have met you," the hostess said.

The sun through the window was hot on Sarah's back, her chest was warm with brandy. She felt recruited from the morning's adventure and could have dozed off in comfort had Wheeler not slapped the table and declared his gratitude for the entertainment.

"Our goal is the tavern in Killingworth by dark," Wheeler said, "and we're only a quarter of the way." He stood up. "I'll get the horses ready."

※

From thence the terrain was more hospitable, so they were able to pace for some time. To her great relief the crossing at Saybrook caused no terror. In over forty years of service the Saybrook ferry had come to meet the requirements of civilized passengers. Sarah's horse was confined in a low box-stall, and she sat on a bench attached to the enclosed sides of the ferry. Seated beside her was a couple going to visit an ailing parent. She kept up a stream of conversation to avoid looking at the water.

When the pair had mounted to resume their journey, Wheeler said, "I've never ridden past Saybrook, so I don't know what accommodations lie on the other side. Perhaps we should eat dinner here. Are you hungry?"

"A stop would be welcome," she said. "Where do we go?"

He motioned with his hand. "Straight ahead from the dock, left at the T and then the first right."

※

Four dogs came running around an unimpressive building. They barked furiously. Squealing pigs and squawking hens scattered in the befouled yard. The door flew open, and a girl began screeching.

"Shut up, you dogs. Come here." She banged a wooden spoon on the door frame. "Bad dogs. Come here." But she commanded no authority over them, and they made a yapping circle around the horses.

Wheeler dismounted and swatted his hat at them. "Go away." They retreated, but continued their protest until the newcomers were inside.

The landlady came into the small social room. "Are you wanting to eat?" Clumps of greasy hair had escaped her bun. Her fingers were webbed with dough; some of it stuck to the hair she poked back over her ears.

"We'd have what's quickest," Wheeler said.

"My pie's not done, but I can broil you some mutton. It'll be six pence apiece." She stood there waiting, so Sarah realized she wished to be paid in advance of her efforts. The hostess slowly counted the coins Sarah had dropped in her dough-covered palm then returned to her kitchen hearth, leaving her two guests to make themselves welcome.

When she came back, they were seated at a table that Sarah had wiped clean with her handkerchief. The hostess placed some bowls and spoons on the table and disappeared. The daughter who had scolded the dogs carried in a tray of meat. The smell of vinegar assaulted their noses.

"What the devil is this?" Wheeler said, but the girl had gone.

"The woman must have broiled some pickled mutton." Sarah bounced her spoon on one of the chunks. "You'll need the jaw of a wolf for this."

Wheeler sniffed, then he pushed away from the table. "It's been in souse. I abhor souse. She probably had the head and feet in the souse barrel too." He stood up.

"I have no appetite either," Sarah said.

They left the tavern and rode off with nothing but a bad odor for their dinner.

"You won't have gotten a true impression of Saybrook by that example. There are people here who could've welcomed you, if we'd had time. Some of the finest men of New England." She was informed of an almanac maker, of a man who repelled Andros, and of the founders of the colony's new collegiate school.

From Saybrook they put forward with all speed. To their good fortune the path was well-trod and easy to follow.

※

At twilight they reached the Killingworth settlement. First was a sheep farm, where two dogs ran to place themselves between their flock and the intruders. Next was a fulling mill, which was quiet from the day's labor. Several houses preceded a small meetinghouse on the town green. Then they came upon a young man who was herding cows in their direction.

"Good evening," Wheeler said. "Could you tell us if the lodgings in Killingworth are on this road?"

"Aye, sir. Before the river ford is Burnham's place. It's the post stage. Where've you come from?"

"We left New London this morning."

"Where are you going?"

"To New Haven. How's the road?"

"Not much of a road at all. There are some Indian paths, but no real roads. Too many marshes and rivers, and some of the farmers have fenced their land, so it's hard to find the way around them."

Wheeler would have asked for specific details, but one cow had wandered off, and the young man ran to catch her.

Half a mile brought them to a weathered building on which was painted a name, not readable in the fading light. Wheeler went in to inquire about the accommodations. It annoyed her that men were able to get on and off a horse when they wanted to. She could dismount only if someone brought steps. They were never left out where she could get to them. She wondered if she could get up onto a man's saddle while wearing a petticoat. Probably not. Men could ride faster astride, and they faced the direction in which they rode. On her sidesaddle Sarah could just as easily look backwards as forwards. Men could ride off and never look back. Further thought about this inequity was interrupted by Wheeler's return with the proprietor, a short man of generous proportion.

"Most welcome, most welcome you are." He lugged the mounting to Sarah's horse and reached for the reins. "You've had a long ride. Come in and my wife will take care of you."

The supper made up for the dinner they could not eat. Almost anything would have been satisfactory, except for souse. Neither of them could resist the pleasant claret the host offered, and after several glasses they were ready for an early retirement.

Destinatio

Saturday, October 7

Raucous honking overhead wakened Sarah. A musket shot raised the pitch, then the honking gradually faded away. The room was gray in the faint morning light. It was much more pleasant to wake in a room with a window. She uncurled from her side to stretch out on her back. Her feet hit a pile that contained her outer garments and shoes. One plunked on the floor. She did not recall going to bed.

A woman called her name and opened the door. "Mr. Wheeler said to wake you. Do you need any help getting dressed?"

"No, thank you." She surveyed the room, which contained nothing but the bed. "Where am I to do my toilette?"

"In the lean-to room off the kitchen. There's a basin and mirror. The door goes out to the privy."

Sarah now recognized the wife of the host. "Tell Mr. Wheeler I'll be out presently."

※

Wheeler welcomed her to a table by the fireplace. Hot

bread pudding was already set out. "Sorry to wake you so early, but we have to reach New Haven before dark. Most towns are strict about no travelling on Sabbath eve."

"I hadn't thought about it being Saturday. I don't want to spend my first hours in New Haven before a magistrate. What's the punishment here?"

"In New London it's usually a fine. For the unrepentant, it's the stocks. But a traveller far from home is often the most suspect and the most harshly treated." His spoon clanked on the bottom of the porringer as he tried to get the remaining bits of pudding.

"I'll settle with the host while you prepare the horses," Sarah said between quick bites. "Do we know the way?"

"Vaguely. The young man last night was right. Mr. Burnham says there's not a road, exactly. We turn at so-and-so's farm, then go a way, then pass by so-and-so's place. With those directions we'll probably have to stop at every door." He left, shaking his head.

Sarah put on her wraps and made her settlement.

Wheeler was waiting at the mounting steps. "When I got the horses at the common field, a man told me low tide's almost over. We'll have to move quickly to cross the two rivers west of here, and one's the Hammonasset." She got aboard her horse, and he motioned for her to go.

They passed the town green and meetinghouse. Several people who were in the road at that hour stopped to watch them. Sarah thought they must be staring in surprise at seeing a female rider, and one in the lead as well. After the burial grounds they slowed to enter an opening in the marsh grass. Ahead, a thin mist hung over a river. In the middle, a man was riding one cow and leading another with a rope.

"What's it like?" Wheeler asked.

"About thirty feet across. The water's only up to the animals' knees." She nudged Athena to wade in. Groups of ducks and geese floated away from the travellers. The man turned to see who was behind him.

"Good morning, sir," Sarah said. She enjoyed his shocked expression.

"Morning." It appeared as though he wanted to ask something.

"Seems like a fine day for a ride to New Haven," Sarah said. She smiled, looked ahead, and continued past him, wanting to give the appearance she had said nothing remarkable, but she wished she could have seen what his reaction was.

At the west bank of the river they again went through the marsh grass. Then they climbed a rocky slope and paused at the top.

"What's ahead?" Wheeler asked.

"The land's cleared. There's a house about a quarter of a mile ahead. Must be the one Burnham mentioned."

"That's where the path bears right and goes up to the next ford. Let's go."

Sarah needed no urging, however. Every moment meant rising water. The previous river had not frightened her. The muddy bottom made Athena's steps sluggish, which she much preferred to slipping and stumbling on a rocky bottom. She was not sure how far the next ford was, but she was riding as fast as she dared. Tenseness in her lower back increased to an ache.

A small orchard marked the bend in the road. A farmer waved from a ladder. Below him, a woman nodded her greeting because she was holding an apple basket. Sarah gave a quick wave with her reins. The ache in her back became a burning pain.

Beyond the farm, bushes and tall grass closed in on the path. When it entered the woods, they had to slow the horses. The path would have accommodated a person on foot; it was shoulder width and head high, but in the saddle, the riders had to use raised elbows and forearms to protect their faces from the assaults of branches.

Sarah noticed the path was deeply worn, in many places a foot below ground level. The young cowherd had mentioned that the way was mostly Indian paths. Since so few people travelled here on horseback, she realized Englishmen could not have worn it so; it must have taken centuries of leather-wrapped feet. She was again in their realm. The last settlement was only thirty minutes back, but she found no mark of civilization here, just the presence of savagery. She glanced around, expecting painted faces to appear.

Trees grew right to the high water mark of the Hammonasset River. This time there was no one crossing the ford who could reveal its depth. It was only slightly wider than the last river and was moving a bit faster.

Sarah turned to Wheeler. "Will you ride ahead this time? I'm afraid to test the depth."

"What sort of embankment's on the other side?"

"Same as here—gradual, gravel. Trees are thick beyond the bank. The path's directly across from us."

Wheeler kicked his horse. "Here we go fella. Easy on."

The first ten feet were quite shallow. Midway, there was a channel where the water touched the horse's underbelly, but in a few steps it was again at ankle depth. He waited there at the edge of the channel for her. "The bottom's firm. Just lift your feet at the middest part."

Sarah gathered up her hems and wedged them between her right knee and the pommel. "Easy on." She repeated Wheeler's instruction. Then remembering the Pollys, she added, "Sojack," although it sounded peculiar—like something one says to a mule. Athena was not offended, however, and carried Sarah to the opposite bank without incident.

After a half-mile ride they emerged from the wood. The path curved southwest and ran alongside a fenced horse meadow. Several dozen draft mares, colts and fillies were occupied with their grazing and paid no attention to the travellers. The path widened. They passed between two farmhouses set back from the road. Five children ran toward them and waved.

Sarah saw a dilemma ahead. "We'll have to stop and ask. The road goes in three directions."

On the right, just before the road divided, was a large house. Part of it was weathered wood, the rest had newer clapboards. Four men were on top, hammering shingles onto a new roof that covered both halves.

Sarah called to a woman who was at a wellcurb drawing

water. "Good morning, goodwife. Could you give us directions to New Haven?"

The woman let go of the wellsweep and set down her bucket. "My husband will have to help you. I'll get him." She went to the ladder and called, "John, there are travellers who need directions. Can you come down?"

Three men came to peer over the peak. The fourth came down a ladder and walked up to Wheeler, wiped his hand on his trousers and held it out. "John Graves. Where are you headed?"

"Good morning. Joshua Wheeler of New London. I'm escorting Mrs. Knight to New Haven. What settlement is this?"

"Madison. To go to New Haven you keep straight ahead to the bridge at the East River." He pushed a lock of hair away from his eyes. "On t'other side's a path that winds down a hill and takes you to a cornfield. You have to ride around it and go south until you find a lane on the right. That takes you to the Guilford town square." Vigorous arm signals had dislodged the hair, and he pushed it back again. "If you come to a saw pit you've gone too far. You have to follow the lane after the cornfield. When you get to Guilford someone can show you the road to Branford and New Haven. It's an easy go from there; it's getting to Guilford that's a tribulation." His arms finally came to rest. "May we offer refreshment? My wife can get you something."

Mrs. Graves nodded in confirmation.

Sarah declined. "Thank you, but we have to reach New Haven before sundown. We plan to ride without stopping. Much obliged for the directions, though."

"Godspeed," Graves offered, and so did his wife.

Sarah and Wheeler departed with her in the lead again. She thought this would cause speculation and debate at the Graves' house before everyone could get back to work.

As they continued it seemed that all of Madison was at work. A man and his black servant were hanging the front door on a newly built house. Two women were busy at a lye kettle that hung over a fire they had made between their homes. A father and his son were skinning a deer, which was suspended from a wooden frame. In a garden where frostbitten stalks and leaves remained, children were gathering pumpkins and squashes. Above the hoofbeats Sarah even heard axes.

After the last house, they passed an ox pasture and came to the bridge. Unlike the one near New London, this had hewn planks that provided a flat bed. It stood in full, midmorning sunlight and was free of algae. Although rocks and boulders encumbered the path on the other side of the bridge, the way down the hill was recognizable until they arrived at the cornfield.

"Now what?" Wheeler asked. "Do you see where to go?"

"I think we should keep to the right and ride around the perimeter until we find the path going south."

As they skirted the cornfield, they startled blackbirds, which rose in strident protest. Their alarm spread like a wave across the field, and complainants joined them until a shrieking cloud completely obscured the sky above the travellers' heads. The skin on Sarah's neck and back contracted. She kicked Athena. They raced along the edge of the field. Sarah's scream was lost in the deafening cloud. It drifted off in one direction, then it shifted and floated over them again. The riders reached the far end. The black cloud settled among the corn rows behind them. Sarah reined to a stop to collect herself. She looked back at the field of quivering, cackling cornstalks.

Wheeler reached out with his hand. "Are you all right?"

Sarah nodded and received a reassuring squeeze before the horses pranced and pulled them apart. She said, "I felt like a black shroud had come over me."

Wheeler looked up. "Around here the sun's often blocked by flocks of pigeons or ducks or whatever."

"Not in Boston. We see migrating flocks now and then, but with a couple of thousand armed households, birds with any sense don't darken our skies. We eat everything that flies."

⁂

They found a cartway that led from the cornfield, so they rode side by side, each in a wheel rut. When they failed to come upon a lane to the right, they decided to stop at a farmhouse and ask directions.

"Hello, in the garden," Wheeler called to someone digging potatoes. A young lad, tall for his years, tossed his garden fork on his shoulder and came to the fence.

"We were told in Madison to turn right after a cornfield to go to Guilford," Wheeler said, "but we don't think the fellow said how far down this road the lane was."

"You didn't come to it yet." One long leg at a time swung over the fence rail. He studied Sarah from both sides of the saddle. "On her own horse, eh? No pillion?"

Wheeler interrupted the examination. "So, how long a ride to get there?"

"Don't know. Don't have a horse." He asked Sarah, "How you stay up on that thing?"

She flipped the end of her reins toward the lad, but he persisted in staring. Ignoring his impertinent question, she asked her own. "Well, if you managed to walk that far, how long would it take you?"

"About ten minutes." He came around where he could inspect her skirts. "You got a hook or something to hang on to under there?"

"You're very bold, you lubber." Wheeler nosed his horse between the lad and Sarah. "We'll thank you to just give us directions. What marks the lane?"

"My Uncle Sam's lot. It's on the corner." The contempt in the youth's voice made it seem as if everyone should know this.

"His lot? What does that mean?" Wheeler flung his hands up in the air. "A farm? A cornfield?"

"Nay, just his lot. He lives in England." He laughed at their ignorance.

"How does knowing who owns a piece of wilderness help us find our way?" The cords in Wheeler's neck pressed on his collar. "Your stupidity's equaled by your rudeness." He turned to Sarah. "Let's go. We can't expect to find civility in a potato patch."

Sarah led, leaving the lad behind and his curiosity unsatisfied. Despite his useless directions, they found a narrow lane near a stand of walnut trees, no doubt Uncle Sam's, and followed it to the Guilford common.

At high noon, the sun gave prominence to every aspect of activity in the village. The two travellers stopped while Sarah described the common to Wheeler. Clusters of pigs, geese, chickens, sheep, and children were in constant motion. Streams of smoke from fireplaces rose to a blue-white canopy over the common. Several men were unloading fresh-cut lumber between two houses under construction. The rasping sound of the saw pits came from a distance to the left.

"Greetings strangers." A man came up behind them. "I'm Deacon Leete. Welcome to Guilford Plantation." He had a broad face and a smile that caused the corners of his eyes to crinkle.

"Joshua Wheeler of New London. This is Mrs. Knight of Boston."

"It's an honor to meet guests from such fine places." He adjusted his neckpiece and pushed the loose folds of his blouse back into his breeches. "How may I help you?"

"We're on our way to New Haven. We hope the path ahead is easier to follow than the one we've just taken," Wheeler said.

"Oh, yes. It's clearly laid and well-travelled. Many brethren from New Haven have holdings on this bank of the Quinnipiac." He pointed across the common. "You see the opposite corner there? That's the road. It goes over Granite Hill and through Branford."

"How many more river crossings?" Sarah asked.

"There's a bridge where Furnace Pond becomes the East Haven River. It's at the iron works; you can't miss it. And about three miles beyond that is the ferry across the Quinnipiac."

"We can reach New Haven before sunset, then?" Sarah asked.

Leete nodded. "You should. Would you have refreshment before you go? We have a woman who keeps a public room."

"Thank you, no." Sarah nudged Athena. "We're anxious to reach our destination."

"Thank you, sir," Wheeler added, and he fell in behind Sarah on a worn path across the trampled common.

※

On either side of the road from Guilford were massive gray boulders that had been thrust out of the earth at sharp angles—granite for millstones and tombstones. The horses' hooves clacked on the graveled path as they descended the hill to Branford. The travellers rode past the settlement and arrived at the East River bridge. Activity at the iron furnace had ceased in preparation for the Sabbath. Farther along they came to the Quinnipiac dock, where they had to wait for the ferry to return from the New Haven shore.

Sarah shielded her eyes from the late afternoon sun. She gazed with anticipation at her goal—the colony of the resolute Puritans, the shelter of regicides, the agricultural port of the colonies, the home of her relatives. In the center of the community the pyramid roof and cupola of a three-story structure rose above the other buildings. It had to be the meetinghouse. She described the opposite shore to her companion.

The afternoon sun and the lack of any breeze made the ferry crossing slow and smooth. Her imagined welcome occupied Sarah's mind the entire way.

At the New Haven dock, Wheeler dispatched a boy to find her relatives. Their homes were nearby, and within minutes she was being embraced by numbers of people whose faces looked familiar to her, even though she had never seen them before. They escorted her to the Prouts' house because it was the closest.

※

During the family reunion Wheeler made arrangements to stable her horse, booked a Monday passage for New London, found lodgings for the weekend and brought Sarah's saddlebags to the Prouts' house.

When Sarah realized what he had done while she was preoccupied, she was embarrassed that she had forgotten her guide. She invited him in to meet her family. "This is my mother's cousin, Mary Prout, her husband, John, and their children." There were four, and she did not remember all their names. Wheeler shook hands with the parents.

"Welcome to our home, Mr. Wheeler," John Prout said. "Have you been to New Haven before?"

"No, I haven't. But from what I can see at the docks, its reputation's well deserved. It's a fair place."

"Let me introduce the rest of my family," said Mrs. Prout. "These are my late sister's children, Thomas Trowbridge, Elizabeth Hodgson and Lydia Rosewell. It's their brother's death that brought Sarah here."

"My condolences to all of you. I'm glad to have been of assistance to Mrs. Knight. I won't intrude on your family gathering any longer."

Sarah went with him to the door, where they determined the amount of recompense he should receive.

"For a half-blind escort you should get a fifty percent deduction," Wheeler said. "You had to find your own way, after all."

"No. No. It was my pleasure to have had your company. Please tell your family I'm most grateful for their parting with it. I hope all's well on your return."

"I'll have much to share with them. Don't forget to call on us when you come back through New London. I want my wife to meet you."

※

As soon as her nieces and nephew had left, Mary Prout installed Sarah on her divan. She adjusted her bodice over the bulge in her midsection and got right to business. "You certainly shocked everyone with your unexpected appearance. We just got your letter last week, and you didn't say anything about coming here."

"I wrote it the day after he died. I had the idea to make the journey then, but I wasn't sure it would be possible, so I didn't mention it."

"Well, you could see the shock when everyone heard there was a will naming the new wife as principle heir. Tell me, what's she like?"

"She's as kind and sweet as you could ever hope to find. I've known her for years, her parents too. She grew up nearby. She was married only six months when her first husband died. Then she lost her parents in a fire. That's when she came to live with me. She had nothing left, just a small inheritance." Sarah stretched to relieve her sore back muscles. "I was so glad when she married Caleb. She said, 'I think I'll have a happy life now.' And then this happened."

Mary Prout shook her head. "Such a tragedy. He was a nice young man. My favorite nephew. Thomas is too stiff. Caleb, though, he could make you laugh. He didn't suffer, did he?"

"He never complained, but he swelled up till you didn't recognize him. Our doctor, Mr. Boylston, tried everything."

"He was delicate of health since he was a child. It never slowed him down, though. He was always going from one venture to another."

"A risk-taker in search of profits," Sarah said, "like everyone else. I've come here to look out for Mary's interests. I'm hoping she'll be provided for. It'll depend on the value of his estate."

"It should be sizeable. Thomas and the sisters will be greatly displeased if it's not. They already had plans for their shares before you arrived. Especially Elizabeth. Go cautiously with her."

John Prout came to remind the ladies that it was nearing time for their Sabbath meditation. Sarah stretched again and gave some groans. She even yawned for good measure. Mary was alert to her guests condition.

"She's too tired from such a journey," she told her husband. "I'll show her where she's going to stay." She took Sarah by the arm. "I'll have cook bring you a tray of refreshment, then you can retire early."

As they climbed the stairs, Sarah was silently thankful she had been excused from the family devotions, but the reprieve was short-lived.

John Prout called after them. "I've decided she should sit in our box at the meetinghouse tomorrow. We leave the house after breakfast. Quarter to eight."

"A quarter to eight," Sarah repeated. Just her luck. Her relatives had turned out to be among the devout Puritans.

Sarah admitted having a religious core and even acknowledged the Great Benefactor's protection on her journey, but she was not one to meditate on a Sabbath eve. And just sitting there this evening would have been an impossible task, anyway, let alone trying to appear pious. She was too full of her adventures. Tired but tightly wound up. She would get through tomorrow's meeting tomorrow.

*

The upper room that was to be her apartment during her stay in New Haven was pleasing. She ate her meal at a table next to the front window. Then she emptied her saddlebags and pockets and found a place in a fine walnut cabinet for all the items. Afterwards she sat at the table to compose her adventures in her journal. Stonington was the last entry.

She began with the father-daughter quarrels of her two unpolished escorts to New London, recording them as best she remembered. Sarah praised her host in that town, calling him affable, courteous and generous, but omitted the wig and emerald satin cassock. She wrote about the rough and terrifying terrain the next morning, but refused to write about the naked Pequots, who touched her. In her journal they got no credit for rescuing her on the bridge. She commended the elderly Saybrook hostess and condemned the souse-maker and the lubber who angered Wheeler. Having penned herself to New Haven, she put away her writing materials and dressed for bed.

Sarah was impatient to explore the town, to have a close look at the houses and find out what was happening at the docks. She was anxious to get the will to the probate officers and was unsure how the relatives would react once they actually read it.

It was exciting to think that all the important personages of Connecticut Colony would be here at the Assembly next week. And Captain Prentice. She now had the time to speculate on what news he might have of her errant husband. At best, she thought, the captain could have word of what business Richard was so successful with that he had no time to write. At worst he would have last seen Richard walk off his ship in London a year ago. And that was a lot more recent than she had seen him.

She went to the window, pressed her face to the pane and cupped her hands around her eyes. There was nothing but blackness outside—no river, no harbor, no houses. She blew out the lamp and went to bed. The bedclothes were cold.

Revelata

Thursday, October 12

The bell on the top of the meetinghouse began calling the members of the General Assembly of Connecticut Colony.

"Let's go. I don't want to miss anything." Sarah helped Mary Prout hurry with her wraps. Mary was puffing, something that happened with moderate exertion because she had much weight to carry. Sarah helped her fasten her cape at the neck.

"I still don't understand what interest the assembly will be to someone from Boston," Mary said. She tugged at the collar of the cape. "They go on and on about fences and tax lists and rates of pay. And this time it'll be about defense plans against the French and Iroquois up north." She opened the door. "Anyway women don't go."

Sarah had expended much energy the previous night trying to persuade Mary to accompany her to the assembly meeting. "I have to do something to amuse myself," she had said. "I nearly killed myself getting here because of the will. I didn't imagine that after I registered it, I'd have to wait over a month for the probate court to collect itself. How do they ever settle anything, if they only meet four times a year?"

Mary Prout just huffed along as they stepped smartly to avoid remembrances left in the road by a herd of horses that had been driven earlier to a waiting ship. The closer they walked toward the meetinghouse the more crowded the way became. When they reached the trampled green, it was filled with men in greatcoats and cloaks, their wide-brimmed hats bobbing as they shook hands.

"Do you see how many women are here?" Mary was panting. "Three. And they're probably widows come for permission to sell land to pay off debts or something."

"Then there aren't three, there are five; you didn't count us. Lead the way."

They wove through groups of men and entered the building. When she first went to Sunday meeting she was impressed by its size for a town so small. But she was amazed that in over sixty years, the residents of New Haven had only managed to build three public buildings: the meetinghouse, a schoolhouse and a gaol. They were still smarting over their loss of independence forty years before, when they were forced to become a county within the larger and more powerful Connecticut Colony. Now her relatives boasted of having the largest town and of reaching an agreement with Hartford three years ago to make New Haven the co-capital. The town had great plans to build a county house, but so far their talk had not produced a board or nail. The two women took a stairway to the gallery, where they chose a bench near the railing. Several dozen other observers joined them.

"You see," Mary complained out of breath, "everyone stares at us, wondering why we're here."

"Nonsense," Sarah replied. As the assemblymen entered and found places to sit, the building rumbled with their boots, which stirred up dust from the dried mud on the floor. She pressed Mary into service. "Who's there in the wig?"

"I don't know, but you can be sure he's from New London. They've taken to wearing them, along with other affectations."

Sarah pictured Gurdon Saltonstall in his elegant peruke. He had such dignity of bearing and was as honorable a minister, scholar and gentleman as she had ever met in an emerald green cassock. She decided to ignore the remark.

"Look there," Mary continued. "Even Governor Winthrop, another New Londoner. A periwig at his age. What might his father say if he'd lived to see this?" Mary shook her head.

From the time Sarah was a girl, she had seen him in the streets of Boston. The last time was about six years ago, when he served on Governor Andros' council. He appeared to be in his late sixties now and looked altogether different in a wig, which he would not have dared to wear in Boston. He would have been severely lectured by Samuel Sewell.

"I wonder who he's talking to?" Mary said. A tall man, whose arms and hands were in constant agitation, finally finished speaking and sat down. Then Winthrop helped an elderly man walk to his seat in the front. The governor called for attention.

Mary whispered, "That's Robert Treat next to Winthrop. The previous governor. How ancient he is now. Came here as a boy. He laid out the Milford settlement when he was only fifteen, but he was always so restless." She paused briefly while the speaker declared the session open. "Once, he left with a rebel minister to found a congregation in Newark, but he eventually came back to his land and mill. He became a distinguished military officer." Mary leaned closer to Sarah's ear. In an even lower whisper she said, "And would you believe he's a recent bridegroom?"

Sarah smiled and nodded. Of course she had heard of Treat. Everyone in Boston knew how he had stood up to Andros. She even knew Widow Bryan, who left Boston last year to marry him. The next time Sarah wrote home she would have to describe the widow's catch.

Half an hour was spent taking attendance. Each deputy rose to give his name, office and town and waited for the clerk to record it. One of them was a sturdy man of fifty some years, who distinguished himself from the others by wearing a beard.

"Captain John Prentice, Deputy, New London."

Sarah had met him the evening before. His stepmother's note had directed her to the Talmadge residence, a block from the Prouts'. She had been invited inside for an interview with him.

"My ship arrived the day after you left," he had told Sarah. "I was a week late. My stepmother was happy to be rid of the waiting passengers." Prentice had fixed his brown, marble eyes on her while his right hand constantly fussed with the bushy, rust-colored beard. "She said you were looking for someone."

"A year ago Richard Knight sent a letter to Boston."

"Oh, Knight. Yes." He had nodded. "He's your relation?"

"A cousin." Sarah had not wanted to admit who he was, and watched the marble eyes to see if they detected her falsehood. "Richard said he was sailing on the *John and Hester* from New York to Barbados and then England, and he would remain there to establish himself in business. The family hasn't heard from him since."

"Knight didn't go to England. I last saw him in Barbados. The day before departure he came on board to tell me that personal matters prevented him from continuing on as purser." Prentice shook his head in reproof. "That put me in a bind to replace him at the last minute."

The captain's hostess brought in a tray of gingerbread and cider and set it on a small table next to him.

"Thank you," he said. "I told him he was acting irresponsibly by deserting a post midvoyage, but he said an important opportunity had presented itself while we were docked there. I have no idea what it was, though."

Since Prentice had not moved toward the refreshment, Mrs. Talmadge pushed it in front of him.

"I don't know what became of him," he said. "If his letter said he was sailing on my ship, then it was a deliberate deception. He came to resign his post the day before I set sail." Prentice then motioned for Sarah to take a plate.

Sarah had thanked him for the information and changed the subject. She would need time alone to sort out the bewildering news about Richard. Over refreshments they had exchanged pleasantries, discovered that she knew his wife's family in Boston, and discussed her journey thus far. Prentice had seemed quite impressed with her account. They had shaken hands when she left. Only then did she notice one finger on his right hand was missing.

She had taken the longest route back to the Prouts' in order to set her wits upon the intelligence she had been given. In the course of a year she had first been puzzled by the lack of correspondence from Richard, then annoyed at his usual thoughtlessness, then gradually grew accustomed to his absence. Now she was angry.

She began to consider Richard's possible motives. By the time she had reached the Prouts', she had come to several conclusions. First, Richard deliberately wanted her to think he had gone to England. Second, he wanted her to think that so if she eventually began searching for him, she would not begin in the right place. Third, he was up to something he wanted concealed—something illegal or immoral. And finally, in a year's time he could have gone anywhere. Prentice's news had kept her mind occupied far into the night.

※

The assembly roll call concluded. Nominations were taken for elections to be held at the May assembly. Mary became animated. "You should be here for Election Day," she whispered. "It's our big holiday. The Assembly meets in Hartford, but we send our delegates off with a feast day. When the young man who accompanies them returns with the results, we fire the cannon. Then we hold a special county market day when the delegates return, so everyone in the county can come hear their report."

A cannon, thought Sarah, herds of farmers with coats of gray, black or brown, ruminating over the news—surely Mary forgot a service at the meetinghouse. That had to be a part of such an exciting day. With an entire county of souls gathered in one place, a minister would never miss the opportunity to deliver an all-day sermon. She had not met Reverend Pierpont yet, but even the most affable and otherwise sensible of ministers was capable of inflicting a six-hour harangue on his flock, with only a noon break for dinner. And in this solemn and pious town such a sermon was a certainty.

There was a commotion when the lower house removed itself to a tavern to take up lesser matters. The fifty-or-so remaining assemblymen began deliberations concerning military affairs. Mary commented in Sarah's ear about the first few speakers, but by the time the discussion centered on how much recompense to pay for horses, saddles and bridles lost in the fighting, her head sank to her bosom and she was dozing. Even Sarah lost interest when a disagreement arose over the number of snow shoes and Indian shoes each town should maintain for its citizens' needs and whether the colony or each individual county should pay for them.

Perhaps the lower house was discussing more interesting cases. Sarah shifted on the bench in such a way as to wake Mary without Mary's knowing she had been discovered napping.

"I've had my fill here," Sarah said.

"How about going to Miles' Tavern for a bowl of China

tea?" Mary asked. "Then you'll be satisfied having seen the lower house as well."

※

"It won't hold another person." Mrs. Miles pointed to the public room. All the women could see were the backs of the men who were crowded in the doorway of the smoke-filled public room. "But won't you come to the kitchen? I have other guests."

Sarah was not the least bit disappointed to be introduced to the governor's daughter, Mary Winston Livingston, and two young women who had accompanied her from New London. Their appearance was a brilliant contrast to the local, drab-colored skirts and longsleeved bodices. They wore belted taffeteen gowns, left unbuttoned to reveal embroidered underbodices, and they had ruffled petticoats. Next to a copy of *Behind the Dressing Room Door* was a curling iron. It explained the three cascades of carefully arranged curls. Sarah glanced at her cousin, who confirmed with a nod that she was right about the proclivities of New Londoners.

Sarah extended her hand to Mrs. Livingston. "We've never been introduced, but I remember seeing you in Boston when you were a girl, which seems to me was just a few years ago. Now I must congratulate you on your marriage."

Mrs. Miles placed two more chairs at the table for her visitors.

The bride said, "I've wanted to travel to Boston again with my husband, but the frontier fighting has occupied most of his time. What brings you to New Haven?"

"The death of my cousin, Caleb Trowbridge." Sarah helped Mary remove her cape. "This is his aunt, Mary Prout. We're related through the Rutherfords. Actually, my theory is that, at this point, most of us in the colonies are related." She gave their wraps to Mrs. Miles. "Where is your husband from?" Sarah knew who the Livingstons were, but she wanted to hear the bride's assessment of the family.

Over tea Mary Livingston imparted with pride the Livingston family story, beginning with their association with the Winthrops back in England. Her father-in-law, Robert, had arrived in the colonies at nineteen. He became immediately successful in the fur trade and political life of Albany because he spoke Dutch and quickly learned Iroquois. Within six years of marrying Dominie van Rensselaer's widow, he was the patroon of hundreds of square acres overlooking the Hudson River.

"I lived at the new manor until John and I built our house in New London. It was an amazing place—a trading post, fort, meetinghouse, bakery and home all in one."

All the while she talked, she twirled one curl after another around her index finger. "Now Father-in-Law is in London trying to convince the English to mount a full campaign against the French in Canada. I guess if he's successful, I'll see even less of John." Mary praised her mother-in-law's kindness, good sense and thrift, and hoped she could also be a valuable helpmate to her new husband. She made it appear that modesty prevented her from giving an account of her husband's fine qualities, making Sarah suspect otherwise.

"If I weren't afraid of water, I'd like to see the Hudson River one day," Sarah said, "but I'm land-locked by my fear of water travel."

"How did you get here from Boston, then?" one of the friends asked.

"She came on a horse," Mary Prout answered for her. "And after her experience, it's amazing she fears something like water. She has more cause to fear her fellow man."

With this *entrée* Sarah was entreated to provide the account of her trip to yet another eager and incredulous audience. Several times her cousin interrupted to remind her of a detail Sarah had left out. Sarah was perfecting her tale. She remembered each turn of phrase that had pleased or amused or shocked her previous audiences. She could feel a distance growing between her experience and herself. Sarah-on-horseback was becoming a character separate from Sarah who was telling the story.

"When the estate's settled, I'll be returning through New London. May I call on you when I'm there?" Sarah asked.

"I'd be pleased. So would my family." The three young women rose to leave. "We're having dinner with Mrs. Pierpont. Please excuse us."

"It was a pleasure to meet you," one of them added.

"I hope I'll also see you in New London," the third one said.

※

The next round of tea Mrs. Miles poured into the bowls was so dark it obscured the small flowers painted inside.

"The Livingstons are lucky not to have gotten their start here as prisoners," Sarah told the two women. "One of Father's consignments fifty years ago was a couple hundred Scottish opponents of Charles II who were for sale. Robert Livingston's father was lucky he was exiled to Holland for his lack of enthusiasm for the crown."

"That's why Robert spoke Dutch?" Mrs. Miles asked.

"Yes. And do you know who John Hull was, the silversmith? Samuel Sewell's father-in-law?" They nodded. Sarah continued, "He was also a fur trader. I once saw Robert Livingston when he was learning the fur business from Hull. He came to Father's shop with him." Sarah put the bowl to her lips but the tea was so hot she set it down again. "I remember his peculiar accent. It was probably a mixture of Scottish and Dutch, I don't know; I was eight or ten. He must have gone to Albany after that because I never saw him again."

"Here, we marvel at his continued survival," Mrs. Miles took a sip of her tea. "He's had to change his political coat each time New York gets another governor, and he nearly had it snatched off his back altogether by Bellomont. Mary said her father-in-law is in London to launch a war against Canada. Ha." Her laugh was more like a horn blast. "That's only part of it. He's also there to get his appointments back and recover enormous sums of money he says he's owed."

"Governor Winthrop rescued the whole family once," Mary Prout added. "He even kept John for a year, when he was ten, to educate him. Later when John came back to New London and wanted to wed Winthrop's daughter, the Livingstons said she wasn't good enough—said her mother was a tavernkeeper's daughter and wasn't even married to

Winthrop when Mary was born. Eventually a Scottish spy of the Livingstons supplied favorable intelligence, and they gave permission for the marriage."

Mrs. Miles spoke directly to Mary. "Some arrogance of Robert Livingston, who left his employer's deathbed to marry the widow and have a child in nine months' time." Mary Prout laughed and Mrs. Miles gave another horn blast.

Sarah laughed too, but shifted uncomfortably and stared at the tea in her bowl. Her own daughter had arrived a few months after her marriage; many betrothed couples married when it became necessary, but she and Richard were not yet betrothed. At the time Richard pursued her he was a successful tavernkeeper. He smiled beautifully and flirted like a rake, and she decided she should have him, but her parents objected to the match. Sarah was determined, however, to have her way and employed her strength to overcome her parents' resistance, even though she suspected that Richard was mostly interested in her father's business and her prospective inheritance. After they married, Richard lost his tavern in a failed trade agreement he had kept a secret from her. Sarah pressed her cousin Robert to find him a position, which turned out to be on Robert's ship. So Richard was at sea for long periods. She moved back to her parents' home. Richard would return for a few months, a year at the most, and Sarah always regarded that as a hopeful sign. Then he would take off after some misadventure, which she and her family would have to set straight.

Sarah wondered how much of this her cousin knew. She did not fail to see the irony of the present discussion.

William Kidd's name drew her back to the conversation. "That's what Robert Livingston gave his daughter and Sam Vetch when they got married," Mrs. Miles was saying. "Captain Kidd's house in New York. And Robert had hardly managed to extricate himself from designing the entire pirate affair with Captain Kidd, when his son and son-in-law had devised their own felony. Ha."

"Have you heard about that?" Mary asked Sarah, who shook her head no.

"John and Sam had bought a ship and were bringing back illegal spirits they'd bought from the French in Canada, when it ran aground off Block Island. Everybody got off to find help, but the tide came in whilst they were gone—"

Mrs. Miles took over, "And the ship drifted across Long Island Sound and washed ashore at Montauk. Of course the fools had left on board all the records by which they could be convicted. Ha."

Mary injected her indignation. "You can imagine our governor's embarrassment when the ship named after his daughter was confiscated."

Sarah agreed. "So the son and son-in-law were trading with the French while the father was organizing campaigns to rid his northern frontier of their encroachments and barbarities. That's a fine piece of work."

The conversation drifted to local intrigues and skulduggery until the topics were exhausted and the women were abuzz with the effects of the strong brew.

Mrs. Miles swirled the leaves around in what little liquid

was left in her bowl. "I still laugh every time I look at the tea leaves. You know what my old auntie did when she received her first package of tea? She boiled it, drained off the water and ate the leaves. Ha. She thought tea was so nasty she never would try it when we told her what to do with it. Ha."

With the second blast of laughter Sarah and her cousin announced their departure.

On their walk home Sarah said, "You know Mary, one could look at our colonial enterprise in two ways. Ministers think we're the new chosen people they've led from the depredations of England to a new promised land. But I think colonization has set loose the forces of self-interest, don't you agree?"

Mary said nothing, so Sarah went on. "We're larcenous, greedy and obsessed with greatness. And the most successful people are usually the least saintly. So what are we then, chosen saints or sinners?"

The two walked on arm in arm. Sarah considered these two possibilities. Her father had traded or sold whatever had come his way, including people. Even though she and Mary Prout and Mrs. Miles had disparaged Robert Livingston's activities, Sarah pictured herself obtaining land in Indian territories and selling it for profit, building a finer house, marrying her daughter to a powerful family. She could see herself conducting business with governors and dabbling in intrigues and diversions like Robert Livingston. She would undertake them all if she found the opportunity. The preaching of ministers competed with the call of New England's prospects. She knew which she would rather listen to.

Inventorium

Tuesday, November 14

Wind rattled the windows and wakened Sarah on the morning that the inventory of Caleb's estate would begin. She never imagined she would languish for five weeks before this first step could be accomplished. She had written home to explain that she was not returning with the next post rider because probate court in New Haven met only four times a year, the next date being the twenty-fifth of November. She had told them that the distribution of the estate would not necessarily occur when the inventory was presented to the probate court. Any question could cause a delay, and from what she had already observed of her relatives' conduct, both questions and delays were very likely.

A knock at the door joined the rattling windows. The young servant girl brought in a bucket of red coals, a bundle of sticks and two small logs to build a fire.

"It's a pity all of you must go to Mr. Trowbridge's today. There won't be any heat." The girl shook her tightly capped head in disapproval. She blew on the pile she had made in the small, shallow fireplace. It was only lit in the morning, when Sarah dressed, and at night, when she prepared for bed. Sarah had been surprised at its size. It was less than a foot deep, causing the hearthstone and irons to extend nearly a foot into the room.

The girl stood up, satisfied that the single thin flame she produced would survive. "I'll be back with hot water."

"Take your time." Sarah pulled the coverlid up to her nose. She would not get out of bed as long as she could still see her breath. If the girl returned too soon, then Sarah had to decide between hot water in a cold room or waiting for a warm room and having cold water.

She was glad her cousins' servant was not a black slave. More families had them here than in Boston. New Haven had become rich from them. A quarter of the town was occupied directly in shipping. They traded with the West Indies sugar plantations. The colony's farm products fed the plantation slaves, and the New Haven traders brought back salt, rum, sugar and molasses. They had credit balances besides, which made them desirable customers for Boston's artisans and importers. She knew the Trowbridges were among the wealthiest, but the wealthiest people in a town of only a hundred and fifty houses was hardly impressive by her standards.

*

After breakfast Sarah and John and Mary Prout put on their wraps and walked toward the harbor on a rutted path, hardened by an early freeze. John led the way.

"I can't believe how much you resemble your two brothers who moved to Boston," Sarah said.

"So we're told," he said over his shoulder. "Timothy and Joseph always mention you with the highest regard. They say your name is to be found on many a court record."

"Joseph's been particularly helpful." What surprised Sarah was that John made it sound like both brothers were still alive. Timothy had gone down with his ship five years ago.

Since her arrival in New Haven, the Prout family had treated her warmly and the Trowbridges had not. Mary Prout and Caleb's long-departed mother were sisters, but Sarah could tell that her Trowbridge cousins regarded her more as a threat than a relative. A veil of displeasure hung between them and herself after they learned she had brought a will that claimed part of their brother's estate for someone they had never met. Their annoyance increased when they discovered it was she who had drawn it up. She would have to watch Caleb's sister Elizabeth sharply. Yesterday Elizabeth told Mary Prout she suspected Caleb's wife had devised a quick marriage when she learned he was ill. Furthermore, Caleb's stepmother had begun making noises about her daughter's entitlement to a share in his estate. Sarah had seen peaceable families in Boston turn nasty in quarrels over estates. It had happened often enough for her to recognize early signs—ones she was beginning to see now.

Sarah and the Prouts turned and walked along the wharf until they reached the corner of what Sarah called Trowbridge Street, because nearly all the Trowbridge descendants lived there. They stopped between the first two houses. On one side lived Caleb's sister Lydia, and on the other, his brother Thomas. Each home contained three generations plus extended family, but only Lydia, Thomas, their stepmother and their brother-in-law came out to join the trio. They were to serve as administrators for the inventory.

"The court officers'll meet us there," Thomas Trowbridge told them. "The appraiser has the key. With the size of Caleb's trade inventory, I imagine this might take two or three days, but all of us needn't remain past our initial appearance. They just want us to attest that the house hasn't been touched since it was sealed."

Although the others nodded in agreement, Sarah knew this little speech was intended to dismiss her, but he didn't know her. He underestimated her resolve. She would make herself present for the appraisal of every single item.

The solemn assembly strode toward Caleb's house.

Sarah's curiosity about it had grown with the length of her stay. There had been few diversions in such a small town—the General Assembly in October and an invitation to the Rev. Pierpont's for dinner. This social accomplishment was followed by visits to a few other homes. She had also undertaken routine inspections of New Haven—checking the wharf each day to see what vessels were coming and going, and surveying the progress of two sloops being built. Gradually she had learned the contents of all the warehouses and knew what each merchant currently had in stock and what prices he charged. New Haven became so familiar she could probably draw a map, including every house and building, without leaving her desk. There was much that was novel upon her arrival—the pyramid-roofed meetinghouse with three front doors, the large number of houses that were painted blue, the plain dress that made each woman resemble every other one, the frequency with which the most savage-looking natives walked the streets of town and the way their cast-out women were in vogue with Englishmen. But all this faded to the background as she became increasingly obsessed with what Caleb's house contained.

The procession passed an apple orchard, which stood between Thomas' house and Caleb's. Here, several weeks ago, Sarah had been caught out peeking in a window by an in-law.

"It lacks a woman's touch, don't you think?" Anna Trowbridge had said, and Sarah had spun around in surprise. Anna was the widow of Caleb's brother John, who had died at a younger age than Caleb. Anna lived with her son directly across the street.

"He sold goods from his chamber closet," Anna had said. "When a new shipment arrived, his place always looked more like a warehouse."

Being discovered had made Sarah's face redden. Her reflex when embarrassed was to strike at the source immediately. "I keep a shop in my own home." Then she realized Anna had not intended any disparagement, so she softened. "I have a stationery and give writing lessons to children, but I'm able to keep my business affairs restricted to one room of my house."

"He had some nice furnishings," Anna had said. "But the constant disruptions exasperated Zula."

"Who's Zula?"

"A mulatta we both own," When Sarah's eyebrows rose, Anna had added, "Caleb sent her to stay with me when he sailed to Boston. She was afraid to be in the house alone. The appraiser said she could live with me until the court decides where she goes."

Now Sarah would finally learn what was in each chamber, closet and chest. The lock had been removed from the door, so Thomas opened it and stood aside to let everyone enter the center hall. They heard voices and went to the kitchen.

"Thomas. John." A portly man of sixty-some years called the name of each family member as he greeted them with a handshake. "Sorry I'm late getting into town."

"It's good to have you back," Thomas said. "You brought an early cold spell with you. I heard you had an excellent crop this year. You keep enough cider to share with friends, or have you shipped it all out?"

"Twenty barrels on the way to Barbados." As he spoke, he tapped on Thomas's chest for emphasis. "And you won't go dry this winter. I have a barrel in my shed."

Thomas nodded approval, then he turned to Sarah. "This is Nathan Andrews, the probate court appraiser. So is John Miles, over there." A squint-faced man, who was holding an old cutlass up to the window-light, glanced at Sarah. He went back to his examination. "And Joseph Winston, there, is the court clerk." Winston was the youngest of the three. He nodded to her from his stool beneath a wall lantern. There was an open record book on his lap, and he had spread his portable stationery case on a chair in front of him because there was no table in the kitchen.

"I'm ready," the clerk said. "Let's get on with it. 'Tis so cold in here my ink will soon freeze." In a rapid monotone he read what he had just written. "*New Haven, November 14th, Anno Domini 1704. Inventory of the estate of Mr. Caleb Trowbridge, merchant, deed both personal and real, taken by us the subscribers as followeth. Imprimis the personal estate—In the Kitchen . . . .*"

The two appraisers had set up the court scales in the center of the floor. They determined the value of the pewter, brass and iron utensils by weight. The remaining items had to be liberated from six months of dust to establish their worth. The family nodded at each decision, and without any disagreements the inventory of the room was completed in two hours.

Sarah had recorded kitchen inventories that took two days, but they were home industries of productive women, not drab and hollow rooms such as this. There were barely enough utensils here to make a proper meal. What could his mulatta have done with only a gridiron, two pots and a skimmer? And no work table. She guessed he must have gone to his family for meals.

The clerk pointed to his inkpot. "Look at this. Ice crystals have formed." He adjusted the long muffler he had wrapped three times around his neck and blew hot breath on the ends of his fingers, which stuck out from the cropped tips of his writing gloves.

"Anna told me we could come warm up at her house any time," Lydia said. "Zula would have a hot drink prepared."

The clerk sneezed. "We should've had her come here early this morning to dust and lay a fire." He blew his nose, then he covered it with his muffler. "In fact, I think she should lay one in the next room while we're across the street. I can't write with frozen fingers and ink." His complaint passed through the three layers of knitted wool.

"We'll have it done," Thomas replied. "And the women needn't spend the rest of the day standing through this. I can fetch them if necessary."

The party stepped out of the house into the midmorning sunshine. The wind had subsided, and as they walked across to Anna Trowbridge's house they agreed the outdoors seemed warmer than Caleb's kitchen.

※

Late that afternoon, Sarah sat at a desk in the Prouts' front chamber with a foot stove under her skirt and a quilt around her shoulders. She was just thawing out from the afternoon's appraisal. Despite the fire that had been built at the court clerk's request, it offered little warmth to anyone but Winston, who planted his chair on the hearth itself. Although Sarah had refused to be dismissed with the other women, remaining for the inventory of the next room had not been very illuminating. Nevertheless, she was writing to Mary because she had learned a packet would sail for Boston in the morning, and she wanted Mary to know the inventory had finally begun.

His house is a typicall four room clapboard with a garret and centre chimney, she wrote. *It's smaller than the Homes of the rest of the Family, and mercifully not Painted brighte blue, as many here are.*

A local Merchaunt found himselfe with a large shipment of Indigo. Although the women Steadfastly hold with the drabbest of clothes, he Convinced them that a blue washe on the Clapboards would bothe preserve the Wood and provide a barrier against diseases of the night aire. Now New Haven resembles a field of cornflowers—a Testament to their Gullibility. Sarah paused to blot up a bead of ink that resulted from her punctuating the sentence too vigorously.

She continued. *The Inventory began today, the coldest I've yet Experienced. Wee had to suffer the complaints of the Poor clerk from Start to finish. He satt with a Muffler wrapped so tightly around his Neck and chin that only his Eyes could move. He had to bee Ever mindful of the drip that kept Forming at the end of his nose, lest It fall and Blur his writing.*

The Appraisers are as competent As any I've witnessed, butt House furnishings in General have low'r value than in Boston. We have finish'd two rooms, the Kitchen and the next Room wch was Full of tables and chairs, the use of which is a Puzzle to mee, since Caleb couldn't have Entertained with such A sparcely Furnish'd kitchen. The appraised Value of the two rooms is only 33 £, 3 shillings and 2 pence. I'd no opportunitie to mount the stairs and examine the Front hall chamber and the back Chamber from wch he Sould his goods. Unless the Chamber Closet and various Chests Contain value ables, I Think their Appraisal will bee as Modest as the previous Two rooms. I cannot at this point offer any opinion of how you will come out in the end.

Yesterday I was told Caleb has a Malata slave, which is a Disagree able discov'ry. Actually hee has but Half, your sister-in-Law, Anna, owning an arm and a Leg. Named Zula, she lived in the Garret, which I haven't Seen yet, butt moved to Anna's when Caleb *left for Boston. It's common to see slaves on Farms here, and even in homes. I was apprized Today of the situation wth them. I'm of the opinion the English are far too Indulgent, especially the farmers. They allow too great familiarity from them, Permitting them to sit at the Table and eat with them, As they say it Saves time.*

There are every where in the Towns I passed, as well as in New Haven, a Number of the Indian Natives of the Country. They Are the most sauvage of any I have Seen. Little or no care is taken to make them otherwise. They mourn their Dead by blacking their faces and cutting their hair, after an Awkwerd and frightfull manner. They trade most forr Rum, for wch they'd hazzard their very lives; and the English fit them Generally as well, by seasoning it plentifully with water.

Thr'out the Connecticot Colony they are Govern'd by the same Laws as wee in Boston, And similar in the way of Church Government. The People are good and Sociable, but as much too Independent in their principalls as the Original settlers were too rigid in Their Administration of justice. Whipping was then counted a Frequent and easy Punishment for those whose Innocent merriment made them Offenders of the Lawes. Winthrop has by his Good services Gain'd the affections of the people as much as any who had bin before him in that post. He is Given to gracious Hospitaity. I dined wth him and his daughter, who accompanyed him here to the General assembly with various of her friends, they all being clothed in the latest of Fashon. He wished me to deliver greetings to his brother when I return to Boston.

The Prouts' servant girl announced that supper was ready, so Sarah wrote a hurried finish to the letter. *I must close wth my* *greatest hope that you remain well since the letter I receiv'd, and that with godspeed I will bee returned to the bosom of my loving family. Sarah*

Since this letter would go by packet, she decided to use her seal. If it had gone by post, someone would have picked off the seal at the first stage. People were eager to read any news, no matter whose it was. She let a drop of melted wax fall on the envelope then pressed it with her brass seal, which produced an ornamental *K* surrounded by decorative swirls. She placed the letter on a stand by the door and went to the dining chamber to join the Prouts for the evening meal.

Divertere

Monday, November 27

My dearest daughter—I write to You in response to the letter You sent me by packet which arriv'd on saturday. I trust You've recv'd my letter of Nov 14 by now. You have inquired about your couzins of which I must report There are too many, ninteen I believe the number to bee if one could manage to gather them all at one time to count them. Only stepcousin Hannah Trowbridge is Your age and a quiet thing the cause of which is—her Mother never stops talking. You've two couzins nam'd Elizabeth; they are both younger. Three of the older Lads I met when they came home from collegiat school in Saybrook during the Genral Assembly. John Prout Jr. is the finest of Character and fair of face and I shall keep him in Mind when it is Time for you to Marry. The youngest cuz is but a Year old and a cheerful boy. If you be not afraid of travel by sea and I bee not afraid to send you; you will visit here when You are eighteen; Mary Prout has invit'd You and made me promis it will be so.

Keep to your studys; I've had cause to Observe the great necessity and bennifitt of Education and Conversation here. Yesterd'y I Being *at a merchants house, in comes a tall country fellow with his cheeks stuffed with Tobacco; for they seldom Loose their Cudd, but keep Chewing and Spitting as long as they'r eyes are open. He advanc't to the midle of the Room, made an Awkward Nodd, and spitting a Large deal of Aromatick Tincture, he gave a scrape with his shovel like shoo, leaving a small shovel full of dirt on the floor. He stopt, Hugging his own pretty Body with his hands under his arms, Stood staring rown'd him, like a Catt let out of a Baskett. At last, like the creature that Balaam Rode on, he opened his mouth and brayed: Have You any Ribinen for Hatbands to sell I pray? The Questions about what kind of pay he would use being answered, the Ribin was bro't and opened. Bumpkin Simpers cryes, It's confounded Gay I vow; and beckning to the door, in comes his Jane Tawdry, dropping about 50 curtsees, and stands by him. Hee shows her the Ribin. Law, You, sais shee. It's right gent. Do You take it? the merchant asks. Tis dreadful pretty; then She enquires, Have You any hood silk I pray? W^{ch} being brought, Have You any thred silk to sew it wth? says shee, wch being accomodated wth they Departed.*

Such country folk Generaly stand speachless a Great while after they come in, and sometimes dont say a word till they are askt what they want, which I Impute to the Awe they hold for these merchants, to whom they are almost constantly Indebted; and they must take what the merchant brings without Liberty to choose for themselves. But the Bumpkins also have their way, making the merchants wait long enough for their pay. These folke have as Large a portion of mother witt, and sometimes Larger than those who have bin brought up in Citties; but for want of emprovements, Render themselves almost Ridiculos, as above. I should be glad if they would leave off such follies, and I'm sure all who Love Clean Houses and floors (at least) would be glad of it too.

Write to me again, for if I am unfortunate to be delay'd here I shall have the Happiness of Hearing from You.

Your loving Mother

Sarah had risen early to complete the letter she had started the night before. Now she was hungry and heard Mary Prout in the kitchen below. She put away her writing materials and went downstairs, where she found Mary huffing around the hearth in the preparation of breakfast.

"Did you notice it's snowing outside?" Sarah asked. "I wonder if it's snowing in Boston." She began filling cider mugs from a kettle.

"Let's hope it doesn't become a storm." Mary leaned across the table to put a bowl at Sarah's place. Sarah noticed her ring as she did.

"I meant to ask you about your ring. Elizabeth received one like it, but we don't know who sent it. One day a package appeared at the post office with just her name on it."

Mary removed the ring and handed it to Sarah. "John brought it to me from New York. He was there last summer."

The ring had two hands that held a heart. Sarah examined inside the band. "This has the very same inscription as Elizabeth's—*hrt in hnd at your c'mand*—and the same initials—*C.K.* The two are just alike." She turned it over several times.

"Those are the initials of the jewelry maker—Cornelius Kierstede. Who would've bought her a ring in New York, your brother?"

"The ring came last spring; my brother died four years ago." And suddenly she knew.

※

Thomas Trowbridge arrived at the Prouts' home after the two women had eaten. He came to tell them he had gone to the docks to see about taking a packet to New York.

"New York?" Sarah asked.

"The probate court can't make a ruling on Caleb's estate until a question concerning 230 acres is resolved." Thomas began pacing, which Sarah suspected gave him something to do instead of looking at her. "An elderly friend named Hitchcock, who moved to New York, had granted the land to Caleb in an oral agreement. Caleb was to drain the low parts, clear it and sell it as farm lots. With the money he made, he was to pay the friend 230 pounds for the property and keep the profit."

Thomas had made three trips across the kitchen. "This is the problem. Even though Caleb didn't finish the improvements, his account book says he went ahead and paid for the land, but we can't find the deed. The court placed the acreage on the inventory list, but the estate can't be settled without they first obtain a written testament from Hitchcock that he made the oral agreement, and they want the deed."

Here he paused and looked out the window facing the docks. "The next packet is scheduled for Thursday coming," he said. "I'll book passage, but I can't be certain Mr. Hitchcock will be home. He has a son in Albany and one in New Jersey. If he should be away for some reason, I'll have to wait until he comes home to satisfy the matter." He turned in Sarah's direction but lifted his eyes to the beam across the kitchen. "I wanted to inform you, so you could return to Boston instead of having to remain here indefinitely."

My cousin is ever solicitous to help me back to Boston, Sarah thought. "Actually, I've just learned of some unfinished concerns of my own in New York, which I could attend to by going there. I'd like to accompany you, but I ask that we travel by land."

That got him to look at her, and he seemed at a loss for words. Mary Prout shifted her glance back and forth between them. Sarah waited.

"Are you—I—but I can't be sure how long I'll be there. It may take me a day or two; it may take a month. I'm returning as soon as I settle with Hitchcock." He swung away and resumed pacing. "If you have your own affairs, then you'll have to hire someone to wait on you there and back. I'm not saying you can't go with me; I just don't want to be detained for anything but this estate matter."

"Will you go by land, then?" she asked.

"Yes, I can go by land, but—but I'll not be responsible for your safety and comfort. The land route's extremely difficult. You'll have to hire your own waiter."

"I'll find a waiter. When would we leave?"

He stopped again at the window. "We'll have to see what happens with this weather. If snow obscures the trail there's no point in departing. The post from New York is dropped off at Miles' Tavern by noon today. I'll go ask the rider what he's passed through."

"I'll see you there, then. I have two letters to post to

Boston. The second isn't written yet, so please excuse me." She hurried upstairs, leaving Mary to deal with whatever second thoughts might occur to Thomas. She was no longer naive about land travel, but if a thousand rivers lay between here and New York, she would cross them because she suspected Richard was there, and she wanted to know what he was doing.

※

Dear Mary, I write to you about the Inventory which was finally compleeted, the Delay due to the delicate constitution of the clerk Mr. Winston who refus'd to emmerge from his House during the cold spell that lasted three days, then he spent two more snuffling in his bed.

The contents of the remaining Rooms in Caleb's house were not apraized at as great a value as I had hoped; his stock contayned in the chamber Closset and linon trunk was just over 60 pownds. His wearing Apparrell being of more value (85 £) than his tradeing stock, wh^{ch} will Be of no suprise to You knowing the attent'n he payed to his Wardrobe. The totall of his Personal estate, incl his stock is 383 £, 3 sh and 3p.

His reall estate is nearly 700 pownds. An unfortunate problem is with the largest piece of land, being 230 acres. It is missing a deed, and your bro' inlaw must needs go to New York to locate the ownner who gave it by Orall agreement. If all this comes right and this Lande can be sold, there will be money to pay the Boston credittor and the estate You bro't to your marriage will not be requir'd to pay Caleb's debtts, which the family is still unawair of.

The Court has appoint'd cousin John Prout, brother Thomas, Sister Lydia, bro'-in-law Hodshon, and stepmomma Hannah Trowb. to be administrators of the estate—And not mee as you can see, saying that not beeing a citizen of New Haven disqualifys Me.

Since I can do Nothing on Your behalfe till Thos. returns I have decided to bear his company to N York and satisfy my curiositee about the city. I must rush this to the Post then find Myselfe a waiter for the Journy; the Chore seems too daunting for cuz. Thomas.

I entrust You wth the task of imparting this news to Mother and Elizabeth in a Mannor that will cause Them the least concern; for I have great confidance in my journey. The ground is hard and small rivers have frozzen. I am of Excellant Health, as I praye all of You remain, untill my retourn.

✼

When Sarah reached Miles' Tavern with her letters, a dozen men were already discussing the rates for their mail. There was no mistaking the back of the man who was putting parcels and letters into his mail pouch. She had spent a day, a night, and part of another day trying to keep his oiled coat and montero-cap within sight. This was the first time she had run into him in New Haven. She stepped around where she could be seen. When he held out his hand to collect payment from the man next to her, his eyes caught hers.

"Mr. Fleer. Still maintaining your commitment to punctuality, I see. I can be assured, then, my family in Boston will receive these letters four days hence?"

He seemed to shift uneasily but covered his nervousness with a sneer. "One and six for each," he said with his hand out.

"I intend a trip to New York. What's the weather between here and there?" She hoped her glare conveyed her disdain.

"The New York rider said there were several inches in

Bridgeport this morning. It's snowed for two days to the west of there. I guess it'll come this way. Snow won't be the problem, though. It's the worst terrain on the whole coast. You'll never make it." He snickered then rifled through his mail pouch, for no purpose she see.

"When the weather permits my departure, I trust I'll not discover travellers who've been abandoned along the roadside."

Fleer had turned away to busy himself with another man's letter, but she knew he had heard her. Again she was constrained from fully venting her anger, since he was delivering her letters to the Boston post rider. Now it occurred to her that he was probably the post rider who comes to Miles' Tavern at noon every second and fourth Mondays. She would be back to have her say one day.

Sarah met Thomas as she was leaving the public room. "The post rider says there's more snow on the way. It may snow for several days."

"Then I'll stop by the Prouts' later in the week to make arrangements with you," he said.

※

Sarah found Mrs. Miles mending some linen in the tavern kitchen.

"What brings you out in the snow?" she asked.

"I came with my mail. Also, I need to ask if you know anyone I might hire to wait on me for a journey to New York?"

Mrs. Miles dropped her mending in her lap. "New York? Now you're going to New York?" She shook her head in disbelief. "You are an amazement."

"I'm accompanying cousin Trowbridge—we have a problem with the estate—but he insists I hire my own waiter. Are you acquainted with anyone suitable?"

Mrs. Miles thought for a moment then rose from her chair. "Let me point out someone in the other room."

They observed the public room from the doorway. Thomas was having a beer with a group of men who had finished posting their letters. Others were reading notices Fleer and the New York post rider had put on the wall. Fleer was at a corner table sipping soup loudly enough for the women to hear. At a far table sat two men.

Mrs. Miles leaned toward Sarah and spoke softly without looking at her. "At the far table. How about him?"

"The gent with the white muzzle or the piece with the tricorn?"

"The tricorn. He has a handsome phiz, eh? He's the old gent's nephew. Came here last week from north of Norwich, searching for employment. No luck yet."

"You think he's reliable?"

"His uncle's as fine a citizen as there is. I've seen nothing questionable in the nephew."

"He doesn't lose himself in drink?"

"Not that I've seen."

"Would you examine them? If the fellow passes your scrutiny, make an arrangement—as much to my advantage as you can negotiate. And see he understands we must stay until affairs are settled. I can't promise a date of return, and I won't be deserted there. That point must be clear."

"Stop by tomorrow and I'll tell you the outcome."

✤

While walking back to the Prouts', Sarah saw Fleer riding toward the ferry dock. If she had known he was the post rider, she would have kept her letters and sent them on the next packet. Then she could have delivered a scalding reproof and exposed him as a rogue in front of everyone. By evening, witnesses would have spread it from lip to lip like a ripple in a pond until it reached the periphery of town.

She would not be caught unprepared like this in New York, if she found Richard. She imagined various scenes in which she might discover him—pulling on a block and tackle at the dock, laughing with a group of men in a tavern, standing at the door of his residence. She would appear. Richard would stagger with shock.

"Where have you been?" she would ask. "Don't think you can get by with abandoning me. Here I am."

Via Volcani et Bacchi

Thursday, December 7

"I didn't think I'd be walking to New York." Sarah had been puffing since the three of them dismounted. The horses lurched and stumbled on the steep path. It was strewn with rocks, which the recent snow had made slippery.

"It's better to struggle by foot than to be thrown off your horse, though," said her waiter, the man Mrs. Miles had engaged. He held her arm to steady her as she climbed the path.

Joseph Bradford interested her. He seemed to be an experienced traveller. He carried an axe and a pistol, a compass and a timepiece. With a rope he had brought, he had tied the horses, one behind the other, so cousin Thomas could lead them on ahead and Bradford could stay at her side. She supposed the bulges in his saddlebags were other useful items she would not have known to bring.

"I have to stop and catch my breath," she said. Although the afternoon was cold, she wiped perspiration from her upper lip and the cleft of her chin. "I wish there were a stream. Our last meal was delicious, but it's left me thirsty."

Bradford took a flask from his saddlebag, removed the lid and handed it to her. He said nothing, just smiled. He had a very appealing smile—and all his teeth.

She did not know what to make of him. He was about her age, had not mentioned a wife, and had taken a waiter's position because he had no other work. But Bradford was no rough ne'er-do-well. She had watched him cut his venison with skill and eat properly with a fork. He even wiped his face with his own handkerchief. The whole demeanor suggested good breeding, but she had not yet pried his family history from him. Perhaps they had lost everything in some speculation. That happened to people.

Thomas called back after he had gone around a curve and could no longer see them. "Are you all right?"

"All right," Bradford shouted. Both voices reflected off slabs of upturned rock through which the path twisted. He put the flask away.

"I was deceived by yesterday's journey," Sarah said. "I thought it would be that easy all the way to New York."

"There's a lot of traffic between New Haven and Fairfield—a lot of settlements close together, so the road's good, but I was told we'd have twenty miles of rugged terrain after that. I didn't know it would be this bad, either."

They caught up to Thomas, who was waiting with the horses at the crest of the hill. He was leaning on a rock with one of the splashes of white paint that marked the way.

From this point they would be able to proceed across a ridge with painful slowness, past huge boulders and massive granite outcroppings. The setting sun reflected their molten origin.

"I've never been in such a desolate place," Sarah said. "It's been several hours since we saw the last house. What will we do when it gets dark?"

Bradford opened a small notebook he took from his coat pocket and studied one of the pages. "It's seven miles from where we ate in Horse Neck to the next ordinary at Rye."

"How far do you think we've come?" asked Thomas.

"We're lucky if we've made a mile an hour." Bradford took out his timepiece. "We left Horse Neck four hours ago."

"Then we may still have three hours to go, if the road doesn't improve." Thomas shook his head and kicked some stones. "What time is it, about five?"

"It's half past," Bradford said. "If I'd known the going would be this slow, I'd have stopped at Horse Neck for the night."

All three of them looked ahead. The sun had just set, but the sky was still light and the horizon was fire-orange. "We'll have about forty-five minutes before it gets dark," Bradford said. "We should go as fast as we can till then." He leafed through his notebook. "December 7 . . . 7. Tonight . . . yes," he found the page he was looking for, "the moon rises at six-thirty, so we shouldn't be in the dark for more than half an hour. It's a waning moon, though. It won't give much light."

They all looked up at the sky.

"At least there aren't any clouds," Thomas said.

Bradford untied the horses and rolled the rope over his shoulder. Sarah stepped up on a rock, from which Bradford gave her a leg up onto her saddle. He broke a limb off a tree, tied some white wadding on the end of it and stuck the other end in his saddlebag. "I'll just have it ready in case we need a torch," he said.

Amazing, thought Sarah. He was so prepared for everything. When she decided to leave Boston for New Haven, she got a horse and saddle and left, unaware that journeys do not just happen on their own. So far, Bradford had anticipated their needs and difficulties—except for the time it would take to get through these hills. But she felt surprisingly unalarmed about their situation. He knew what he was doing, even though he had never ridden this way before. His total attention was devoted to waiting on her. And unlike her last guide, this one could even see where he was going.

✤

Lights shone in the first building they had come upon since they left Horse Neck. It was the inn they were looking for. Bradford knocked on the door, which was opened after some moments by a short, thin man with a neck and head that stretched out from his full-cut blouse like a turtle's from its shell. It bobbed up and down after each *oui*. The proprietor came with Bradford to help Sarah down from the saddle.

"This is *Monsieur L'Éstrange*."

The head bobbed in greeting. "*Voudriez-vous quelque chose à manger?*"

Bradford turned to Sarah and Thomas. "He wants to know if you want something to eat?"

"Of course," Sarah said. "I've heard people speak of French *fricassée*. See if our host can make that."

"What's *fricassée*?" Thomas asked.

"I don't have any idea," she said, "but it sounds interesting."

"*Nous voudrions de la fricassée, s'il vous plaît,*" Bradford said.

The head had bobbed back and forth as each one had mentioned the dish. When Bradford relayed their request, the little turtle beak expelled a pouffing sound.

"*Ce n'est pas facile,*" he said. His head now bobbed with disapproval, but he went inside to prepare it.

⁂

Sarah waited in the public room while the two men attended the horses. They joined her at a table she had taken, where she could watch the Frenchman prepare the supper.

"You studying the art of making this mysterious dish?" Thomas asked.

Sarah nodded. "He hacked a chunk of salted rib meat to pieces with a cleaver. Then he tossed the shards in that skillet to brown."

They watched him pour in boiling water from a kettle. His *sabots* clacked on the floor as he went to a barrel in the corner of the room and exhumed some shriveled potatoes and some carrots with withered tops. He clacked back to his skillet, dropped them in and put on the lid.

"*Fricassée* seems to be nothing more than poorly made stew, seasoned with the dried dirt that clings to the vegetables," Sarah said.

The daughter of the host brought a bottle and three glasses to the table and poured some wine. The three lifted them for a toast.

"To our journey," Thomas said.

"*A notre santé*," Bradford added.

"How do you come by your French?" asked Sarah.

"In a Canadian prison." He said it no differently than if he'd said "At school."

His statement sent a buzz through Sarah's head and chest. When it subsided, she tried to decide what she might say next, but it had taken so long that breaking the silence felt more awkward than saying something.

Thomas rescued her. "How far can we get by tomorrow evening?"

Bradford consulted his pocket notebook again. "We're seven miles from New Rochelle, and it's twenty-three more to New York."

"But what about the road? We spent nine hours going twelve miles this afternoon." Thomas said.

"*Monsieur. La route à New York, est-elle difficile?*" Bradford asked.

The old turtle removed the lid and gave the *fricassée* a stir. "*Je crois que oui.*"

"*Ça prend combien de temps pour y arriver?*"

"*Une dizaine d'heures, peut-être.*" He dropped the lid back on the pot.

"He says he thinks it's a rough road that'll take about ten hours," Bradford said. "If we leave by seven we can get there before dark." He refilled the glasses then asked Sarah, "How was your journey from Boston?"

Since they were waiting for stew, she had time for her unabridged version, which allowed her to present the entire cast in detailed anecdotes and to fully exhibit her humor. Finishing the first bottle of wine enhanced her storytelling and their appreciation of her wit. The trio was halfway through the second bottle by the time she reached the episode with the Pollys. Her well-primed audience thought it was more hilarious than any others had. Her entry into New Haven coincided with the arrival of the *fricassée*. Into each bowl *monsieur*'s ladle deposited a heap of jagged bones held together by stringy meat and some remains of the long-expired vegetables.

"This undertaking is contrary to my notion of *cuisine*." She leaned closer to the bowl and sniffed. "It smells like dirt."

Even this comment struck the two men as funny.

"Will you ask where I'm to sleep?"

"*Madame est fatiguée. Où est son lit?*" Bradford asked *monsieur*.

"*Punaisette*," he called to his daughter. "*Amène-la à la chambre.*"

"She'll show you," Bradford said.

Sarah raised her glass. "If you're really going to eat this, then I'll drink again to your health." She finished her wine.

"I've eaten worse food," Bradford said. "And I've gone a

few days with nothing at all, which is even worse than the worst meal." Both men laughed.

Sarah shook her head and followed the daughter.

The girl took a few steps up a steep and narrow stairway, then turned and said, "*Soyez prudente, madame.*"

Only half of Sarah's shoe fit on each step, which had a rise of about twelve inches. There was no handrail.

"A ladder would be easier to climb than this."

She tried to pull up her petticoat, but there was no room to move her arms. By turning sideways she was able to grasp a step above her and pull herself up. Then she saw that the stairway turned a corner. She hollered down to the men.

"If I get stuck here by the bulk of my body, you'll have to wait a couple of days for me to lose weight."

She heard their laughter.

The dim light offered by the girl's candle mercifully revealed only the larger items of rubbish in the lean-to chamber: a rough bench, a long table with one of its legs split, a chair with most of the woven rush strips broken. The foot of a low, single bed extended under the table. Resting on high legs was a double bed.

"*C'est pour vouz, Madame.*" Punaisette pointed to the smaller bed, which was only an empty box-like frame with a wooden plank bottom. "*A moment, s'il vous plaît.*"

She rustled through an open chest under the high bed and came out with a ticking to spread inside the frame. Further burrowing produced some coarse wool rugging for a cover. When she departed with the candle, she said, "*Bonne nuit.*"

"Bun-you-eat?" Sarah said to herself. "What's that mean? Bun-you-eat. Something to eat?" She groped for the edge of the table. "It must mean good luck. Good luck finding the bed in the dark." She stubbed her toe on the table leg. "Good luck not breaking your foot." She removed none of her clothing, not even her shoes, laid back on the bed and arranged the rugging. "Bun-you-eat," she mumbled. "It means break your back. Bed of bricks."

Last night's lodging and entertainment in Fairfield was as good as any in Boston. Her bed had been of horse hair, which cushioned the stiffness from being in the saddle again. The torture rack where she now lay magnified each aching muscle. She could still feel the pommel under her knee.

She heard steps on the stairway. Little Miss returned with the candle and was rummaging through the chest again.

"What are you doing?" Sarah wanted the girl to detect her annoyance at being disturbed, even if she did not understand her question.

The girl spread a coverlid on the double bed. "A bed-uh foo-er zee men-uh," the girl said slowly. Their boots clomped on the stairs.

"I'm glad I'm not doing this with a skirt on," Sarah heard Thomas say, and Bradford laughed. They crowded into the room.

"You'll have to share the double bed," Sarah said, "unless one of you wants to sleep on the broken table."

Bradford told the girl to leave him the candle. When she had gone, he held it up to examine the bed.

"It's sturdy enough to hold both of us. Notice the French craftsmanship—every joint held together by cobwebs."

Sarah could not believe that Thomas actually giggled.

The fluttering candlelight made the dirty smudges on the coverlid seem threatening.

Bradford bent close to the bed and sniffed. "Smells like bedbugs. We'd better leave our boots on and tie our sleeve and pant cuffs." He produced a hand full of ribbons from his pocket, and they tied each other's wrists. Then they did their own ankles.

"They can still crawl down your neck," Sarah said.

"I have a Mohegan ointment I learned to make. It usually helps. Do you want some? Do you want your wrists tied?"

"They're tight enough, but I'll try some ointment."

When they finished their preparations, Bradford set his tinderbox next to the candle and blew out the flame. The double bed creaked.

"This might be long enough for the little Frenchman," Thomas said, "but it's about a foot too short for me."

"We needn't have tied our pant cuffs," Bradford said. "The bugs won't crawl all the way out there to find a way in."

They laughed. It was quiet for a moment, then one of them snickered, which infected the other two.

"My poor tired carcass isn't used to such lodgings," Sarah said. She shifted in her bed, causing a great cracking and rustling.

"What's that?" Bradford asked.

"It sounds like my ticking is filled with corn husks."

They laughed again.

"A-o-o-w," she groaned. "And some corncobs too."

This sent them into spasms. Eventually they quieted. Then one giggled, setting off a new round. In the next interlude there was a scratching. A small clawing.

"Now what?" Bradford asked.

Thomas whispered, "She's hungry after all. She's nibbling on her bedding."

The two men fairly roared, and their shaking bed creaked even more.

"I'm not doing anything," Sarah said over the laughter. "Be still. Listen."

Their suppressed mirth escaped in snorts.

"It sounds like a rat." Sarah said.

Bradford felt for his tinderbox and lit the candle. "I'll chase him off. Four's too many in such a small room."

Thomas rolled over to bury his laughter in the bedding.

"Be serious," Sarah said. "I'm the one with the edible bed. Find the damned thing."

Now Thomas was squealing, and Bradford was struggling to appear sober-faced. He pulled the table out from the wall and kicked a couple of boxes underneath. They could hear the intruder scurry down behind the wall.

"Here's the hole in the floorboard. What can we stuff in it?"

"Look in the box under your bed. That's where the girl scratched up our kennel."

Bradford stuffed a piece of tattered linen into the hole. "That should do. Let me check to see it's the only hole." He leaned over to examine the six-inch space betwixt her bed frame and the wall. "Nothing here."

Some melted wax fell on her shoulder, but Bradford did not notice.

"We can get to sleep now," he said.

※

The room was finally quiet, and Sarah heard their slow breathing. Although her back pressed hard on the bed, her mind was floating from the effects of the wine. Cousin Thomas had proved not to have such a stiff collar after all. She had expected him to remain annoyed about her coming and about having to suffer the overland route. And had it been just she and Thomas, she was certain the journey would have been unpleasant. But Bradford's manner and skill had tempered Thomas.

So far during the journey she felt Thomas had watched her narrowly. When he spoke to Bradford, he referred to her as Mrs. Knight. Was he making sure Bradford was reminded of her marital status? Was he reminding her?

She felt her shoulder for the wax Bradford had dropped. She would pull it off in the morning after it was well-hardened.

This had been the most enjoyable evening since she left home, but she wished she had gone to the outhouse before she came upstairs.

Lex Talionis

Friday, December 8

"What's that?" The elderly gentleman at the door held a cupped hand to his ear. His servant, who had opened the door, looked as though she did not understand what was being said and neither did the elderly woman standing behind him. Sarah tried at greater volume.

"I'm Sarah Knight from Boston. My cousin John Prout has recommended you to me."

The man's wife related what she thought she heard directly into his ear. "She came last night from Boston. There was some kind of wreck."

Sarah felt they were examining her up and down for further clues as to what had befallen her and why, of all the doors in New York, she had knocked on theirs to reveal her misfortune.

"How can we help you?" the man shouted.

"You don't understand," Sarah shouted back. She turned to Bradford, who just laughed at her from the gate at the end of the path. People passing by him in the street were also looking her way. The whole neighborhood could hear.

"May I help you?" A middle-aged woman joined the trio in the doorway. "My parents don't hear so well, as you can tell."

"I'm Sarah Knight from Boston. I've been in New Haven at my cousin John Prout's, and I've come to New York on business. He recommended that—"

"Oh, John." She leaned toward her father. "She's John Prout's cousin. She's just arrived here."

"Ah. Ah," both parents repeated and nodded. "Won't you come in?" the older woman said. "What's your name again, please?" She turned to the daughter. "What's her name?"

Sarah gave a brief description of the nature of her visit, and the daughter relayed the information to her parents. Bradford brought her saddlebags to the door and left to secure a stable for the horses and a room for himself. He would call for her in the morning. The Burroughs family welcomed her into their home, where she was given a pleasant room and invited to join them for supper.

※

"You rode from Boston to New York on horseback?" Mr. Burroughs' fork hung in the air as he shifted his glance from Sarah to his wife to his daughter. "She went on horseback?" he asked his daughter, who confirmed it with a headshake. "How is that possible? There's no road. Post riders complain about towns that haven't cleared a way for them."

"And well they should," Sarah said.

"What did she say?" Mrs. Burroughs asked her daughter.

"There was no road from Boston," the daughter explained. "I'm afraid they can't believe anyone, except a post rider, would do such a thing," she said to Sarah. "I'm amazed, myself. Why didn't you come by packet?"

"I've a great fear of water."

"Were you with a party?" Mr. Burroughs asked.

"No. I left Boston in the company of a post rider, but he deserted me in the Narragansetts the second day. I was able to hire guides from there."

"What party did she travel with?" Mr. Burroughs asked his daughter.

"She traveled by herself, Father. With hired guides." Then she addressed Sarah. "This is very difficult to explain."

"I've kept a journal. I can get it, if they'd like to read it."

"That would be wonderful, but in the morning. They go to bed directly after supper." She leaned toward her father. "You can read her journal in the morning."

"What's that?" Mrs. Burroughs asked her husband.

"We're going to read her journal. She's kept a journal."

"Ah, a journal."

⁂

It was only six-thirty, so Sarah went up to her room, where the servant had prepared a fire and a lamp. Sarah sat at a table with her journal. She had written only one sentence for the date, December 6th. *Being by this time well Recruited and rested after my Journy, my business lying unfinished by some concerns at New York depending thereupon, my Kinsman, Mr. Thomas Trowbridge of New Haven, must needs take a Journy there before it could be accomplished, I resolved to go there in company wth him, and a man of the town wch I engaged to wait on me there.*

Sarah had stopped here and was staring at her words, while the previous night played again in her head. She had fallen asleep in a swash of French wine. When its power diminished, the hard bed had roused her. As quietly as possible, she had quit the room, but Bradford must have heard her on the stairs because he had come down, built up the fire and sat with her until the others woke at daybreak.

In whispers they had revealed how each had come to be at *L'Éstrange*'s fireplace. She confessed she was going to New York, not so much in the interests of her best friend, but to learn the whereabouts of the dissembling truant she had married, to discover what he had been doing while pretending to be in London, and to apply the law of the talon to whatever offense she uncovered.

And Bradford—he had come because it was the first employment he had found since being ransomed by Connecticut Colony from a French prison in Canada. He described the attack on his settlement by Abenakis, the death of his wife on their march to Canada, and his being traded to the French, who held him for three years before Connecticut completed negotiations.

"I haven't talked about this until now," he had said. He had not taken his eyes off the flames in the fireplace the whole time he spoke.

"I've told no one either—about what Captain Prentice disclosed," Sarah had said. "At home we hardly mention

Richard's name anymore."

— *a man of the town wth I engaged to wait on me there.*

She noticed she had not written Bradford's name in her journal.

After Thomas had risen this morning, she had discharged their ordinary, which was as dear as if they had been given far better fare, and they had taken leave of *monsieur* without eating. They had an ample breakfast in New Rochelle and had reached New York late in the afternoon. During the ride she had been preoccupied with her own thoughts, and her two companions had said little.

Now she stared at the blank space on the page and realized that, except for some wretched bridges, there was little she recalled about the journey, no sights inspired her imagination, no people left impressions. But vivid in her mind were the crackling sounds from the firewood, the smell of burning oak; the orange cast to the walls and every word she and Bradford had exchanged in the public room.

It was useless to try to write when she could not concentrate. She put away her stationery and prepared for bed. When Bradford called for her in the morning, she would divide their tasks. He would investigate the docks, check with shipping agents and visit the taverns. She would locate Kierstede's jewelry shop and inquire at city hall about searching court records. They would meet before supper and call at the house where Thomas was staying to see if he had found Mr. Hitchcock. She hoped not.

Saturday, December 9

"His wife!"

Bradford nodded.

"I can't believe it." Sarah stared at him.

"That's what she said when she answered the door. I said, 'Is Richard Knight at home?' and she said, 'He left in September. I'm his wife. What do you want?' Then I asked when she was expecting him home, and she said, 'I don't think I am. His ship came back without him, and if he does come back here, I'll probably strangle him.' Then she slammed the door."

Sarah shook her head. "I figured he'd been here all along. I thought of a dozen schemes he could be involved in, including the pursuit of—of some petticoat. But I never imagined this. Never." She smacked the Burroughs' front gate with the gloves she had in her hand. "That bastard."

Bradford took her gloves, stuck them under his arm and held both her hands. For a moment, fury fixed her stare on the spot where she had hit the gate. Then she became aware of his hold, and she looked at him.

"I'll go with you if you want to talk to her," he said, "but wait a day or two. You should uncover as much about them as you can first. And you shouldn't do anything while you're this angry."

She stood there, unable to construct a response and not wanting him to withdraw his comfort. But he let go and returned her gloves.

"I don't have a couple of days to sit and contemplate this situation, do I?" Even to herself she sounded like she was hissing. "Thomas could get his business accomplished and be ready to leave in a couple of days."

"Tomorrow's Sunday, though," Bradford said. "You'd probably be expected to stay in anyway. Why don't I come for you early Monday morning?"

"Sundays exasperate me." She took a deep breath and exhaled very slowly. "Fine. It'll give me a whole day to imagine what my replacement is like. Time to make battle plans."

Bradford just shook his head.

"And would you keep watch where Thomas is staying? I wouldn't like to discover that he'd settled with Hitchcock and started back to New Haven without me. I don't trust anyone anymore."

"I'll keep an eye on him."

She started up the path to the door. "Thank you, Joseph," she said without looking back. He did not reply, but he was there because she had not heard him walk away. She had never said his given name before.

Monday, December 11

"I'm also Mrs. Richard Knight. I've come from Boston to find out what has happened to my husband," Sarah said to the young woman squinting at them in the setting sunlight. "We should talk."

The woman's eyes darted back and forth between Sarah and Bradford, whom she recognized. She retreated into her house and indicated they should come in.

"No, I'll wait by the well," Bradford said, and he pointed

toward the wooden frame in the center of the street.

She and Bradford had been productive in their research into Richard and the other wife, and she had had time to devise alternative strategies, depending on the various reactions the woman might have.

She offered Sarah a chair at a table in the single room that occupied the downstairs of the small house. It was wedged in-between others on a street leading from the main docks. Sarah guessed they were about the same age, but the new wife was thinner and had darker hair. At least she was not a beauty. The woman sat tentatively on the edge of a chair and had a wary expression, as if she were anticipating a blow but was not sure when. That meant Sarah could begin with the strategy for the stunned, silent reaction.

"My waiter and I have spent an entire day investigating the circumstances of my husband since he arrived here in New York. A year ago he brought you here from Barbados. He has had four occupations, two from which he was dismissed and one that failed. In May he sent our daughter a ring made by Kierstede the jeweler. He sailed for Hispaniola, September fourth, on the *Blue Dolphin*, but he didn't return with it last week. He said he'd come back in the spring. Rent for this house is three months in arrears."

The woman turned away from Sarah and buried her head in her skirts. While Sarah had been running through Richard's activities, she had watched this woman's face. She had never seen anyone go gray before. Sarah stood up, walked over to the sobbing woman and placed her hand her shoulder.

"You didn't know he had a family in Boston?"

The woman shook her head no.

"Were you married in a legal ceremony?"

She nodded yes.

"In Barbados?"

Another yes.

"You're from there? Your family's there?"

Yes.

Sarah rejected duplicity on the part of this woman, who just sat and wept. Sarah forgot about strategies altogether. With her hand on the shaking shoulder she asked, "What's your name?"

After a few moments the woman answered, "Arabel."

"So, what do you suppose he's up to in Hispaniola, Arabel?"

"I don't know. The landlord came two weeks ago to threaten me. Richard hadn't paid the rent before he left. He'd told the landlord he'd pay when he got home, but he didn't come home." She wiped tears off with the backs of her hands. "I was afraid that man with you was sent by the landlord, so I shut the door in his face." She blew her nose on the corner of her apron. "The *Blue Dolphin* only makes two trips a year. I don't know if he'll come back with it in April, but I had to use the money he left me to live on. I can't pay the back rent, or the rent until next April, and if the landlord turns me out, I don't even have money for a ticket back to Barbados." Her last words quivered up an octave.

"Well, let's just sit here for a while and figure out what to do next. I'll come up with something. I've been doing this a lot longer than you have."

Arabel blew her nose again. She stared at Sarah for a moment with soggy, red eyes. "How long?"

"Fifteen years."

"I'm sorry. I didn't know he was already married."

"You have no need to apologize."

Tuesday morning, December 12

Across from the shipping office, Sarah waited for Arabel. Snowflakes as large as moths flew about her head.

"Arabel, I'm over here," she called. "We'll have to wait inside."

Arabel glanced at the sign above Sarah's head—The Boisterous Oyster—and looked concerned.

"I looked in. It's alright," Sarah said. "We have to wait for Bradford before we go to the shipping office. He's trying to find some of the crew from the *Blue Dolphin*. He thought they might know more than the captain about why Richard jumped ship."

Sarah chose a table by a window at the front of the tavern. "You look weary-worn. Would you like some China tea?"

"I didn't sleep much," Arabel said. "But for all the time I've spent thinking, I still don't know what to do."

Sarah hailed a dozy waitress and ordered the tea. "We'll figure something out after we talk to the captain. We should go to the magistrates too. I don't know what the law is here; I don't know what a woman's position is."

"I don't either." Arabel looked down at her cold, chapped hands and quickly stuck them under the table. "But I've heard that it's been common practice since New York was Dutch—that men from other colonies had second wives here . . . you know, that the laws where they came from didn't apply here."

"We'll find out."

The waitress brought the tea in brown bowls, so Sarah could not see if it had been made like Mrs. Miles'. She and Arabel blew on the steamy surfaces and took several careful sips between glances out the window at the three-story shipping office. Sarah considered the least awkward way to ask Arabel about her marriage.

"You said you married in Barbados, correct? It might make a difference," Sarah said.

"In Barbados. I hadn't known him long. He pressed his proposal to me with such great urgency that I was quite flattered, but I know now it was just the money."

"Wealthy parents? I always suspected that's what attracted him to me."

"Well, they're dead, so it was my inheritance. If they'd been alive, perhaps they would've seen his true intentions and disapproved the match."

Sarah uttered a snort of self-censure. "My parents' disapproval just strengthened my resolve; I was so determined I should marry him."

They drank for a while then Arabel said, "It didn't take me long to see my mistake. Within weeks he'd backed a privateering adventure, and my inheritance was sunk by a

French cannon. We moved to New York with the last of our resources." Her eyes filled with tears.

Sarah patted Arabel's hand. "I promise you by the end of the day we'll have a plan for dealing with . . . uh, with our. . . with Richard."

They had not noticed Bradford coming up the street; they only saw him approaching their table with vexation on his face and snow swirling off his greatcoat and hat.

"I found two crewmen who shared quarters with him onboard. I had to bribe the truth from them. He found a rich widow in Hispaniola—"

Arabel cried out, and Sarah reached for her. Bradford waited, but Sarah said nothing so he continued.

"He told these crewmen some old widow was desperate to bestow her treasures on him. He thought with some luck he might wear her out in short time—those were his exact words to the crew—and then he'd reap the rewards of being her widower."

"Three wives?" Arabel could hardly utter the words.

"Why just three?" Sarah said. "He's been away ten of the fifteen years I've been married to him. There could be half a dozen." She pushed the tea bowl away with her elbow, put her chin on her hand and stared out the window for a few moments. She turned back to Arabel. "Ah, well," she said slowly, "perhaps we can think of some appropriate wedding present to send to the happy groom."

※

"What a reptile!" Captain Tanner roared. The two wives of Richard Knight jumped when the captain sprung out of his chair to his full height. "I'd have whipped him, had I known. I can't abide that sort of indecency on the part of my crew."

"Well, what we came to find out," Sarah said, "is whether he indicated to you that he might return here in the future. The two of us need to seek relief from this intolerable situation."

"I don't know; he was very vague. He wouldn't give me a reason for not returning to New York. He just said that if I hadn't heard from him by the time I set sail again, that I should bring some things he left with me." He sat back down at his desk. "I've encountered situations like this, though. Very few thankfully. Go speak to the magistrates. I've known them to dissolve bigamous marriages before, but I don't know what procedures are required."

All during the discussion, Sarah had been studying an embossed metal casket with a curved lid, which sat on top of a cabinet behind the captain's desk. She could not be mistaken. It had sat in her own house years ago; she had dusted it too often not to recognize every detail.

"May I inquire about the box up there?" she asked. The captain looked up at it. "That? It's his. That's what I was telling you he left here. You recognize it?"

"It was mine," she shot back. "My father had it made for me when we married. It disappeared with my husband."

"A reptile," the captain repeated.

She did not dispute his assessment, but the captain's assumption that Richard had stolen it was not correct. Richard had told her he needed a strongbox like this at one of the places he had set up a shop, and she had agreed he could take it, but she was not about to tell the captain this.

"He left it here before we sailed because he said he had no permanent residence here in New York."

Arabel had looked at Sarah. "How could he say that?"

Sarah improvised as she spoke. "I'm sure there's little of value in it. My husband never sustained a single adventure he undertook. But the box, itself, is valuable to me because it was the last thing my father gave me before he died. Could I take it?" Sarah had thought this sounded convincing, but she decided to add a final touch. "I have a key to it in Boston."

As the captain lifted it down, he said, "I'm going to give it to you. When he finds out he's been exposed, the last thing he'll try to do is challenge me for it." He set the box on his desk. "Go ahead and take it home with you."

※

"That the table in the corner—by the fireplace." Bradford motioned with his head to a place they could hardly see through the blue smoke of the tavern where he was rooming. Sarah and Arabel went ahead of him. He set the metal box on the table then took their cloaks, shook the snow off on the hearth and hung them on nearby pegs. He brought back an iron poker to the table. The three of them stood with their backs to the men, who were already drinking before midday.

With one pry the lock and hasp broke off.

"That was easy. There you are." Bradford pushed the casket in front of the two women and scraped a chair up to the table so he could sit and watch.

Sarah opened the lid. "Now," she said, "let's discover what, if anything, our mutual husband has hidden from us." She took out a leather pouch that was on top. The three of them fingered the coins that fell out. "They're all Spanish *reales*, aren't they?" she asked.

Bradford shook his head in confirmation.

"Do you know how much they're worth to the pound here?"

He did not.

Arabel shook her head.

"We'll find out when we exchange them," Sarah said.

"What are these papers?" Arabel asked.

Sarah mumbled as she scanned through half a dozen sheets. "Ah-ha. Trade credits." She studied the bottom of each one for the second time. "Eleven pounds, thirteen pounds, six, fourteen, eight, and another eight. They're extended by two names here in New York." She looked at Arabel. "He must have come back from a voyage with a small inventory he didn't want you to know about."

"What do they mean?" Arabel asked.

"Two merchants didn't pay him for the goods yet. They owe him these amounts in money or in equivalent goods."

"They're no good to us then." Arabel sounded disappointed.

"Oh no, you're wrong. They're not made out to him. Unspecified credits leave no record of what they were issued for. That means the goods were probably ill-gotten. At least he was clever enough to know that. So these credits can be redeemed by the holder." She waved them in the air. "And we're holding them. We can do what we please with them." She shuffled through them again. "Sixty pounds. We owe Richard an apology for thinking he was worthless. Sixty pounds. Shall we take thirty each?"

Sarah saw Arabel look happy for the first time. Her teeth were decayed, but her smile was pleasant.

Meum et Tuum

Wednesday, December 13

Sarah walked up King Street, which ran north of the Burroughs' residence. The busy foot traffic had ground the snow into the paving stones, and they were slippery, so she had to attend her steps while trying to admire how well-stocked the shops were. She was to meet Arabel outside the dry goods shop of Elizabeth Jourdain, where they were to begin taking advantage of their husband's endowment. She saw Arabel ahead, studying a window display. Sarah joined her in examining some gloves and hoods.

"Here we are like wistful children," Sarah said.

"I've stood here many times and watched women come out with new clothes. All I have is what I'm wearing and a five-piece gown that I brought from Barbados." She opened her cloak. "Look where I've had to sew on elbow patches." Then she lifted her apron. "And I haven't been able to get this candlewax stain out, so I always have to wear an apron over it."

Sarah nodded. "I've been in this bodice and petticoat since

I left Boston, and that includes sleeping in them." She cupped her hands around her eyes and looked into the shop. "I think if I can find something that fits, I'm going to just toss out what I'm wearing."

"You've had to sleep in your clothes?"

Sarah looked at her and smiled. "Just when I was on the road. One of my guides warned me to keep them on overnight, so I'd still have them in the morning."

"People would steal your clothes while you're sleeping?"

Sarah nodded again. "Clothes are hard to come by in some places. It's the Navigation Acts. Some people can't afford what England forces us to import. That doesn't leave them many choices—make their own or keep wearing what their great-grandparents brought over. You should see what people in the wilderness are wearing."

A woman with a large parcel came out of the shop. Arabel held the door for her then waited to follow Sarah in. They were drawn immediately to three headless mannequins, who were now the only other occupants of the shop.

"Do you know how long I'd be locked in the stocks for wearing one of these in Boston?" Sarah said.

"In the stocks? Why?"

"All the lace here," she held up one sleeve. "And this one with ribbons. Even the colors might get me arrested."

"May I help you?" The proprietress, who stood in a doorway at the back of the shop, was remarkable for the India night gown she was wearing. An entwined leaf design circled the bottom of the shift. From that, snake-like patterns rose up to her shoulders and continued in the turban that coiled atop her head.

Unperturbed by serpents, Sarah said. "We're determined to walk out of here with new clothes. It may be easier for my...," Sarah glanced at Arabel in an attempt to decide what to call her, "uh, for my friend Arabel. She won't run afoul of the law, as I would, if she wears clothes like these."

Mrs. Jourdain seem unamused. "These three are the latest gowns from London. And on this shelf," she pointed behind her, "I have others folded up. I also have yardgoods if you want something made." She opened a tall cabinet. "I have patterns for all the clothes on these dolls. And they're not all English. The ones on the bottom shelf are French and Italian designs."

While Sarah and Arabel studied the fashion models on the four shelves and whispered a few comments to each other, Mrs. Jourdain shook out several of the folded gowns and spread them on a table in the center of the shop.

"Are you from Connecticut Colony, then?" she asked Sarah.

"Massachusetts, but the same applies," Sarah said. "Nothing to offend the sobriety of the magistrates and clergy. No ostentation, they say. The young girls try to keep up with the current century, though. They wear slashed sleeves with modest insets and even trim their cuffs with lace. But when they go to meeting, they have to tuck it under, so they won't be lectured in front of the congregation."

"Well, I have black goods you could make a shift from, or a petticoat and bodice," said Mrs. Jourdain.

"I'm not that somber. Help my friend, first. I'll give some more thought to what I can get by with."

Arabel had returned to one of the mannequins and was fingering a gentian blue sleeve.

"It's three pieces," Mrs. Jourdain said. "Bodice, stomacher and petticoat. That color would go nicely with your dark hair."

Arabel looked closely at the fabric.

"It's a lightweight silk damask," Mrs. Jourdain said.

"I guess it wouldn't be too warm. I'm going home to Barbados."

"Silk is very suitable to warmer climes." Mrs. Jourdain unhooked the stomacher and held the triangular piece up to Arabel's chest.

Arabel looked at Sarah. "It's beautiful. Do you think I should?"

"How much is it?" Sarah asked.

"Two pounds. Two and six if we need to re-hem the petticoat."

Sarah nodded and Arabel said she would have it. Mrs. Jourdain removed the petticoat from the mannequin and held it to Arabel's waist. They determined that it would not need altering. Then they turned their attention to Sarah's plight.

"I've decided I'll have some color," Sarah said. She picked up the bodice of a mulberry gown from the table. "This is beautiful fabric."

"It's a medium-weight druggett, mostly wool with some silk. The twill weave catches the light nicely." Mrs. Jourdain held the petticoat by the window and made it shimmer in the sunshine.

"And the lace whisk, does it remove?" Sarah asked.

"Yes. See the buttons here, around the collar? When the whisk is attached the collar stands up. When you take it off, the collar folds down over the buttons." She removed the offending ostentation and held up the bodice. "This has such a nice cut that it's pleasing even without the whisk."

"You should have it Sarah." Arabel said. "Don't travel in it, though. But be sure you put it under your pillow at night."

Mrs. Jourdain looked startled at these suggestions, but Sarah laughed.

Arabel selected a simple linen sacque and some cotton drawers, and Sarah took a great while choosing some items for her mother, Elizabeth and Mary, which Mrs. Jourdain said she would send on the next packet. Arabel and Sarah asked that the purchases for themselves be delivered to their residences in the afternoon. Outside the shop they assessed the damage to their found-money.

"I have twenty-two pounds sixteen," Arabel said. "What about you?"

"Twenty-one and two."

"This still seems like a fortune after what I've lived on the last few months." Arabel looked up at the sun. "Do you think it's time for our appointment?"

"It looks mid-day enough. Lead the way."

They walked to the corner and turned south along the waterfront to the town house. The magistrate of the civil court, who was expecting them, was in his chamber at the front of the building. Sarah noticed that from his desk he could look out at the green and see the stocks and several cages that served as public gaols. The three of them got straight on with the business of the mutual husband, and after an exchange of information the magistrate called in his clerk to record his decisions on the matter.

"We'll draw up a complaint here in New York because it's his last residence." The magistrate scratched his chin. "Well, he may try to claim new residence in Hispaniola, but he's let a house here until April and left a wife in it, so it's my opinion he should still be considered a resident."

He handed his clerk a piece of paper and said, "Use the standard opening paragraph of a bigamy complaint with these three names."

He turned back to the two women. "I'll state that the date for him to respond in court shall be the day after the *Blue Dolphin* returns from Hispaniola in April. If he doesn't return with the ship or respond in any way, I'll notify the courts of Boston and Barbados that Richard Knight has engaged himself in bigamous relations with Sarah Kemble Knight and Arabel Lyons Knight so that said women can be relieved of the intolerable condition with which they are presently bound through marriages performed in those respective places." He looked at both of them with raised eyebrows.

They approved.

He rose to see the women out. "So as soon as you return home, you'll have your magistrates send me testament to your marriages. Then I'll have all the documentation prepared for the April complaint to be heard."

They assured him this would receive their immediate attention and thanked him.

When the two women stepped into the street again, Sarah pointed to the stocks. "It will be a matter of satisfaction, when I'm back in Boston, to be able to picture this street in New York and imagine Richard in that very spot."

Arabel laughed.

"Let's go book your passage home," Sarah said.

※

"Now I'm down to fourteen pounds, sixteen shillings," Arabel said as she placed her receipt for a berth on the *Shearwater* in her purse. "You don't know how relieved I am to know that it won't make any stops between Charleston and Barbados."

"Why's that?" Sarah asked.

"Because Hispaniola is in-between them."

"Really?" This geographical discovery made Sarah's mouth slowly curve. "That would have been a stop with delicious possibilities," she said.

"I wouldn't have dared to set foot off the ship. I'm not as bold as you."

"I'm not so bold as you think, either. I wouldn't even set foot on the ship to begin with. But just the thought of stalking Richard in Hispaniola is delicious." Sarah linked her arm with Arabel's. "Oh well, let's celebrate what we have achieved with a beer. Is there some place interesting nearby?"

"I've only been in the old brewery. It's nice."

They made their way from the shipping agents' office up

Dock Street, past the ten-gun battery. They turned left at the blockhouse where Wall Street began.

Sarah wrinkled her nose. "Slaughter houses?"

"On the other side of the stockade," Arabel said.

"Even in the cold you can smell it." Sarah pointed to the remains of a structure at the edge of a gaping hole in the dirtbank and wooden pilings. "This doesn't look like it's of much use as a fortification."

"The town's grown much further north of here, so they don't keep up the wall and batteries any more. In fact, they used the wood from this hole to build the town house where we just were." Arabel stopped at the first corner on the left. "This is the tavern. Do you know where we are?"

Sarah looked left, down the street. "Is this the end of King Street?"

"Yes. Mrs. Jourdain's is down a block." A shout and some laughter came from inside Pettijohn's. Arabel shrugged her shoulders and smiled. "They're doing what New Yorkers do best," she said.

They joined the drinkers and took a small table so as not to be molested in their conversation. A hostess came immediately.

"What beers do you have today?" Arabel asked.

"Oat, persimmon, birch and walnut." The woman wiped her puffy red hands on her apron then used it on the table top.

Arabel looked at Sarah. "Walnut's very nice."

Sarah nodded, so Arabel ordered two pints.

"This was the first brewery in the colonies, they say. It's

named after him." She pointed to a soot-darkened portrait above their table.

Sarah read the sign affixed to the bottom of the frame. "J Vigne. First child born here in 1614." She looked at Arabel. "This place is older than Boston. The Dutch must've stepped off their ship and built a brewery."

Arabel laughed.

"Not the Puritans." Sarah added. "First they put up a meetinghouse then a gaol."

Into their second pint Arabel was bold enough to ask Sarah about her journey to New York.

"Did you come all this way just to search for Richard?"

"Partly. I went to New Haven to attend to my cousin's will on behalf of my best friend, who'd married him. But I made a couple of discoveries that led me to believe Richard was here. Then there was a complication with the inventory, and my cousin had to come here and sort it out, so I decided to make the trip as well."

"How far is it? Wasn't it difficult? Dangerous?"

"I've ridden two-hundred and seventy miles so far. Some of it's been boring, some exasperating. I've ridden to exhaustion, and a lot of it's been terrifying. It's been hell, actually."

"Why go through all that again? You should sail back."

"Never."

They both sipped their beer.

"You know what's annoyed me the whole way? Being stuck on the side-saddle." Sarah could see Arabel did not understand. "You need steps to back your bum onto the thing, and you can't get down until someone helps you. I hate being stuck like that. Men get on and off as they please."

"That's because they have pants. You don't." Arabel giggled.

"Pants." Sarah finished the second pint. "This is fine beer. Dare we have another?"

Arabel nodded and giggled again.

"Pants," she said again, while waiting for the third round to appear. "You've given me an inspiration. I need a divided petticoat—one that has a skirt for each leg, so I can ride a man's saddle. Look." She traced the outline of a skirt on the table. At the center of the bottom hem she began a narrow, inverted V that ran halfway up the front. "Stitch along here," she said, "then cut up between the stitching. A leg would go in each side."

"You're outrageous." Arabel clapped her hands and laughed.

"I'm serious. I should have something like this made here, where it won't cause a hurried convening of the council. At home they'd nattle it apart stitch by stitch."

"Outrageous."

Sarah sipped her beer. She had begun in jest, but she just ought to have such a garment made. She could test it on her own, when she got home. She would make Robert lend her a saddle and teach her to mount and ride. Outrageous? He probably wouldn't even protest. After all she'd done, there would not be much point in it.

Bradford arrived at the Burroughs' residence shortly after the arrival of the shimmering mulberry gown, which had attracted the attention and approbation of the entire household. The servant took the gown to Sarah's chamber and the Burroughs left Sarah to consult with Bradford in the front hall.

"I wanted to let you know that I saw Thomas near the dock this afternoon," he said. "He was leaving for Perth Amboy because Hitchcock still hasn't come back from his son's house, and he wants to persuade him to return immediately."

"Did he say he'd contact you as soon as he got back?"

"No."

"Then keep a sharp eye. I don't want him claiming he couldn't find us and then leave."

"Our horses are all stabled at the same place. I'll bribe the stable mate to keep me informed. What happened with the magistrate?"

"He's made the arrangements for the complaint to be heard in April, so Arabel and I will just have to wait. She got her ticket today. She's sailing home on Friday. And we went shopping. Richard provided us with new wardrobes."

"How thoughtful."

Sarah saw a slight wickedness in his smile and appreciated it.

"What's Arabel going to do about her landlord?"

"I told her, 'Don't cover Richard's debts.'" Sarah shook her finger as she spoke. "I said, 'Just leave and let *him* face the landlord when he gets back.'"

"But he may not come back."

"That's what she said, but I told her it's the landlord's

problem. He'll have to figure out what to do about Richard. She should say nothing—just walk out the door and get on the ship and take her fourteen pounds and sixteen shillings with her."

"What's she going to do when she gets back to Barbados?"

"That's just what she asked me. She's wondering what's to become of her. She said she'd be able to live with an aunt, but she knows relatives don't want to support a single woman forever. And she'll have a hard time attracting another husband without a dowry."

Bradford nodded.

"I told her to keep what's left of Richard's money and buy some goods—anything—at a modest price and sell them at a profit and to keep doing that until she could buy some property or land. I explained how I've managed with my two enterprises. I said that whatever she invested in, to be sure it wasn't dependent on someone else who could lose it for her. I cautioned her about speculation. One shouldn't speculate unless one can afford to let someone else lose the whole investment."

"You've been very decent to her, very helpful."

Sarah shrugged her shoulders. "Why should I have been otherwise?"

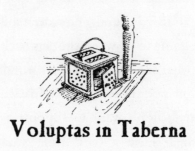

Voluptas in Taberna

Friday afternoon, December 15

Sarah sat at the table in her room at the Burroughs'. She still had three hours until a late afternoon reception for the Governor of New York. He had returned from Jersey, and the mayor had devised some entertainment for him. She was sorry to have missed the Governor's arrival ceremony, but she had been on a thoroughly enjoyable excursion to the *bouwerij* with the Burroughs.

She rose a little in her chair, smoothed her petticoat underneath and sat back down carefully. She did not want to appear at the reception with the back of her new mulberry gown all crumpled. She picked up her pen. How could she adequately describe a town so different from her own? And what should she disclose of what had transpired here?

Dearest Familie, I send you greatings and Best Wishes from the Cittie of New York. It is a pleasant, well compacted place, situated on a Commodius River with a fine harbour for shipping. The streets are paved in Pebblestones and graded to Allow drainage. The inhabitants

Sweep the filth to piles and the cittie's cartmen colect it each Satturday. Along the Water front are the fasheonable houses. The Buildings are Brick Generaly, very stately and high, though not like ours in Boston, the gabled wall facing the street, and having stepps along the roof line. The Bricks in some of the Houses are of divers Coullers and laid in Checkers. Being glazed, they look very agreeable. The inside of them are neat to admiration.

The House where I attended a Vendue had the hearth laid wth the finest tile that I ever see, and the stair cases laid all with white tile which is ever clean, and so are the walls of the Kitchen wch had a Brick floor. They make their Earnings very well by these Vendues, for they treat customers Liberally with Liquor. The Customers Drink and Bidd up Briskly, after the sack bottle has gone plentifully about, tho' sometimes good penny-worths are got there. For me I bought 100 Rheem of paper wch a Dutch flyboat had retaken from some foreign ship. The goods from pirate, privateer, English or Dutch beeing all the same to local merchants. I payed only 20£ for the lot and have sent it by ship to Boston.

Sarah made some quick calculations and realized she had been able to stock her stationery for well over a year with her half of Richard's assets. She continued with her letter.

They are Generaly of the Church of England but there are also Dutch, Huguenot and Divers Conventicles as they call them, viz. Baptist, Quaker, &c. They are not strict in keeping the Sabbath as in Boston and other places where I had bin, But do conduct affaires with great exactness so farr as I see. They are sociable to one another and Curteos and Civill to strangers. At the Vendue I made acquaintances amongst the women of the town, who have curteosly invited me to their houses. Today I go to Mrs. Peartree's whoose Husband is the Mayor and will offer a Reception of their Governor, Lord Cornbury, who has returned from the Jerseys.

I have also had a wonderfull Diversion. In winter it is the Habitt to Ride in Sleys about three or four Miles out of Town, where there are Houses of entertainment at a place called the Bouwerij. My host, Mr. Burroughs cary'd his spouse and Daughter and myself out upon the snow that fell recently to one Madame Dowes, a Gentlewoman that lived at a farm House. She gave us handsome Entertainment of five or six Dishes and choicest Beer and metheglin, Cyder, &c. all which she said was the produce of her farm. I believe we mett 50 or 60 slays during the day.

My Hosts are cuz'n. Prout's friends of long standing and have extended a gracious welcome to me although they are quite Deafe. They depend on their maiden Daughter to interpret for them, or all who converse with them must shout. Their sense of humour is quite in tact and they remaine Younger than their Years (and Eares) do suggest.

Thomas Found Mr. Hitchcock not at Home, being gone to his son's in Perth Amboy. The man not retourning at the time expected, Thomas has taken a boat there to persuade him to return and compleat the bussines about the deed which should be accomplished by weeks end. While I regrett leaving such a fine place it does bring me closer to my beloved family and home.

Sarah read what she had written. She had decided to omit any intelligence of Richard and was not sure in whom she might first confide, even after she returned home. She dreaded having to tell her mother, because of pride, and Elizabeth, because it would only hurt. But Robert would appreciate the turnabout she played on the one who had stung both of them many times. She signed her name.

※

In the entry hall of her home, Mrs. Peartree presented Sarah to Mr. Peartree, who in turn introduced her to Mrs. Burger. She had also come to the reception without an escort.

"My husband's the constable of Dock Ward," Mrs. Burger explained. "Since two ships just arrived, he has to stand duty. He's sorry to miss any party, especially here at the mayor's."

The two of them waited in the hall while a servant hung the wraps of other guests. Sarah offered no excuse for coming alone, but she thought of several that sounded interesting: My husband's other wife says he's still at sea—My host couldn't bring me because he goes to bed at six-thirty—or—The man I'm travelling with didn't bring any evening clothes. "I don't know many of the people here," she said. "Could I keep company with you this evening?"

"Of course."

They gave their cloaks to the servant.

"The reception is this way, where the noise is coming from," Mrs. Burger said.

Sarah had to turn to take in the entire high-ceilinged room. "This hall is bigger than my house."

"Mine, too," Mrs. Burger said.

The great hall was filled with milling people, and the movement of so many colors made Sarah dizzy. "I could never have imagined this," she said to Mrs. Burger.

Sarah saw her companion's lips move, but her words were

drowned out by a great cackling. Mrs. Burger took no notice, though, of the robust woman from whom it issued. In fact everyone, except the unfortunate few in this woman's conversation circle, seemed oblivious to her. She again shrieked with laughter.

Sarah was compelled to stare. The woman was extraordinary. A hooped petticoat spread out from a full belly. Her mantua had puffy sleeves with ribbons exploding from the shoulders, and it was fastened with bows down the center of her flat bosom. Her hair rose a foot above her head. Sarah had seen pictures of wire commodes that covered the head with every imaginable ostentation, even birdcages. This particular one employed ringlets of white hair, red ribbons and a fan-shaped lace arrangement at the top with matching lace panels that hung from her temples down to where her breasts should have been.

This woman's humor was again excited, and she slapped the arm of a gentleman with her fan. Then she whipped it open and spared the group the view of her open mouth as she whooped.

"Since it's the middle of December," Sarah said, "the fan must be for drama."

"Pfff," Mrs. Burger puffed. "It's all for drama."

Sarah pulled on Mrs. Burger's arm. "I want to move nearer for a better view. I've never seen such a woman."

"The reason being, that's not a woman," Mrs. Burger said. "That's Lord Cornbury, our governor."

"Good God," Sarah whispered. She had got close enough

to see that the woman's beard was reappearing since her morning shave.

Mrs. Burger then removed Sarah to the opposite corner of the room, where a servant offered them claret in glass goblets. "You mustn't remain where Lord Cornbury's wife can see you. You're wearing a lovely dress, and if she fancies it, she'll have her carriage sent 'round tomorrow to fetch it." She took a sip of claret. "But you'll have fair warning, because it's the only one in New York. When we hear it rumbling along, we hide whatever she admired the day before. What she does is send for a dress, saying she wants to have a pattern made of it, but she never returns it. She adds it to the wardrobe she's already collected at the expense of the women she's met."

"That's appalling. And if she finds a larger size, does she dress her husband?"

Mrs. Burger nodded. "Can you imagine the shame of seeing your gown coming at you on such a monster? You see, he bears resemblance to the Queen."

"No." Sarah looked hard at Mrs. Burger to detect a jest.

"Yes. She's his cousin, and since he represents her in the colony, he thinks his vain masquerade will remind us how close he is to the throne."

"He looks like Queen Anne?"

"They say it's uncanny."

"God have mercy on her," Sarah said.

"But how he dresses is of little consequence compared to his monstrous behavior. It's united all New Yorkers, even enemies from our recent civil war. They've all joined in hating him with equal fervor."

"More than Bellomont?"

"Pfff. More. This man's without conscience or character. Let's sit and I'll tell you about an outrageous occurrence."

They passed into an adjoining salon where numbers of people were seated. "It's a beautiful room," Sarah said. "The whole house is beautiful. I can see wealthy New Yorkers aren't constrained by the clergy's influence, as they are in Massachusetts. Our leading families can get by with a solemn kind of elegance, as long as they stay with simple lines and sober colors."

"I guess it's the difference between the English and Puritan churches. Although I can't say that any church has much sway over the people here." Mrs. Burger indicated two seats near a window. "Our governor attends faithfully, but he learns very little from the time he spends there."

"What was the outrage you referred to?" Sarah asked.

"Right after he arrived two years ago we had a yellow fever epidemic. He fled with his household to Jamaica, on Long Island, but the only house he thought suitable was the Presbyterian minister's. The minister felt it was his duty to vacate for the governor, but after the epidemic, Cornbury decided he liked it so much he chased the minister off and claimed it for himself."

"The minister didn't go to court?"

"Pfff. Lord Cornbury bends the law to his own purpose. He said since the house was built with public money—which it was because the community of Jamaica built it—that it now belonged to the Crown, and therefore the Church of England."

"And by extension, to him as governor," Sarah added.

"Exactly." Mrs. Burger was growing increasingly agitated as her story progressed. "The Reverend didn't want to lose his church, in addition to his home, so he and his congregation occupied the church and refused to leave. Then Cornbury had the door broken down and drove them into a nearby orchard. They say the defiant Reverend finished his sermon there. The last straw was when Cornbury replaced him with a minister of the Church of England and fined the Presbyterian for preaching without license from the governor. And the travesty of it all is when Cornbury first arrived here, there were only ten members of the Church of England in the whole of New York City."

"So this gave you a taste of things to come," Sarah said.

"He's a vile man. Arrogant. Has a violent temper. He accepts bribes, appropriates money for his own purposes, and he even embezzled the money he was granted for raising his own troops. Our Assembly has recently forced him to submit to a treasurer they elected, who's now in charge of expending funds."

"Sounds as though he's tried everything men usually devise to make themselves odious to people."

"Pfff. I've told you what I'm able to discuss in public. On his watch my husband has witnessed debaucheries and dissipations he can only hint at in my presence." She seemed unable to continue.

"In light of the governor's conduct, it's surprising to me the Mayor holds this reception. And why does everyone here seem to treat Cornbury with deference?"

"We haven't any choice," Mrs. Burger said.

"He wouldn't get by with such behavior in Massachusetts."

Mrs. Burger smiled. "Ah, well, this colony has always been used. It began with patroons and the Dutch government. Actually, the people permitted themselves to be robbed. The British have simply imitated the corruption of their Dutch predecessors. People like Cornbury wouldn't consider asking for an appointment in Massachusetts, when they can squeeze all they want from here."

They sipped the rest of their claret and looked around at the gathering. At last Mrs. Burger said, "We've spent too much time on a detestable topic. Let me introduce you to other people."

In an hour's time Sarah found some ladies she had met previously at the Vendue and met a score of new ones. Most of them asked, as their first question, what brought her to New York, and as their second, how her voyage had been. This provided for a dramatic disclosure of her means of travel. By the time she chose to leave, several ladies of the Dock Ward had arranged an entertainment for her later in the week, when she could relate the events of her journey to them without, as one woman put it, the distractions attendant on a political reception. And Sarah knew what that meant.

*

"You're where I left you," she said to Bradford. "Did you wait here with the servants the whole time?"

"No. After you went in, I walked over to the Hudson embankment for a while. When I started back at sunset, they were lighting the lanterns on the Broadway. If it's not too cold for you, you should come see it."

"I'd like to, regardless of the cold." She put her hands inside her muff and Bradford held her under the elbow. At the end of Beaver Street, where the Mayor lived, they came to Broadway.

"What a nice idea. Lanterns on both sides of the street." Sarah stood and looked up the street. "The light on the snow is lovely."

"We could walk as far as Wall Street then come back down to Dock Street," he said.

"Fine."

"A nightwatchman told me the city requires every seventh house on the street to have a lantern on a pole, but the expense is shared by all the households. The city even requires the planting of trees."

"Yes, I see. Summer must be pleasant too. I'd like to come here in the summertime."

"We rode in to New York on this street, but it was afternoon," Bradford said. "I didn't notice any of this, did you?"

She shook her head. "How could I have missed a mansion such as this?" She pointed.

They were the only pedestrians on Broadway. Their footsteps crunched on the packed snow. After they reached the crumbling fortification at Wall Street they turned around.

"I was told many of the Dutch live here on Broadway," Sarah said. "I like the way their lace curtains look behind the hoarfrost." They remarked upon such interiors as they could see on their walk back to the fort.

"It's impressive, isn't it?" Bradford said. "The fort and the stockade are higher up an embankment than you'd imagine.

Over a hundred feet in some places." Torches were fixed to the opening in the fort wall where a turnstile gave entry to the gate. "I walked inside today. They have thirty-eight cannon."

"From the layout of the town and the fort, you can tell they figure all their enemies will come by sea," Sarah said.

"If we'd had fortification like this up the Connecticut River, we'd never have been wiped out." They walked around the gun mount that stuck out into Broadway like a wedge.

"What else is inside?" Sarah asked.

"The far side's all barracks. On the other side of this wall are the chapel and the governor's house."

"He lives in there? A smart idea considering what I've just seen and heard about him. He may need the fort to protect him from attack by his own people."

"I was going to ask if you had a chance to talk to him at the reception."

"You'll have to hear the whole story, but my feet are frozen. Is this Dock Street we've come to?"

"Yes. Where I'm staying's around the corner."

"Good. I'm hungry. I only had a glass of wine, and if I go back to the Burroughs' house now, they'll all be in bed."

※

Sarah watched Bradford fill a foot stove with coals from the fireplace. A ring was pressed into his hair from the band of his hat. Without his greatcoat and tricorn he looked smaller. Under his clothes she could see the shape of his arms and legs and body. She watched them move.

Bradford flipped the door of the small stove shut with his

boot and brought it to their table. She lifted her petticoat so he could place it under her feet.

"Oh, that's excellent," she said. But more than the warmth, she felt a ruffle with his attention, not because she was unused to attentions accorded her. She expected them. At home people attended her because of her position in the community. Even here, if she had come into this tavern alone, someone would have got a foot stove without her having to ask for it. However, she did not think duty or regard for her standing motivated him. She thought it was more personal. He fetched the foot stove because he cared about her being warm.

A serving girl came for their order. They decided to start with a glass of flip and watched while she poured molasses in the beer then stuck a hot poker in it to make it froth.

Sarah told Bradford about the governor.

During their first course of raw oysters, the two discussed where they had seen the highest mounds of shells along the coast and how long it must have taken for the natives to amass them.

Next they had pigeons with sweet marjoram and roasted walnuts. They talked about her occupations in Boston and about the trading business he had begun and lost.

"And you aren't bitter? You certainly have good cause," Sarah said. "For me, the loss of a husband will be a gain in the end, but I'm so angry because I've wasted fifteen years."

He thought for a moment. "If I were still angry with the French and Abenakis, it would be like trading one prison for another. Anger would control me; what they did would still have power over me. Do you understand what I mean?" He took the last bite his supper. "They already destroyed all I had and stole three years of my life, and that's enough. They can't have any more. But I learned one thing—Don't have a business that can be carried off or burnt. I want to deal in land."

She told him how Robert Livingston had acquired his empire. They talked about where new land might open up next, about which tribes were most likely to sell it, and about how much cleared and virgin lots had sold for recently.

While talking, she wondered what his face would look like in ten years, or twenty, when he had become a wealthy landowner. She hoped he wouldn't don a wig like other Connecticut patricians. Dark hair suited his almond skin. A white peruke wouldn't.

They had peach wine after supper and laughed about having the same ambitions. They even envisioned a future partnership in land speculation, when each had marshaled enough wealth. They drank a toast to it. Bradford and Knight, Incorporated. The future had the aroma of peaches.

They shook on the deal, but they never let go. His clasp caused her pulse to quicken, and looking into his eyes made her quiver inside. The desires she had suppressed for years now arose in a flood. She wanted words whispered in her ear. She wanted an arm wrapped round her back, a hand in her hair, breath on her neck. She wanted the weight of a body on hers. Could he see all that in her eyes? They filled and stung.

He reached up with his left hand and slowly wiped away the tears that ran down her cheeks.

"Would you come to my room?" he asked.

Dies Frigidi

Sunday, December 24

Sarah opened her eyes and saw a window. She looked around the room trying to remember what tavern this was. She shut her eyes and drifted, half awake, through images of several different taverns, the signboards hanging outside, meals they had eaten, numbing hours aboard Athena, and through a confusion of blowing snow. Even with another look at the room, she could not picture this tavern from the outside.

On the second day of their return trip to New Haven, she, Bradford and Thomas had arrived in Stratford late in the afternoon. They had waited four hours until the ferrymaster decided the ice floes had cleared enough for them to cross the river. From there the journey to New Haven was only twelve miles, but she felt too miserable to go on, so they had stopped at the first town after the ferry.

Sarah sat up and looked out the window. Fine, light snow was falling through empty tree branches, she was alone again and covered with silence. Then she remembered this was not a tavern but the home of someone Thomas knew here, a cousin's widow. Sarah hopped about to dress in the cold room. She walked to the window and looked down at the front of the house. There were still tracks the horses had made last night—three that came to the house and two that left.

Someone knocked on her door. She opened it and recognized the woman, whose arched eyebrows furnished her with an inquisitive and solicitous expression.

"Good morning, Mrs. Knight. Have you slept well?" Her voice was soft and high, like a warbling bird.

"I feel much better. I wasn't in such good condition last night."

"Of course not. I still can't believe you came from New York on a horse in this weather."

"Everything froze, even my mind. I just woke up and couldn't think where I was. You'll have to forgive me, but I don't remember who you are, either."

The woman chirped in amusement and patted Sarah on the arm. "Mrs. Winston, and you're in Milford. But I'll explain downstairs. I have a hot breakfast for you."

※

Sarah worked on a sticky mound of boiled oats in hot milk, which her hostess had served in a piece of plain crockery.

"My husband was a cousin of Thomas' wife," Mrs. Winston said. "Mary was a Winston before she became a Trowbridge." She offered no information about her late husband. She gathered her skirt in front, perched on a bench at the table and folded her hands in her lap. Mrs. Winston was dressed more plainly than anyone Sarah had seen so far—a black cap and gray dress without collar or cuffs, like a perfect gray catbird. She seemed to be about fifty.

"Thomas and the other gentleman were eager to keep riding last night, so I didn't quite understand what all of you were doing. You rode from New Haven to New York? And now you're on your way back?"

"We went there several weeks ago to take care of some business," Sarah said. "We left New York Thursday, but the weather's been so bad it took us three days to get this far. The last two nights have been the most woeful I've suffered in my entire journey from Boston."

"From Boston? You've ridden from Boston?"

Sarah nodded. "And I've felt every stone under my horse's feet."

"What an amazement. I haven't been ten miles from my birthplace. When did you leave Boston?"

"October second."

A drum commenced to beat, causing Mrs. Winston to jump up. "Oh dear, it's meeting time. I have to go, or I'll be fined. You're welcome to come with me."

Sarah affected a cough and rubbed her arms, as if still chilled. "I think I'd best stay in. I'm still not recovered from my ordeal." She coughed again to emphasize the point.

"Of course, poor thing. Here, use my double-wool whittle." She removed the fringed blanket from a hook by the door and arranged it over Sarah's shoulders. "You stay by the fire until I come back. It'll be about two hours. I always hope for a shorter sermon, when the meetinghouse is so cold."

"May I write in my journal at your table?"

"Yes, yes." The drum's steady beat kept Mrs. Winston aflutter. She tied the strings of her cloak at her neck and pulled up the hood. "Lay on another log if you want." She opened the door. "And there's plenty of hot water in the kettle if you need it. *Au revoir.*" Mrs. Winston shut the door.

Sarah sat huddled, watching the fire, which crackled and flared because of the draft. When the drum ceased, she looked around for her saddlebags. Bradford had left them draped over a chest near the stairway. She arranged her stationery items on the table, put two logs on the fire and lit an oil lamp. She sat with her back to the fire and arranged the whittle over her lap and legs. Whittle? In Boston a shawl had not been called a whittle since her grandmother died.

Sarah dipped her quill and began to write. *Having here transacted the affair I went upon, and some other that fell in the way....*

She chuckled at what "some other" meant then continued writing.

... after about a fortnight's stay there I departed New-York with no Little regrett, and Thursday, Dec. 21, set out for New Haven wth my Kinsman Trowbridge, and the man who waited on me, about one in the afternoon....

"With no little regret." She could not have dreamed of such a stay, as it had turned out, or envisioned such an interesting place—houses made of brick and tile, lanterns in the streets, the confusion of tongues and dress, social life unfettered by religious dogma, fully stocked shops and warehouses along the dock streets. And crowded, boisterous taverns.

Bradford stayed in one of these taverns. After they left his room that night, the gratification and warmth in the deepest part of her began to fade with each stairstep. The public room had filled with sailors and the women whose livelihood it was to entertain them. It had reverberated with crude language, shouts and raucous laughter. She had cursed under her breath at a man who was squeezing the half-exposed breasts of a giggling whore. Sarah's sense of pleasure had eroded in the atmosphere of the room. Outside the tavern door, the cold air had hit her face. When she had inhaled, it sank into her chest.

They had walked the first block in silence. What remained of their interlude was the carnal residue. She had said, "I can't reappear in Boston carrying a souvenir of my visit in New York."

He had said nothing. He knew, as well as she did, what price the guardians of public morals exacted of a woman who bore a child when her husband was away. Even a husband such as Richard.

Snow had fallen during the next few days, so she had not quit the Burroughs' house, although Bradford had come to collect her safeguard to have it waxed for her journey back.

The following Monday morning she had been relieved to find evidence she had not acquired a souvenir. She had lingered abed with the excuse of feminine discomfort, until late in the afternoon, when she had been entertained by some of the women of the city at a Mrs. Rombout's house.

Bradford had called on Tuesday to report that Thomas

and Hitchcock had returned. Their business was completed the following day, and on Thursday morning the trio had packed and left.

※

Sarah looked at the last two lines she had written before she had lost herself in reflection. She wrapped Mrs. Winston's whittle tighter about her, dipped the quill in the ink and wrote on.

Thursday, Dec. 21, started for New Haven wth my Kinsman Trowbridge, and the man who waited on me about one in the afternoon.... She dipped her quill, added a comma, then she continued *... and about three come to a halfway house about ten miles out of town, where we Baited then rode forward, and about 5 come to Spiting Devil, Elsewise called Kings bridge, where the man that keeps the Gate at the end of the Bridge gets three pence for crossing over with a horse.*

We hoped to reach the french town and lodg there that night, but unhapily lost our way about four miles short, and being overtaken by a great storm of wind and snow which set full in our faces at dark, were very uneasy.

But finding a Cottage thereabout, we were invited to sit by the owner's fire. He had but one Bedd and his sick wife was in it, or if we prefered he would go to a House with us, where he thought we might be better accommodated—thither we went, But a surly old shee Creature, not worthy of the name woman, would hardly let us into her Door, though the weather was so stormy none but shee would have turnd out a Dogg.

So we struggled next dorr to her son who Invited us in his house. He shewed me two pair of stairs, one up the loft and tother up the

Bedd, wth was as hard as it was high, and hee warmed it with a hott stone at the feet. I lay very uncomfortably. Insomuch as I was so cold and sick, I was forced to call them up to dispense something to warm me. They had nothing but milk in the house, wch they Boild, and to make it better, sweetened wth molasses. I knew this not until it was down and coming up agen, wch it did in so plentifull a manner that my host was soon paid double for his portion. But I believe it did me service in Cleering my stomach. It was a sick and weary night.

Sarah rose and arranged another log on the fire. Through that night Bradford had sat in a chair by her bed. He had dozed between the times when he had tiptoed down to the fireplace to exchange a cooled stone for a hot one. Thomas had slept on a table down by the fire, and in the morning he had expressed that Bradford should surely ask for more wages than he was being paid, because of all the attention his employer required. Bradford had only shrugged his shoulders. Thomas had not been aware that the attention included strokes on her head after Bradford had tucked the hot stone under the bedclothes and even a kiss on her forehead when he must have thought she was asleep.

Sarah felt flushed and rushed on to the next day. *The morning weather on Friday the 22d Dec. being now fair, we departed East Chester (a most miserable poor place). Being come to New Rochell we had good Entertainment and Recruited ourselves very well. This is a pretty town, well compact with handsome houses, Clean and passable Rodes, situated on a Navigable River, an abundance of Cleerd land, all that caused in me a Love of it, wch I could have been content to live in.*

So were Bradford's words when they rode through there. "I

could be content to live here," he had said. "I wonder what lots cost?" They had not looked at one another.

We Ridd over a Bridge made of one entire stone of such a Breadth that a cart might proceed with safety, and some room to spare–it lay over a gorge cutt through a Rock to convey water to a mill not farr off where they were cutting ice. After wee baited at Hors Neck we took leave of York Government, and Descending the Mountainos passage that almost broke my heart in ascending before, we come to Stamford, a well compact town, but wth a miserable meetinghouse.

We had many great difficulties from Bridges which were exceeding high and tottering and of vast Length, steep and Rocky Hills and precipices, (Buggbears to a fearful female travailer.) About nine at night we come to Norrwalk, having crept over a timber of a Broken Bridge about thirty foot long, and perhaps fifty to ye water. I was exceeding tired and cold when we come to our Inn, and could get nothing there but poor entertainment and the impertinant Bable of one of the worst of men. A host could not have bin one degree Impudenter. And this I think is the most perplexed and Intolerable night's Lodging I have yet had.

Saturday, Dec. 23 wee hasted forward. Having Ridd thro a difficult River wee come to Fairfield where wee Baited and were much refreshed. We rested our wearied Limbs and enquired about the town. It is filled with wealthy people but they are Litigious, nor are they inconcurance with their minister. They have abounance of sheep, whose very Dung brings them great gain, with part of which they pay their Parsons sallery, And they Grudg that, prefering their Dung over their minister. They Lett out their sheep at whatever price they agree upon for a night, And the sheep will sufficiently Dung a Large quantity of Land before morning. But the folk were once Bitt by a sharper who had the sheep a night and sheared them all by morning.

From hence we got to Stratford, in which I observed but few houses, and not fine ones, but the people I conversed with were civill and good natured. Here we waited to cross a Dangerous River ferry, the River at that time full of Ice.

Now she was brought up to the present lodging, and she felt cold just recalling her journey. She put away her stationery and poured hot water from the kettle into a mug. For flavor she broke off some dried herbs that hung from a beam. The leaves did not look familiar; she sniffed them but did not recognize the smell either. It was pleasant, though, so she crushed them in her cup, sat down and rewrapped herself again.

Mrs. Winston returned from the spiritual refurbishing.

"It seemed so long today, especially since I knew you were here and I wanted to get back home. Have you entertained yourself? How are you feeling?"

"I've brought myself up to date in my journal and made some tea. I don't know what I put in it. I hope it's not a physic or suchlike." She laughed. "It's from there." She pointed to the beam.

"Lemon verbena," she chirped. "I use it for potpourri, but it won't harm you."

"Well, join me then, and I'll describe New York and Boston and wherever else you'd like to hear about."

✼

The early afternoon passed rapidly for the two women. About two o'clock there came a knock on the door, and a young man entered without waiting for an answer.

"This is my son, William. He lives next door," Mrs. Winston said to Sarah. "I told him about you at meeting. Come join us," she said to him, "You're just in time to move the kettle from the fire."

Mother and son ladled turkey stew with steamed dumplings into three bowls.

"He shot it yesterday. There was a large flock on the beach. When the snow covers the ground in the winter, they come peck in the surf for shrimp."

"All of Milford is probably eating turkey today," William said. "Everyone ran down to the beach when we heard them. What a commotion. We had to organize ourselves so we didn't shoot each other. We couldn't even tell who shot what, so we just divided them up at the end, and everyone took home at least one. I don't think but a couple of turkeys got away."

Sarah mentioned some of the animals she had seen since leaving Boston, and the conversation about her travels resumed. Then she raised the matter of getting to New Haven.

"Thomas said your waiter wanted you to recover for a few days before resuming your journey," Mrs. Winston told Sarah. "Thomas said he'd send the waiter later in the week. Thursday, maybe."

"I really want to go as soon as possible," Sarah said.

Did Thomas have in mind hurrying home to attend the matter of the deed, while she recuperated at a safe distance from New Haven? She and he had come to enjoy the other's company in the course of their travel, but she knew him well enough to understand that any deal in his own interest came before all else, even family. He had not acquired his wealth otherwise. "Could you escort me there?" she asked William.

"I'm only free at weekends," he said.

"I could go today, after we eat."

William and his mother looked at each other, then at her.

"It's the Sabbath. It's not allowed," he said.

"Please don't consider leaving now," Mrs. Winston said. "You had a terrible journey. You've got chills. You've been coughing, and I promised Thomas I'd care for you."

"You have, and I'm much improved." She turned to William. "We could go after sunset. Would that satisfy the law—no travelling from sunset Saturday to sunset Sunday?"

"I don't know," he said. He looked at his mother again. She shrugged.

"I'd pay you well," Sarah offered. "You could escort me to New Haven and come home in one evening, couldn't you?"

"It's but nine miles. I could do that, and it's nearly full moon; it would be light." He thought for a moment. "But there's the ferry. The ferryman would have to consent to a round trip on a Sabbath evening."

Mrs. Winston tried again. "I'm so glad of your company. Another few days would make you much stronger. How will I explain myself to Thomas, if you arrive in New Haven with a fever or pneumonia?"

"I'm really quite fit, and I'm grateful for your kind ministrations, but I've travelled a long way on the business of an estate. If I'm not present when Thomas appears before the magistrates, I'd have done it all for naught." She turned to William. "Should we inquire with the ferryman, then? Would it help to offer double the fare?"

When his mother gave no further protest, he pulled on his coat and went to speak to the ferryman.

After the two women spent another hour talking, the sun set and Sarah departed with the good woman's son. She vowed that if some delay in New Haven permitted her a couple of days to visit, she would ride back to Milford and have another mug of potpourri.

Disputatio

Sunday, January 21, 1705

Sarah sat in her room at the Prouts'. Her table was by the window. With the lid of her writing box, she scraped a hole in the intricate swirls of hoarfrost that covered the windowpane, but she saw nothing happening on the street that led to the long wharf. She watched the frozen shavings melt on the window sill.

On the morrow the repulsive Fleer would appear at Miles Tavern to collect the post again, so she decided to spend the afternoon composing a letter to Mary and her family, one that would attempt to explain the exasperating behavior of Caleb's relatives. In the last few weeks her frustration and anger were hardly containable under a veneer of civility that was so thin it was almost transparent. Added to the bickering about the estate was a longing for her family.

My dear Ones, I sorely miss You and would enjoy some comfort if I knew my retourn to Boston was imminent. After my jorney to York my Hostess enforced a lengthy rest, during which time I Occupyed myselfe wth books I borrow'd from the minister, who has the only library. In this Rising star of merchantilism, hee is aparrently the sole One Who devotes time to reading. He offered me "Wonders of the Invisible World," he beeing an admirer of Cotton Mather and not having to live in his midst and be witness to the extreemes of his passion. The piece was too hysterrical for mee to accept as an explanation for the sadd events in Salem, but my praise of its clarity and thoroughness pleased the kind Minister. I read about Josselyn's voyages and "New England's Prospect" by William Wood. Both men came from England and with foreign eyes describe not their own home but a foreign Lande. But I could not discern much of their jorneying here. Did they have no bad meals, meet no Rude hostess, sleep on No hard bedds with buggs? I much more enjoied readding the "Voyages of Hakluyt" who suffered not the Discomfourt of travalling here at all, but Stayed at home and penned Instructions for how others should settle here. And by staying home he, no doubt, never miss't a meal served by his wife. Although drama is eschew'd here as in Boston, The Minister had two volumes of Shackspeare, the playes of Henry and Richard being accept'd as histories.

Then finding Myself Recruited and fitt for business I discoursed the family and court that we might finnish the Matter. The family chooses not to honor the Will, and Each One disputes the shares of the estate the others feel entitled to. You shoud know there are 25 blood relations—but Caleb's brother and two sisters have the strongest claim here, And issuing from them are 14 nieces and nephews, all But one being minors. The Familie endevors to exclude Caleb's stepmother from their negotiations, except when shee learns of their meetings, so I suppose she'll petition the court on behalf of her daughter, because she's quite determined for her to have a Portion.

Elizabeth H has not relinquished her thought that Mary scheemed to marry Caleb on his deathbed. Upon receite of this letter go ask Mr. Boylston and the reverend Mather for letters of confirmation of Caleb's good health prior to youre marriage and some words on his sudden incopacitation. Have the letters sent with the next post or packet. The family is thick wth the members of Probate court, so I can only hope that these Letters will quiet her complaints. She is the most Formitable oppostion.

I suspect the familie hopes their Wrangle will tire my Patience. But I'm resolved to stay to the End of the affare, no matter how much to my displeasure it is to remayne. The court had finally set a meeting but the death of someone's Uncle caus'd delay. Then Last weekend new amusements were contrived, so yesterd'y I implored that good holy Gentleman, the Rev. Mr. Pierpont to mediate.

I will propose what I believe is the Best Offer wch is this. Mary will retain the 230 achres and relinquish any other claims as wife. (It's the single larg'st piece of the estate and could doubel its worth) Tis less than 20% of the estate and I think They'll be happy to be ridd of Mary at much less than the usual wifely Share. The family will then bee the sole Heirs. The court has set six months time for claims ag'nst the estate. The familie knows there are no Credittors in New Haven who will take a bite from their portion (and they haven't tho't to question mee about Boston) This is their only small sorce of Contentment so I'll not disturb it. But when the Boston Credditor comes round, it will be They, howev'r, and not Mary, who will proportionaly have to satisfy the Claime. And if they desire to quarral foreverafter over his pots and clothings and barrels of salt, I'll not be present to hear it.

Reguarding the 230 achres, they're Removed upriver from the

Towne but in the direction where the newest homes have been bildt. Caleb Finished draining one Section and began cleering some parts for farming. I have someone to compleat the work, divide the Lotts and manage it for Mary. If hee returns from Hartford before I leave I'll reach an agrement wth him subject to Mary's aproval. New Haven has just been made the secnd capital of the colony and Thomas has recently buildt a wharf that extends 300 ft from the harbour. I antecipate speedy growth in the pop. here. Since Mary hasent a pressing need for money I sugest Holding on to the land for a year or so untill it has doubled or trippled its valeu.

Pierpont meets wth us Tues to mediate. If hee should suceeed I could leave that night. The moon is full-faced on the 23d, but that Escort of Travallers and Mistress of Tides is also the prod of Lunacy, and I hope Her effects fall not here on the family that grows less reasonable wth each passing day. My love to you all and wth longing to see you I send this letter in hopes I will follow it.

She sealed the letter then re-opened the one that was awaiting her when she had come back from New York almost a month ago. Robert had told Elizabeth to write in French as a practical application of her lessons. Although Sarah could have struggled with her lapsed French and probably arrived at an approximate understanding of its contents, she had promptly written a note to Bradford, asking him to come to the Prout residence. She had wanted him to read it to her.

"You have dark circles round your eyes and your face is pale," he had said. "You were supposed to remain in Milford until I came for you."

"I was afraid I might miss something."

He had shaken his head.

After introducing her waiter to Mary Prout, Sarah had led the way into the kitchen where Mary had installed her on a truckle bed. Mary had it moved downstairs so she could supervise Sarah's bed rest while she worked. "You're not to be trusted," she had chided.

"My warden has allowed me this interview with you," Sarah had told Bradford, "so you could read a letter to me. It's written in French."

He had translated it, and they all agreed how clever Elizabeth was. Bradford had commended her grammar and idiom. Then Sarah had asked to hear him read it in French. It had sounded beautiful. She did not have to worry that she displayed too much fascination with hearing him read because Mary's praise was effusive.

"What a gift you have," Mary had told Bradford. "I could listen to you read all day."

So could I, Sarah had thought.

Before Bradford had left, Sarah brought up the fact that she had not yet paid him for waiting on her during her New York journey. It had been awkward. He had looked as though he might refuse the salary, but it was not possible to say anything in front of Mary. He had blushed. Sarah felt peculiar giving him money, but she had managed a formal commendation. "In my need of escort, I couldn't have found a more competent or considerate person."

He had said nothing—just acknowledged her with a nod.

"My cousin's estate should be settled soon, and I'll

require a guide to Boston. Would you undertake the journey?" They had never discussed this, and she observed the surprise on his face.

They had not spoken of their liaison afterwards. The temptation to arrange another was too great. Except for the night she was sick, they had not been alone together again.

Then she needed to arrange for a guide to Boston. She knew hiring Bradford would be unwise, but she had found herself asking him anyway.

After turning his hat in his hands he finally said, "I'd be happy to, but I have to leave for Hartford in a few days."

"Hartford?"

"My uncle heard the government in Hartford might offer reparations to victims of attacks on the northern settlements. But I have to apply in person. He's urged me to go as soon as possible. It may take a week or more. Will you be ready to leave before then?"

"I doubt it."

"She won't even be out of this bed for a week," Mary had added.

The arrangement had been left vague, and Sarah realized that gave her a chance to change her mind if she wished.

That was nearly a month ago. Now she studied every sentence of her daughter's letter before she translated it aloud in English. Then she folded the letter, tied it with the others she had received from her family and stared at the window, where the hole she had scraped was once again covered with hoarfrost, and the world outside was obscured from her view.

Tuesday, January 23

In the best room of the Prouts' house, the New Haven resident of sound judgement and great personal charm stood before the contentious heirs of Caleb Trowbridge. Sarah thought James Pierpont's appearance conveyed the force of character she hoped would extricate her and Mary from this lengthening drama. Pierpont's long, straight nose directed attention down to a steadfast chin. He parted his hair in the middle, and it flowed over his ears to his shoulders, offering a high and distinguished forehead. Even his brows arched impressively above penetrating eyes. Sarah's confidence rose when he cleared his throat and grasped the lapels of his unbuttoned coat.

"I beseech you to consider the character of your departed brother, who held you in the highest affection before his untimely death, so far from you. He was honest and fair in his dealing with all people." He extended one hand toward them. "I also entreat you to accept the marriage into which they entered. It should be honored. And to honor Caleb's last wishes is to honor his judgement and wisdom." He picked up a small volume. "Hear what the great minister Mr. Wigglesworth tells us."

> *Vain, frail, short liv'd and miserable Man . . .*
> *Learn what deceitful Toyes, and empty things,*
> *This World, and all its best Enjoyments bee,*
> *Out of the Earth no true Contentment springs,*
> *But all things here are vexing Vanitee . . .*

And what are Riches to be doted?
Uncertain, fickle, and ensnaring things;
They draw Men's Souls into Perdition,
And when most needed, take them to their wings.
Ah foolish Man! that sets his heart upon
Such empty Shadows . . . .

He paused to let them absorb this message.

Well done, thought Sarah. They all looked uncomfortable. This was the opportunity to make her proposal.

"Your admonition's given us much to reflect on, Reverend," Sarah said. "Mary wouldn't want her marriage to Caleb to cause discord. As her agent I suggest she surrender her position as wife and major heir." Sarah saw she had stunned everyone.

"Mary's desire not to create divisiveness within the family is commendable," Pierpont said, "but I'm sure no family would want a widow, even one of brief duration, to be without provision."

Most of the family members nodded, some a little reluctantly, it seemed.

Sarah continued, "Most of Caleb's estate consists of properties that would burden her so far away: like his house, his trade inventory, the farm, the orchard, the animals, even his personal effects. All these would bring advantage to the family here, but Mary can't know what each of you could best use. She should withdraw and leave it to all of you. I suggest she take the two-hundred-thirty acres. It's a small portion of his total estate, but it's something I could hire a manager for."

"A thoughtful suggestion," the minister said. He looked around at everyone. No one was willing to disagree. "What's necessary to effect this change and to have the family divide up the rest?"

Thomas said, "The court would hear Mary's request. And if we don't object, there's no reason why they should. As far as the rest, I propose that all of us submit a list to the court of what we'd like to have. They could negotiate any conflicting claims."

"Is there objection to this plan?" Pierpont asked.

There was none.

"Let us pray. Bless those gathered here, who in their willingness to please thee, ask for continued strength to choose the righteous path. Amen."

Amen, Sarah sighed to herself.

Thursday, February 1

Sarah had just departed the final meeting with the officers of probate court and walked along the dock. She stepped onto the tilted bow of the ferry, which had been dragged partly ashore. Ice stretched out twenty feet. Beyond that, the surface of the river rippled until it reached the opposite bank, which was also opaque. There were hundreds of ducks. Scores sat still on the ice; a few honked while they walked around aimlessly. A couple of them slipped into the water; others waddled onto the ice and shook themselves violently.

"I'm so happy this has concluded," she had said to several of the female cousins, when they left the court. "I'd leave tomorrow if my guide were here." And Lydia had seemed overly pleased to tell Sarah about the river.

"You must not have been down to the wharf lately," she had said. "We call this between-times. You can't travel when the river's between-times. The ferry's frozen ashore by the ice, but the river's not frozen in the middle, so you can't go by horse either."

Sarah should have been aware of this, since water surrounded Boston. She looked at the dock on the opposite shore. How did Fleer manage to keep his precious schedule when rivers were between-times? Then it occurred to her that each one of the rivers and streams that she had crossed to get here was a potential for delay. How many were there between here and Boston? Every mile or so it seemed.

Maybe that was why Bradford was not back yet. Last week she had begun to worry that he would not return. As a precaution she had looked for another guide, but the only man available was slovenly, his teeth were ringed with green scum, and when he spoke, spittle formed white parentheses at the corners of his mouth. She decided she would travel with no one but Bradford. They would just have to keep their distance from one another.

Sarah watched several seagulls rise from a nearby pier and fly across the river. Having to stand there inflamed her nerves and made her jumpy, so she walked from one end of New Haven to the other, up and down every street, until she felt thoroughly frozen—her hands, feet, face, even her nerves and her lungs. When she was numb, she went back to the Prouts' house.

Valete Dolor

Tuesday, February 20

Sarah stepped out the door and with the first breath her nose hairs froze. She had no complaint about the cold, though. Since Bradford's return, they had been waiting for the river's decision to thaw or freeze. The last four days were so bitterly cold that the surface finally appeared solid. At sunrise Bradford and a port officer had walked across with their horses. From the sound of the hooves and by using a drill, they determined the ice would support traffic. The port officer raised a safe-passage flag, and by the time the party attending Sarah on her departure had arrived at the river's edge, dozens of people were coming and going.

"It's a blessing the sun's strong and there's no wind," Mary Prout said. Her arm twined round the arm of the houseguest she was sorry to lose. John was on Sarah's other side. They, the Reverend Pierpont and nearly all of Caleb's relatives were walking toward the ferry dock to see her off. Missing were the smaller children, for fear the weather would harm them, and missing was Stepmother Hannah Trowbridge, who had pressed so hard for her daughter to be named an heir that the rest of the family was not speaking to her.

The group came to the shore, where Bradford waited with the horses. Behind him a band of noisy boys was running and sliding on the ice.

"The Dutch have a passion for *schaats*," Sarah told the group. "They're metal blades they put on their shoes. Every patch of ice in New York has a Dutchman on it. They fairly fly on the frozen rivers. It looks terrifying."

"Burroughs told me about it," John said. "Even people his age use them."

"We saw some women doing it. Remember at Harlem?" Thomas asked Sarah. "They had fur hats and fur on their coats. They looked like dancing bears."

It was finally time to say their last good-byes and for everyone to give Sarah messages to take to family and friends in Massachusetts.

"It's so cold; you should wear your mask. Where is it?" Mary Prout fussed with Sarah's garments. "Let me help you put it on."

Sarah removed it from her muff. She and Mary had altered it the evening before. It had come with a mouthpiece, consisting of a couple of glass buttons attached to short cords, and Sarah had to keep the mask in place by holding the buttons with her teeth. "How am I supposed to talk with a mouth full of buttons?" she had complained. So they had sewn on two strings to tie around her hood. Mary fastened it and gave Sarah a hug.

"Don't cry, Mary. You promised not to. Your tears will freeze," Sarah said. "I'll miss you. Thank you for your many kindnesses." Then she shook the mittened hands of each relative.

Bradford helped her up the mounting steps that were at the ferry landing. He decided to walk between the two horses. If a hoof should slip on the ice, he could better steady things.

They began their crossing. Sarah waved to everyone. Bradford had reins in both hands so he nodded his head. When they reached the east side of the river, they looked back and saw the tower of the meetinghouse, the blue houses, which stood out against the snow, and the tiny cluster of relatives, who were waving their last farewells.

✣

Winter made the journey different from the one in October—naked trees, the absence of outdoor activity, snow obscuring the distinctive features of the landscape. Sarah recognized nothing. There was advantage in the snow cover, however. Tracks clearly marked the route. Still, they made slow progress because they often stopped to warm themselves with a drink, and they stopped earlier in the evening because it was too cold to travel without the benefit of the sun.

Bradford looked at his timepiece then over his shoulder at the lowering sun. "We'll need to stop at the next ordinary."

Within half an hour they came to a house. "I'll go ask where we can find accommodation." They rode to the door, and he dismounted. At his knock a man and woman came to the door.

"Yes, friend," the man said.

"We're travelling to New London and need a place to stay. Is there an ordinary we can reach before dark?"

The man leaned outside and looked at the sky. "No, I don't think you can make Clinton. You can stay upstairs here, if you want to. The inside isn't finished yet, but we can fix you a pallet by the chimney." He turned to his wife for approval.

Sarah thought the couple looked familiar. She looked more carefully at the outside of the house. Part of it was weathered wood, the rest was new. Then she remembered stopping here with Wheeler. Some men who were putting on roof shingles had watched her. This was the woman at the wellcurb, and there it was with snow drifted against one side.

"Tie your horses under the lean-to on the barn," the man said to Bradford. "Come in, madam. You must be very cold."

He could not recognize her, of course. She still had on her mask. She decided to say nothing but was not sure why. The wife went to put something in two bowls for the guests' supper. After Sarah had removed her outer wear and put it on a hook by the door, Bradford came in. They sat at the table and ate by themselves. The couple had already excused themselves to attend sick children in the next room. Later their footsteps and voices moved up a staircase.

※

Sarah and Bradford were thoroughly warmed by the time the host brought an oil lamp for them to take upstairs. Then he went back to his children's bedside.

The guests climbed the narrow steps to the second floor.

Tools, sawhorses, stacks of shingles and piles of boards cluttered the area, which smelled of new wood and sawdust. They stepped around studs that would frame the rooms.

The chimney went up the center of the house. On the other side of it they were startled to find a single pallet for them on the floor.

"They think we're married," Bradford whispered.

Sarah sat on the edge of the pallet. "Well, one of us is, anyway." She picked up a curled wood shaving and rolled it between her fingers. "By April the magistrate said I'd be—how did he put it?—I'd be relieved of the intolerable condition with which I'm presently bound. But I know how the courts work. This could drag on for a year or so."

Bradford sat down beside her and struggled out of his boots.

"I've never been good at putting off what I want." She crushed the wood shaving and tossed it away.

Bradford took both her hands and she looked at him.

"Richard's still my. . . ." She could not finish. "It seems men do what they please in New York. I should have hired an assassin. It would have been quicker."

He smiled then kissed her.

"We haven't talked since that night," he said. "I wasn't sure how you felt."

She wrapped her arms around his shoulders. He pulled her close, as they lay back on the pallet, and he buried his face in the cleft of her neck, below her ear.

"You said nothing," he whispered, "I was afraid you'd—"

She stopped him with a kiss because his whispering sounded so doleful.

He looked at her. "I wanted to be with you so much, but I was worried about what to do—you know, about how to protect you." He held her close again and spoke into her ear. "There's a way to keep you from carrying home a souvenir, as you put it." He paused and looked to see if she understood what he meant. "I bought something. From the tavernkeeper in New York. He was experienced in these matters."

That night she learned what the English meant by "tiny French hats" and what the French meant by "little English hoods."

Saturday, February 24

The rekindled feelings and pleasures were all the harder for Sarah to part with when she arrived in New London. Bradford would not be able to escort her to Boston. He had to travel north to his home county to claim the compensation the Hartford court had granted.

"If they give me land, then I'll have to stay and clear it before I can sell it and go to New Haven," he said. "But if I'm given money, then I'll go right to New Haven and start working on Mary's property. I could be the first one to purchase some of her lots."

They did not know when they would see each other again. He left her at the door of the Saltonstalls', where only a formal handshake and thank you were appropriate. The Saltonstalls bore her into their hall with eager greetings, but Sarah hardly noticed. Through the window she could see Bradford ride away, and she was trying to pretend she was not feeling wretched.

⁂

A rise in temperature detained Sarah in New London for five days. The ice on the river was too thin to ride on and too thick for the ferry to push through. She had to wait for the ice to refreeze or to break up and go out with the tide.

The social calendar of New London benefitted from this delay. Sarah's fame as a traveller had preceded her arrival, so social engagements helped keep her mind off thoughts of separation from Bradford. Half of the population, she discovered, was born in Massachusetts or was married to someone from there or had relatives who either moved there or came from there. It had been the same in each town she had visited. While she was in New London, all these people made claims on her presence, which had no small effect on her self-esteem.

The condition of the river had not changed by Saturday afternoon, so she would have to stay through the Sabbath and hope for a departure on Monday. That evening Sarah read to Saltonstall and his family from her journal. She selected passages she hoped were most interesting and edifying. "I apologize for the prose," she said. "Many times I wrote in haste. My words could be better turned."

"Not at all," the minister objected. "It's fascinating. I don't know of any men who have ridden your path and recorded such experience."

"They wouldn't have had her experience anyway," added his wife. "They're not women."

"A good point, Elizabeth. What will you do with your journal?" he asked Sarah. "It doesn't sound as though you've written it just for your family. Do you have another audience in mind?"

"I don't know. When I began, I suppose I had some vague pretension my odyssey would interest people. Then after I read some travel books I borrowed from Reverend Pierpont, I thought more seriously about it. But I realize how rough my notes are, having read them aloud to you. I'd have to turn them into more refined prose."

"It has great possibility, though. You should prepare it for printing," he told her.

"Hmm." Sarah smiled and nodded. "It's tempting."

"I'm enormously interested in having a printing press here." He got up and began pacing. "How many printers have you in Boston? Any chance of luring one here?"

"He's talked of little else lately," added his wife.

"It's intolerable to be without one. Do you know our colony has no means of printing its own public acts? And my congregation—they have nothing to read, except their Bibles and common prayer books." He continued back and forth across the room. "In Boston, Mather gets his sermons in every household ere they're off his lips. I'm afraid New London won't attain any maturity of thought, if those who can write have no means of provoking readers."

"We don't know how fortunate we are in Boston," Sarah

said. "There are several bookshops and presses as well. If you'd prepare some proposal or some offer, I'll take it home with me and see what I can do about a printer."

Saltonstall stopped and regarded her.

"But in the mean time," she said, "you should just order a small press from England, whether you have a printer yet or not."

"You're right. We should have one here on the ready."

"If we can't hire a printer to come here," Mrs. Saltonstall said, "maybe we could send an apprentice to Boston."

The evening ended with much optimism for the printed word in New London.

Sunday, February 25

Despite invitations from all the leading families to join them in their seats at the meetinghouse, Sarah decided the most diplomatic choice was to sit with Elizabeth Saltonstall and her children. The Reverend Saltonstall now stood before them in a long black coat with a short muslin tie at the neck. Watchful Bostonian eyes would probably not have noticed the trespass of lace peeking out at the cuffs because their eyes would have been fixed on the transgression of his wonderful wig. They would not have heard a word he said.

He seemed to look at each person in the meetinghouse before he began speaking. An effective device to make them attentive, Sarah observed.

Be merciful unto me, O God . . .
Mine enemies would daily swallow me up:

For they be many that fight against me . . .
Every day they wrest my words:
All their thoughts are against me for evil . . .
They gather themselves together,
They hide themselves,
They mark my steps, when they wait for my soul . . .
When I cry unto thee, then shall mine enemies turn back.

"Psalms, fifty-six," he said, and again he looked over his congregation. His analysis focused on the words *they wait for my soul*, which taught that one must be ever watchful for perils to the soul. Next he asked them to reflect on the victims of the Deerfield Massacre. "One year ago at this time, the residents of that settlement were sitting, as you now sit, in their meetinghouse. Their minister, no doubt, was reminding them to be vigilant toward the safety of their immortal souls, as I am asking you to be today. And whilst they sat unawares, the bloody alliance of forest savages and popish agents was stealing upon them. Four days later, fifty-three residents were slain and ninety-five were taken captive."

He scanned the congregation again. "Were an axe to rend thy head tonight would thy soul fly to God?"

Saltonstall could not have chosen a topic that affected Sarah more. The attack on Bradford's settlement was probably similar to the Deerfield massacre. She gave her full attention to the two-hour sermon, one considerably shorter than what she heard the good minister was capable of.

✼

Being invited to Sunday dinner at Governor Winthrop's home was the high point of Sarah's stay in New London. At the table he and his guests carried on with the morning's sermon topic of the Deerfield massacre and captivity.

The governor's daughter appeared more solemn than she was when Sarah had met her at Miles' Tavern in New Haven. "My husband just wrote me from Boston." She removed a letter from an envelope and began reading.

John Sheldon and John Wells have come from Deerfield to seek license to travel to Canada. Sheldon's wife and baby were slain and four of his children carried off. Wells' mother was taken captive. Sheldon remained in Deerfield through the summer to supervise its defense and uphold the shattered church, whose minister had also been carried off. A chaplain was finally sent from Massachusetts in November to relieve him. Also by then, autumn made bare the cover in which the enemy could hide, so the danger to the settlement lessened. Therefore, he and Wells came to ask the Council to redeem their loved ones. They received credentials and a letter to Marquis de Vaudreuil. I offered my service, being familiar with the way, so they engaged me for one hundred pounds plus expenses. We depart on the morrow for Hatfield, by way of the Bay Path. There, Colonel Partridge will outfit us with snowshoes, packs for our backs, dried meat, etc. From there we will go to Albany and head north. I know not how long it will take me. I leave Sam . . . .

Here Mary Livingston interrupted herself to explain that Sam Vetch was her brother-in-law, who owned a ship with her husband.

Sarah already knew that and more. It was the ship Mrs.

Miles had said was involved with the French trading debacle.

The young wife continued.

I leave Sam on the ship. He will go on to Bermuda and return to Boston by May. If I have not arrived yet, someone in Boston may have word of our mission. I will try to send a letter to you by post via Albany as well.

She refolded the letter.

Sarah had to revise the opinion she had formed in New Haven of a brash John Livingston. "He's to be commended most highly for offering his service," she said to Mary. "I know the pain and suffering of those who've lost everything in such raids. If I learn that your husband's come back to Boston, I'll extend all possible courtesies to him."

"God grant them all safe journey," the governor said. "And may they return with all who were carried away."

"Amen," said everyone at the table.

Domi

Tuesday, February 27

Captain Saxton and his wife both spoke at once, expressing their pleasure at having the lady traveller from Boston at their table again. Sarah had left New London that morning after high tide had broken the ice and the outgoing tide had launched the fragments out to sea. She and her guide, a man Saltonstall had found, had ridden as far as Stonington and were enjoying a supper of roast beef and pumpkin sauce at the Saxton's Inn.

"Of the places you've seen, where could you live besides Boston?" the captain asked.

"I'm not sure. I saw many towns with pleasant aspects. But I'd have to consider the business possibilities above all else." Sarah set down her knife and fork. "Right now I have a stationery shop, and I give writing lessons, but if I decide to do something else, I believe I'll deal in land. Where are the best prospects for acquiring land here in Connecticut?"

"Not so good around here," the captain replied. "What do you say Mr. Rogers?"

Sarah's guide was familiar with the Connecticut Colony. Two of his ancestors could probably claim to have produced more descendants in New London than any other couple. There were few families who were more contentious, either. Most of them, with the exception of Sarah's guide, formed a religious sect that provoked the established congregationalists daily.

Samuel Rogers wiped his chin with his napkin. "New Haven and New London will grow the most because they're parent congregations, and they negotiate for land. New Haven usually deals fairly with the natives. They sign agreements with them and pay the prices asked. New London's not so scrupulous, so people get land for less and make more profit when they sell it. But the tribes north of New London don't like being treated that way and often cause trouble."

Perhaps this had caused the tragedy in Bradford's settlement, Sarah thought.

Wednesday, February 28

The next morning, while they waited for low tide, Sarah sent Rogers down to the waterfront to a shop Mrs. Saxton recommended. He was to purchase a bedrug, scissors and sewing notions, several yards of woolen duffel, four pewter cups and a poppet or other plaything such as might delight young girls. Sarah paid Mrs. Saxton for a bag of cornmeal. With all these items tied onto the backs of their saddles and a letter to the captain's relatives in Boston in Sarah's pocket, she and Rogers got underway.

It was five miles to the Pawcatuck. Low tide left the dead stalks of water plants protruding from the mud.

"This is the river where Mr. Fleer left me." She described the episode while searching the underbrush of the opposite bank for the rude hovel where she had been given shelter.

"Is that smoke rising down there?" Rogers asked.

The wisp was so thin it would twist and disappear, then reappear. "That's it. We're farther upstream than where I crossed last time."

Rogers went ahead, leading Athena by the reins. The water reached just under the horses' bellies.

"Hello the house," Sarah called as she had before. When the father emerged, he shielded his eyes and squinted from the sudden brightness.

"You're back," was all he said.

"I wanted to repay you for helping me at the worst moment of my journey."

Rogers had dismounted and untied the parcels. He handed them to the man.

"Thank you right kindly," he said. "You coming in?"

"No. We're trying to reach Havens' Tavern before dark. How are your wife and daughters?"

"Doing all right, but they can't come out. Got no coats. They're probly looking out one the cracks at you, though."

Sarah smiled at the house, waved slightly, then felt silly having done so. "Give them my greeting."

"Thank you, again." He nodded his head good-bye because his arms were full.

❧

Since most of the Narragansett country was flat and unremarkable, they were able to ride hard, stopping every hour to relieve themselves of the strain.

"I must have developed callouses," Sarah said. "No more sore spots on my legs. I don't even have the pain in my back that I had before. I'm just tired and a little stiff."

"If you're accustomed to the saddle, you should keep it up after you get home."

"Maybe I could be a post rider."

"We could call you Knight Rider." He laughed.

"Actually, I'm not surprised Fleer is so cantankerous. A large part of the journey is simply boring. Even if you have a companion, you can't talk while you ride hard. And at the places where you stop, some people are so rough they make you glad of just your own company in the saddle."

❧

The kindly Mrs. Havens seemed so pleased to welcome Sarah once more. "I can't believe you're here. When Mr. Fleer returned this way in October, I asked about you, and he said you'd made it to New Haven."

"Yes, but I'm sure he failed to say he deserted me on the embankment of the Pawcatuck—just rode off and left me there to find my own way."

This brought a gasp from the hostess.

While Mrs. Havens prepared a special supper of roast fowl, Sarah recounted her abandonment, the ride to New Haven with a blind guide and her trip to New York.

"My gracious. You've had quite a journey. I don't know any woman who'd do what you've done." She served Sarah then carried Rogers' plate into the public room, where he had joined a group of men. When she returned, she asked, "Have you recorded your adventures?"

"I've kept a journal."

"You should have it printed. If you do, I'll be a subscriber. Then I can say, 'She stayed at my place.'" She laughed. "And for years, people will talk about that Boston woman who rode to New York."

"I think that's unlikely," Sarah said, but the idea appealed to her vanity.

Thursday, March 1

Mrs. Havens had tears in her eyes when she waved goodbye to the guest she thought would be a legend. By afternoon the travellers found the ford at Weybosset Neck. It was low tide. Sarah saw nothing of her young canoeist. The crossing was so easy she began to think the rest of the way to Boston would be the same, but after riding across the Providence Neck, Sarah could see and hear roiling water. By the time they reached the river embankment, she was highly agitated.

"I don't remember anything like this. Where are we?" she asked.

"This is the Seekonk."

"I don't understand. It was just low tide on the other side of Providence Neck." Her voice was rising.

"This doesn't have anything to do with the tide. The

water's rushing down from streams upland because the snow cover's melting."

"It's a flood?" Her heart started pounding. "What do we do?"

"I guess we'll borrow the canoe over there." He pointed to an overturned craft with tapered ends, a bark canoe, not a dugout like the one she had previously ridden in.

"How can you paddle a canoe through this? We'll be swept out to sea."

"No we won't. I'll paddle about fifteen yards upstream then turn and paddle for the other side. The current will carries us over."

"I don't believe it." Her voice quavered.

Rogers drew in his breath and tried to explain the manoeuvre to her in several ways, none of which was satisfactory. Bradford would not have had to struggle, as Rogers was now struggling, to remain patient.

"I'll show you," Rogers said. "If I ride across and come back, then will you try?"

She agreed to nothing, but he proceeded anyway.

Completing his demonstration, he disembarked and said, "I'll take you, come back, send the horses across, then paddle over with the saddles."

She was not proud of her cowardice, but she could not help herself. An hour had passed on the bank of the Seekonk before she was persuaded into the canoe. It wobbled so when she stepped in that she sat immediately. She held on to the sides with all her strength. Her arms were rigid props to keep her from being tossed. Rogers gave a great heave, grunted with several strides that thrust the canoe into the current, hopped out of the shallow water into his seat and began paddling with much force.

The noise she heard herself emitting was less than a scream and more than a moan. It rose on every swell and with each spray that washed over the sides.

She thought they were making little progress upstream. Her head was swollen with fear. I've travelled this far, now I'm going to drown. I'm almost home. She heard Saltonstall's voice. "Were the river to rend thy canoe, would thy soul fly to God?" Then Rogers let the canoe turn to run the current. He began paddling furiously toward shore. Before another fatal thought could inflict her, the canoe struck the bank. She jerked forward and screamed. Rogers hopped into the shallow water and pulled the canoe partly ashore. He pried one of Sarah's hands off the gunwale.

"You can get out now. You're alive. I'm deaf, though. How have you managed to go from Boston to New York and back without dying of fright?"

She got out of the canoe and went to sit on a log while the great flapping inside her subsided. Rogers reversed his manoeuvre and landed near the horses. He removed the saddles and bags and placed them in the canoe. Then he swatted each horse on the rump and whistled. As soon as they stepped into the water, he pushed off in the canoe and started paddling. He whistled and hollered at the horses as he turned to shoot toward the shore.

"Hey-ah. Come on." He whistled a second time. "Call your horse," he shouted to Sarah.

She had already jumped up at the sight of Athena thrashing in the river. "Come on," she also called. "Come on." She did not know how to whistle.

Rogers was out of the canoe by the time the horses reached the bank. He grabbed their dangling reins and turned away while the horses shook off water.

After tightening the cinch on the second saddle, he leaned on the horse and sighed. "I'm ready to find the next ordinary and call an end to the day."

"I'm with you on that," Sarah said.

Unfortunately, the first building was the shabby Attleboro Tavern where Sarah had met Fleer. A horse was tied outside.

"You wouldn't want to stay here, trust me," she said. "The woman doesn't even have a lamp."

"I'll go in and ask where we can be accommodated." He returned with the young Bristol post rider who had brought Sarah here from Dedham.

"Well, Ma'am. You're still in the saddle. You just coming back from New Haven?"

"I am," she said.

"Seen anything of Fleer? I been waiting since yesterday for him."

"No, I have not."

Since she said nothing more, Rogers helped with the conversation. "Rivers have been a problem the entire way from New London. Thawing and ice floes. The worst was the Seekonk. It's flooded. We came across in a canoe. If you've been waiting for someone, then he must be behind us."

Ha! Now he is the one stuck on the wrong side of a river, she thought. The terror of her canoe ride was worth the delay it would cause him.

"Since we left the canoe on this side of the river," Rogers said, "he may have to wait until the water goes down."

The post rider shook his head.

"How do we get to the nearest lodging?" Roger asked.

The post rider gave them directions, and they arrived there within minutes.

*

After an early supper Sarah brought her journal and writing box to a table. January eighteenth was the last entry—a brief comment written a month and a half ago. Why had she become so negligent? She thumbed through the pages. Nearly half the book involved her five-day trip to New Haven in October. There was a lengthy description she wrote about New Haven, itself, several pages about the journey to New York and only a few lines that described the last two months back in New Haven. She was aware there was no reference to Bradford, and there were reasons for that. She was not going to tell anyone about him yet, not even Mary. And they could not be together now, anyway. She had her obligations in Boston, and he had his recompense to deal with. Then he had to return to New Haven and begin work on Mary's property. Even if Sarah's marriage was terminated in April, she was not about to get aboard a horse and go through this journey again—not as long as her memory of it was so sharp. So she just left him out. It was a way to live with the separation and the uncertainty. It was a way to live in Boston and not spend the time in painful remembrance of him.

Sarah dipped her quill and added several uninspired comments about settling the estate. After Mary's future was assured, Sarah had lost interest in the whole matter. Perhaps it had not been the reason she undertook the journey after all. She had set her mind to travel and had dismissed every attempt to dissuade her.

She should have learned something about her impulsiveness. Look what it had gotten her. A worthless husband. A bigamous marriage. A torturous journey and separation from her family. A lover. Well, she had at least faced the consequences of her some of her impulsiveness, but facing consequences was not the same thing as curbing the impulses to begin with. These were two different matters, and she did not entirely trust herself concerning the latter.

She wrote of her stop in New London and her journey to Boston. The Seekonk crossing occupied her for a while. She filled a whole page with the frightening events, giving credit to her guide for their safe passage. Then she read it aloud and noticed how clearly she portrayed her fear. She reread the passages about her first canoe ride and the bad river crossing in the Narragansetts, about her abandonment and about the mishap with the Indians on the bridge. Sarah had learned from retelling her journey that her audience was most pleased when they heard how she felt about things that happened to her. So maybe other colonists would like to read about her journey. Hakluyt, Josselyn, Wood—they wrote for English readers. But

New Englanders did not need a foreign traveller's description of what the country looked like or what opportunity it offered. They wanted to know what everyone else was doing—how everyone else was managing. Those who never travelled from town to town wanted to hear what travel itself was like. She had Saltonstall's encouragement to publish her journal. Perhaps she would. She even had one customer for it.

Friday, March 2

Sarah woke well before sunrise and spent the time, until the others rose, wondering whom she might see in the streets of Boston. What would she do first? Maybe have a bath? In just a few hours she would sit at her own table for supper and sleep in her own bed. Maybe on Saturday she would take the ferry to Charles Town and surprise Robert, now that she was an experienced water person.

Sarah and Rogers set out at a hard pace following breakfast. By late morning the horses became lathered, so they decided to stop at the next stream.

"There's a man ahead watering his horse," Rogers said.

When they came closer Sarah thought she recognized him. "Aren't you John Richards?"

"Aye. Do I know you?" He came around his horse, closer to her.

"Sarah Knight. I've seen you at the town house. It's wonderful to see someone from Boston. Makes me feel like I'm almost there."

He shook her hand. "Are you returning from a journey?"

"Yes, and you? Are you headed to Boston?"

"Aye, but I wanted to water and rest my horse. I came down this way yesterday. The road's dreadful in many places."

"Why's that?" Rogers asked.

"Sorry," Sarah said. "This is Samuel Rogers of New Haven. He has some business in Boston, so he's accompanying me home. Samuel, Captain John Richards."

The two men shook hands.

"The road's a slough," Richards said. "We've had warm weather. The ground has thawed and some places are like sponge. Very slow going. Very tough on the animals. Look at my horse's legs."

She had already noticed they were crusted with mud to a point above the knee.

"We'd best be going then," said Rogers. "We want to be in Boston by supper."

When the road permitted it, the trio pushed even harder than hitherto. Occasionally the horses' legs sank in the mud or in sodden layers of decayed vegetation, and they strained to free themselves. On a hill just outside Dedham, Athena began to wheeze and her chest heaved. She staggered near the crest, slipped on a mass of wet leaves and sank down onto her front knees.

"Athena," Sarah cried as she slowly slid from the saddle.

Athena's back legs collapsed and she rolled onto her side.

"Oh, God, I've killed her." Sarah fought with her skirts and struggled to her feet.

Athena squealed and panted, lifted her head then dropped it. One frightened eye stared up at Sarah.

"What's happened?" she asked the men, who were at her side.

Rogers bent down and patted Athena to calm her. "She's windbroken."

"Is she dying?"

"No, she'll survive, but she can't be ridden now," Richards said.

"What should we do with her? How will I get home?" Sarah asked.

"I'll ride up to the next farm for help," Richards said.

✤

It was late in the afternoon by the time the men left Athena with the farmer and prepared the borrowed horse. The new mount galloped roughly. In a very short while Sarah's bottom felt as though it had been beaten with a board. She recriminated herself mercilessly for nearly killing Athena and spoiling her return to Boston. She might be relieved to arrive home, but rejoicing would be impossible.

Her tears made a blur of everything, and she hardly noticed the water pouring over the Dedham causeway. Richards went first, then Rogers took her reins and led her onto the flooded causeway bridge. Halfway across, the current carried a branch toward them. It hit the side of the bridge and flipped onto the planks, striking Sarah's mount in the chest. The horse reared and tossed her off. Sarah gasped when her hands and feet hit the icy water. She thrashed about as she struggled to stand up against the current and keep from being washed off the bridge. Rogers, still on his horse, grabbed her by the hood. She clung to his leg and ran along side him. They reached the end of the bridge that way. Richards had captured the frightened horse and ran to help Sarah.

"Thank God you grabbed her hood," Richards said. "We'll have to get her inside quickly. Drapers' Tavern is just up the road."

Sarah did not remember being put on the horse, but soon the men were taking her down again. She was aware of a flurry of attentions. The hostess helped her out of her sodden clothes and into a gown of her own. Someone wrapped her in a bedrug and set her in a rocker by the fire. A hot drink was placed in her hand.

"Are you warming up now?" the hostess asked. She was rubbing Sarah's other hand.

"Yes, thank you," Sarah said. She emptied her mug and set it down.

"Your clothes and shoes will be dry by morning. There's a bed ready, but if you think you'd be warmer, you can sleep with me."

"I'm fine here," Sarah said.

"In the rocker? You don't want to sit up all night, do you?" the hostess asked.

"After five months I was going to be in my own bed tonight." She wrapped the bedrug tighter around her. "I'm not going to sleep in any other."

Saturday, March 3

Sarah and her companions left the tavern at dawn. The muddy road made her think of spring. It was March now. And then it would be April. April when the *Blue Dolphin* was to return from Hispaniola. April when the court would hear the bigamy charges. In April would she be free?

The three travellers shared the soggy way with farmers carrying the products that sustained Boston through the winter. They followed egg baskets, butter tubs and milk jugs and passed a small cart with lumpy bags of root vegetables. One man had slaughtered chickens dangling by their legs from strings tied to his saddle.

Sarah searched the horizon for the outline of Boston. As they approached The Neck, she could see Trimountain. The three hills were blue against the rising sun—permanent and reassuring. She wanted Boston to be the same as when she left because she felt different. At the foot of Trimountain, although she could not see them yet, were the registry and probate offices, her shrill minister, her nosey neighbor, Moon Street, Mary and the boarders, her stationery, fifty reams of new paper, her writing desk, her mother and daughter.

They all awaited her.

Afterward

Sarah Kemble Knight never published her journal. The real reason for her journey has never been proven, and little is known about her apart from what she recorded in her journal. She was born in April 1666, the daughter of Elizabeth Trerice and Thomas Kemble of Charlestown and Boston. She had several brothers. Her marriage to Richard Knight occurred sometime before 1689, but his exact identity is unknown; there were a number of Richard Knights in Boston at the time. Knight's daughter, Elizabeth, was born in May of 1689. A census in 1707 does not show Richard Knight as a member of the Knight household. It does, however, include Mary Trowbridge and three male boarders.

Knight lived on Moon Street in Boston's North End, where she was a neighbor and contemporary of Cotton Mather. When she moved from Boston, she sold her house to Captain Peter Papilion. A later owner was Rev. Samuel Mather.

Captain John Prout, the court registrar of Boston, was a relative of Knight. Probably through his influence she obtained employment at both the registry of deeds and the probate office. Her name and her handwriting appear on Suffolk County court documents between the years of 1695 and 1714.

The journal of Sarah Knight remained in family hands until 1825, when Theodore Dwight Jr. claimed to have obtained it (minus a few pages) from Mrs. Icabod Wetmore. Dwight finally published it for the first time, one-hundred-twenty years after her journey. Fortunately he made a fair copy of it because he said his maid used the original journal to kindle a fire in his home. Its publication caused the usual speculation of the time—that it was a fictitious journal written by a man. The journal and the controversy surrounding it interested William R. Deane, who collected information about Knight for a biography he never wrote, although he did publish his findings in a preface to an 1858 edition.

Regarding the nature of Knight's business, she mentioned being detained because of delays in the settlement of an estate and said she left after the distribution. Tradition has held that it was the estate of Caleb Trowbridge. This presents some interesting puzzles. The inventory of Trowbridge's estate was taken November 15, during the time Knight was in New Haven, but her name does not appear on any documents. There are no references to his widow. Although no will appears on the record, there was a bond signed on November 22 and the administrators were appointed on November 25. No action by the probate court is recorded by the time Knight left New Haven at the end of February 1705, however. The estate was still being contested in October of 1705 by Caleb's stepmother and was not heard before the court until May of 1706.

Several problems remain with the connection to Caleb Trowbridge. Most accounts suggest that he had come to Boston a month or two previous to his marriage and died there on September 19. No one making these claims offers any public record of his conducting business there or of his death. Caleb's name appears on the list of those buried under the First Church of New Haven. If he were, it is probably because he died there. If he had died in Boston, it is very unlikely that his body would have been shipped back to New Haven. Although the church lists Caleb as being buried in its crypt, there is no tombstone for him, and he is not listed on the church roll as a member.

The admission of a Mary Lillie to the church sometime after August of 1704 is also a puzzle because his marriage to Mary Emmes Lillie of Boston took place in Boston on July 19. In August she would have been Mary Trowbridge. All that is verifiable to date is that Caleb was in Boston in July, Knight was in New Haven from November through February, and Mary Trowbridge was still a member of Knight's household in 1707.

Subsequent generations of interested readers have filled in the scarcity of facts about Knight's life with tradition. She has been described as the first writing teacher of Benjamin Franklin and Samuel Mather. She has been credited with keeping boarders, with keeping a stationery shop as well as a shop for women's goods, with owning a tavern and farm, with being a public scrivener, and with being the colonial version of a real estate agent. Whether or not her readers have created her personal history, they have maintained an appreciation for her writing for nearly three hundred years. There have been numerous editions of the journal printed to the present date, and her journal is included in most anthologies of early American literature.

One ironic twist to an episode Knight mentions in her journal concerns Governor Winthrop's daughter, Mary. Knight met her and was entertained at the Winthrop home in New London. Nearly ten years later, Knight's daughter had attracted the attention of Mary Winthrop's husband, John Livingston. He was the son of the first Robert Livingston of Albany and Alida Schuyler Van Rensselear. Mary was still lingering on with a fatal illness when John wrote to his family requesting permission to marry Elizabeth Knight. His sister wrote an angry letter to her father, objecting to both the prematurity of John's request and to the inadequate social standing of Miss Knight. The only copy of an existing letter by Sarah Knight was written to Robert Livingston, promoting the match of her daughter and his son. Mary died, John prevailed and Increase Mather married the couple in October of 1713. They moved to New London, followed shortly by Knight.

It is known that Sarah Knight owned property in the New London area; some of it she owned jointly with Joseph Bradford. Her named is mentioned in Joshua Hempstead's diary, and there is a record of one conviction for selling whiskey to Indians. She was apparently an astute businesswoman, judging from the £1,800 estate she to left her daughter.

Sarah Kemble Knight died at the age of sixty-two and is buried in New London next to her daughter.

To order a copy of this book
ask your local bookseller
or
send the following to:

Colonial American Press
P.O.B. 1416 Sta. A
Dept. B
Rutland, Vermont
05701

Name_____

Address_____

_____

City_____ State____ Zip_____

Paperback ISBN 0-9647752-0-4
    Number of copies_____ $19.00 each
Hardcover ISBN 0-9647752-1-2
    Number of copies_____ $34.00 each

Total amount of enclosed order $_____

Special discounts are available to historical societies
and organizations or businesses
for the purpose of fund-raising or promotion.